LITTLE ROBIN

Vera's Story

By

Barry Boughen

ISBN-13: 978-1977801623
ISBN-10: 1977801625

To Jill
Enjoy the Read
Barry

For those who encouraged me to publish my book.

CONTENTS

In my other professional career, I have come into contact with many elderly people who are cared for in nursing homes. It is so wrong to write them off and say their lives are over. They are only over when they are over and every day of their lives is as special as ours.

It is through caring for these people and learning from them that I have gained the knowledge to write this story. Each and every resident within a nursing home has a story to tell if only anyone will take the time to listen to them.

This story is Vera's story.

We may have to get old but we do still have our memories.

1.

Vera is sitting in a comfy brown reclining chair by the large picture window of her nursing home's main lounge. Her right leg is bandaged. The lounge is a modern extension built onto what is otherwise a transformed former country house set in large and picturesque grounds of gardens, trees, shrubs and lawns.

Being in the home is not Vera's first choice of course. No one ever asks to go there, but 'needs must' as they say. In no way did Vera ask to lose her home and the great pride she held in it. She didn't ask to up and leave most of her highly treasured possession, some worthless to others but priceless to her. In no way did she ask to lose a certain amount of her pride and dignity either, but Vera is sensible enough to realise that, yes, 'needs must' has to be right and she makes the most of her new life and tries hard to keep a smile on her face and a joke on her tongue.

She is no longer alone and that is a bonus to be appreciated. Around her she has other residents, or 'those old people' as she would call them and she has staff to assist her in all of her daily tasks, needs and routines rather than have to struggle helplessly and, often, haplessly on her own. Staff are there to help but they are also there to be seen as almost a kind of sport for Vera's naughty mind.

She knows that life will never be the same again but she also knows that she has had a life; a long one. Times haven't always been good and sometimes times were definitely not good at all but she loves a smile. She loves life and she loves to be loved. She has been loved, true, tenderly and utterly.

She is sitting on her own in a corner while staff are busy caring for others. Vera likes being there, in her corner, in her chair on her own. People are around if she needs them but she does like to be left to lose herself in her own thoughts, imaginings, ramblings and reminiscences.

She is dressed in a blue and white flowered dress and light blue cardigan with comfy slippers and talks to herself, and us.

Vera

Albert's out there again. He's the gardener here they say but he shouldn't be out there, should he? He's seventy five or even eighty if he's a day. He's only a few years younger than me, even if he's that. Poor man. He could even be older I suppose, now that I look at him properly, through my specs rather than over them. He should be in here with us, not out there. Still it's a nice sunny day to be outside. I wish I could be outside taking in the warmth and sounds; seeing the birds and smelling the smells. They'd be better than the smells in here I must say. We had cabbage, meat and gravy for dinner and we all know what that does to old people. And most of them are old, really old. I told the girls I wanted to go outside today.

"But you can't Vera," they said. "You can't go out. Not today sweetheart. You haven't been well, have you? You've had a touch of the flu."

"But I haven't touched anybody," I told them, pretending to be cross. "Not me."

"What do you mean?"

"You said I'd touched Flo. I haven't even seen her today. Is she dead?"

They did laugh. I pretend to be deaf sometimes but I'm not really. Only sometimes. It's all good for a laugh though. We all need cheering up. You can catch depression in here.

"No you silly old sausage," the nice girl with the long wavy hair and blue eyes said, loudly. "You haven't touched Flo. They said you've had a touch of the flu, Vera!"

"I have," I told her. "I've had a touch of the flu, you know. I haven't been well and had better stay indoors today."

"That's a good idea," she said. "I wish I'd thought of that."

I told them I'd just look out of the window instead.

Albert is bending over in the rose garden. He's dead-heading and pulling out a few weeds. It's a shame to see the roses going over but they have been good. The weeds are things like chickweed and dandelions and things like that and he's doing his best pulling them out. Well, pulling them out one at a time anyway, the poor old soul. Maybe I shouldn't laugh but he does look funny on those big feet, huge light brown shoes and skinny legs. It takes him ages to bend down, ages to pull a weed up and then ages again to stand up and drop it in his wheelbarrow. He must have nearly six in there by now. He's been at it for over an hour. He's got a little rip in his trousers. Probably caught it on something. Barbed wire perhaps.

I don't think he really needs a wheelbarrow. He'd make far more use of a walking frame like mine. Mind you, mine's got purple ribbon on it and I don't think Albert would like that. Can you imagine a man walking up and down the corridor using a walking frame with purple ribbon on it? Perhaps he'd better stick to his wheelbarrow after all. I don't use my frame much these days. It's in my room. Room 29, down by the shower. These days they help me to a wheelchair and then into my chair, this chair. I sit here so much and for so long it's almost my home in a way, but it hasn't always been my chair. I sort of inherited it after Mr Graham, the vicar man, died in it while he was writing a sermon. He was old and didn't preach any more but he still did like writing his pieces on a Saturday ready for Sunday. Then, by Sunday he's forgotten what day it was anyway. I don't think he left anything behind it. The chair does seem clean. He may be frail, old Albert, but he does dress well for a gardener, apart from that rip in his brown trousers, and he's a proud man. He wouldn't want to be seen with purple ribbons, would he?

The robin has just landed again. Look. He's right by Albert's big feet, looking for food. He's looking around. Albert loves that robin, and so do I. Especially me. Albert nearly trod on him yesterday. I think it's my robin come down to see me again, bless him. He's found something to eat and now he's turned around and is looking straight at me. Straight at me. He seems happy enough, thank goodness. He always does. I think he knows it wasn't my fault. It wasn't my fault, was it?

Vera loses herself for a few moments; a tissue in her hand and her hand on her chin, and just concentrates her gaze on her robin until it flies off.

She then continues to speak.

It's all happened in here this morning you know. There seems to be something in the air, or in the food. Must be the meat, cabbage and gravy. A little while ago I sat here, watching Albert and the robin, and minding own business, when suddenly there was a deafening scream, or more of a cry, from the other corner of the room. Over there by the rubber plant that no one seems to water. Whatever happened to Baby Bio? It looks dreadful. Where was I? Oh yes. What a commotion. Frightened the life out of me it did. One minute I was lost in another world, my own world, and then suddenly I was brought back to reality by old Sid from Room 12 upstairs, screaming for help. Well, the girls in their white tops, and one in light blue, came running down the corridor and went to him. One was the nice girl with the long hair and the other one was that Norma, the one whose eyes are too close together. She's the coarse one, always swearing. I couldn't really see what they were doing and I couldn't hear what old Sid was saying but they quickly helped him up and ushered him out towards the lift.

A while later Norma came back in the room and she came over to me and told me what had happened. I don't think I really heard her right. I try to say it isn't but my hearing is bad sometimes. I do have to admit it.

"Well," I said. "I didn't hear the shot."

"What?" Norma said, looking down at me in my chair as if I was stupid.

It would be much nicer if they came down to my level.

"The shot," I repeated to her. "I didn't hear it. Did you? And what's he doing with guns in a place like this anyway? Has he even got a license?"

Norma looked at me again and then laughed.

"Your hearing is getting worse Vera Betts," she said, beaming from ear to ear, pointing her finger at me and shaking her head. "I didn't say he'd 'shot' himself, did I?"

"I should have known, shouldn't I?" I said to her. "The smell should have given it away shouldn't it?"

Vera smiles to herself and then, with her wiping the corner of her mouth with her tissue, her head bows and she drifts into a quick sleep until she hears a tap on the window.

"Is….is that you my little Robin?"

I look up and see that it's Albert, the gardener again. The silly sod, beaming from ear to ear as well he is, and in his hand he's got a huge worm. Silly old sod. The silly old sod woke me up just to show me a worm?

"You're a silly old sod!" I tell him but he never hears me. These windows have got double glazing and Albert's got no hearing so I just smile. Do you know, he isn't a bad looking man from through double glazing. He gestures that he's going to give the worm to the robin.

"What?" I say, loudly. "Give it to Robin? No. You can't do that. It's bigger than he is. It might eat him. Either that or it'll tangle itself round him like an Annie condo."

I'm sure Albert never hears what I say. What are them snakes called? They crush things and then swallow them whole. They're not Annie condos are they, but you know what I mean I'm sure? You know, don't you? Anyway, Albert can't hear what I say and he throws the worm to the little robin. It lands right by his tiny feet and frightens the life out of him. He jumps up and lands on the gatepost. It looks frightened out of its feathers and I don't like to see Robin frightened. He's been through enough as it is.

I must tell you soon about Robin. I'm old now and I do jabber on a bit but Robin is important, bless him. So important. They say God needed my Robin more than I did but I can't believe that. Surely he could have given me some time with him. He took him so quickly.

I'm old and I need help with getting around. I did get along a bit with my frame but I couldn't get too far. If I overdo things now my head starts spinning and then the corridors start spinning and then I fall down. Happened three times it did. Look at my forehead. I've still got a bruise from last week. Haven't used my frame since. Came out in a ruddy great welt it did. Looked like I had a pinky red molehill growing on my head. It's gone down now but the bruising's still there. I do bruise easily these days but bruises heal. Well, the ones on the outside of your body do anyway. The ones inside sometimes don't. Some of them never heal at all.

My memory isn't too good either and I have to pee in a bag. It's strapped to my leg you know and it's connected to my, my 'thingy', by a tube. It came out the other day and I soaked my chair. The cleaning girls had to get this posh looking machine out to clear it all up. It's a big noisy blue thing with pipes everywhere. The chair was left wet from the machine and I couldn't sit on it all day and had to sit on that red one over there but then Mr Tidy, or whatever it is they call him, he said it was his chair and I had to get out. He got quite nasty because I didn't move. I couldn't move, could I? How could I move? It's alright for him. He just stands up and away he goes, up the corridor like a scolded cat, but not me. I have to have two of the girls in white tops help me up and they weren't around were they? So you see, I wasn't being awkward was I? Mr Tidy couldn't see it like that though. To him it was his chair and I should just clear off. It is nice here with other people but sometimes other people can be a pain.

What was I talking about? Let me think. Hang on. Ah that's it! Yes, memory. Mine isn't too good you know. Not these days. It's strange really. I can't remember being born, but then again who can? I can remember my first day at school though and I can certainly remember my first kiss. Oh, I did love him. My Jonny. That kiss and starting school were so many years ago that I can't even work out what years they must both have been and yet I can remember them so clearly, but if you ask me what I had for dinner I couldn't tell you. I can if it was sprouts though. They seem to boil them for days in here and then you can taste them all afternoon and right up 'til bedtime. They ask me what I had for dinner and I just have to swallow to be reminded. Ah, I say, with a smile on my face and feeling smug, and them thinking I've remembered. It was sprouts, wasn't it? Well done Vera, they say. I never did really like sprouts but they say they're good for you and I need all the goodness I can get at my age. I asked for a bath yesterday.

"Heh Norma!" I said. "I haven't had a bath for ages."

She laughed.

"You are a silly old so and so," she said. "You had one this morning. Don't you remember? Me and the new girl, Betty, gave you one and you splashed us up. You remember that, don't you?"

"Of course I do," I said. "I splashed you two all up didn't I?"

"That's it," Norma said. "You remember."

I didn't remember did I? But I just didn't want to look stupid so I said I did. Then I lifted my arm to my nose and sniffed and I could smell that stuff they use these days. Not soap. No, not soap. Soap is what we used to use in our day. Lifebuoy or Pears or Camay and things like that. What they use today is called shower gel and it comes in a bottle; liquid. They pour it over your back and then rub it in. That Norma is a bit rough sometimes and I do complain but only lightheartedly. To tell you the truth, her rough hands on my old back is lovely. It does get itchy sitting here all day in this chair that used to belong to the vicar. Anyway, I lifted my arm up and smelled it. It smelled gorgeous so I knew I'd had my bath.

What was I going to tell you about? I do forget things and my mind does wander these days. Please help me out. Ah yes. Thanks. It was Robin, wasn't it? My Robin. My sweet little Robin.

It happens willy-nilly these days. Even my own granddaughter did it. I say granddaughter and I call her my granddaughter but really she was my husband's daughter's daughter, not mine. It happens and little is said but back in my day something was said. It was said strongly inside the family but nothing was ever said outside of it.

"It's our secret," they'd say. "It's happened and we'll have to deal with it but nobody must ever know."

They never said it nicely. Things got irate and people hated the ones that did it. I did it.

I used to go to school. Yes, they did have schools, even back in my day thank you. Ours was only a smallish school in a smallish town and they didn't teach you half the things they do now but we got by. They taught us one and one makes two and what the capital of Moscow is and things like that but these days they teach them everything. They even teach them about sex. I wish they'd done that in my day. I do wish they had.

2.

"Vera!"

A voice from somewhere.

"Vera!"

I'm asleep aren't I?

"Vera! You getting up! It's school today. Remember!"

I shake my head to bring myself around.

"Ok mum!"

It's been holiday time but the weather has not been good. Rainstorm seemed to follow rainstorm with only sharp gusts of wind in between seen as any temporary respite from it. I'm actually looking forward to going back to school after more than a couple of weeks of staying indoors with mum as my main company. My best friend, Kathy, has been round but we stayed mainly by the fire. Yes, it's May and we had a fire. Not every day but we did have a few. At least we can afford fuel, even in late spring. A lot of people don't have that kind of luxury. We're lucky because my father is the owner of the local hardware shop in our town and he's doing well. We've got our own car, a big black Hillman, and our own big townhouse when most of my friends live in rough little houses and ride around on rattly and rusting bicycles.

School, in the sunshine that has now decided to show itself at last, just as the holidays are over, seems hugely appealing. I shake my head again and get out of bed, looking forward to seeing Kathy and all my other friends.

As I say, it's May now but is still quite cold despite the appearance of the sun. There's no heating in the bathroom, or anywhere else apart from the fire downstairs come to that, and my morning routine has to be quick, or 'cheap and cheerful' as my mother always calls it. My father never calls it anything. He's not really into talking, let alone humour. He does smile a lot though but, ninety nine times out of a hundred, it's when the customers in his shop hand him their money.

I run into the green painted bathroom, take off my pyjamas, rinse quickly, brush my hair in front of the slightly chipped wall mirror and then retreat back to the bedroom to get dressed. It honestly feels more like the middle of winter. I take a quick look into my bedroom mirror and am still amazed that, although some of my friends have started to fill out, I'm still skinny. My face seems to have grown up slightly but my body is still that of a ten or eleven year old. I can't look too much as I've got goose-pimples. Get dressed girl. I do. Even the stair carpet seems cold under my feet.

"Morning Vera," mum greets, cheerfully from the kitchen. She seems in a good mood. Probably because dad is just leaving and she is to have the whole day to herself. Even without me.

Dad, who, looking at him closely, is a tall and proud well-built and balding dark haired man, dressed for work in a green suit. He just grunts as he leaves through the front door. At least a grunt is something I suppose. For him there's never time for pleasantries. Never time nor inclination that is.

'He's a proud man,' mum would always say. Proud of being miserable?

Sitting at the table, the pine one in our kitchen, a cup of sweet milky tea is soon placed in front of me, followed by two slices of buttered toast served on a side plate which depicts a lady dressed in a crinoline dress, standing by a cottage door with roses growing over it. The jam is standing there by me but I don't bother today. Both the tea and the toast are warm and slide down beautifully but there's no time to linger. School beckons and there are friends to catch up with and stories to hear.

"See you later mum!" I shout, grabbing a jacket from the pegs in the hallway and still chewing my last mouthful of toast.

"And don't dawdle on the way home," I just hear her say as I shut the door behind me. "We're visiting Nanny. Remember?"

I'm thirteen years old and life feels great. Especially as I'm nearly fourteen. I've always been quite a happy child and, luckily, people seem to like me and I like them. In the new sunshine, I walk with a light step under trees full of cherry blossom which has obviously suffered slightly in the rain as petals lay everywhere beneath them. Nothing much has happened during the holiday, apart from a dull visit to my aunt's farm which is stuck out in the middle of the woods, miles from anywhere and anyone, so it's good to be out again.

"It's not a farm Vera," mum would say, trying to sound posh. "It's only a smallholding."

We're quite well off but mum doesn't like the thought of anyone having more than her. Calling auntie Gloria's farm only a smallholding does seem to make things better for her to accept. It's a run-down farm owned by a run-down woman and is certainly nothing to be jealous of. I call it Cold Comfort Farm. Aunt Gloria's on her own these days after uncle Fred dropped down dead in the pigsty years ago. They say he had a heart attack. Gloria has managed on her own since then, just, but it is a struggle for her. Mind you, she likes a struggle. She's always been struggling with life and seems to enjoy a good moan.

I quite like the farm, or smallholding, which ever one it is. Especially in the springtime when all the new animals are being born. Chickens, pigs, lambs sometimes and wildlife. Aunt Gloria is a strange one though. Always has been. You can tell she's dad's sister. They both dislike smiling unless they're getting paid for it. Dad when he sells a bolt or a nail and Aunt when she sells an egg.

Walking down the hill and by a row of small terraced cottages with roofs and chimney stacks that badly need mending I spot a familiar figure and a strange feeling sends waves through my stomach. It's

Jonathan or Jonny as we call him. He's a couple of months older than me but is in our class. He's a tall lad and is quite well built. He could really comb his hair more but all the girls like him and one or two even say they love him. They're just being girls and silly, aren't they? I don't think anyone can simply love someone just because he's good looking. I may fall in love one day but not for years to come yet. Most people do, but not yet. Not even with handsome Jonny. He is nice but I'm still a girl whose body is skinny. Some of my friends have got breasts but I'm even more flat chested than him. There is this feeling inside me though. These waves running through my stomach. I tell myself it's just the excitement of going to school.

Jonny hasn't seen me and is quite a few yards in front but there's Kathy, coming from a small side street on my right. Where's she been? That isn't where she lives.

"Kathy!"

She looks both ways up and down the street and then runs over to me.

"Vera!"

"Where have you been?"

"Mum's having her troubles again. She had serious pains in her stomach last night so they took her to hospital. I stayed at aunty Pauline's. Dad called in this morning and said she's feeling much better."

"Say hello from me and tell her to get well soon."

"I will."

Kathy looks ahead and smiles.

"There's Jonny. I haven't seen him for two weeks," she says. "When I do see him I get butterflies in my belly."

Butterflies? Is that what they are? I've got them too.

I can't tell her I feel the same. Kathy is a bit more outspoken than me. I'm not too shy but I am the quiet one of the two. Kathy suggests we run and catch up to Jonny but I decline. I can feel my face going red just at the thought. He's only a boy but I've got these 'butterflies' as Kathy calls them and now my face has gone red. Strange feelings. Perhaps I am growing up after all.

In my changing mind, I watch Jonny stride off in front of us but wish in a way that he had noticed us and had held back.

"I like your house," Kathy says.

"Pardon?"

"I said I like your house. It's posh compared with mine."

"Do you?"

Kathy stops and then puts her hand on my shoulder to stop me. She looks at me.

"Vera, you're not really listening are you?"

I turn around and look into Kathy's eyes. I wasn't listening was I? I was looking at Jonny.

"You were looking at Jonny," Kathy says, smiling broadly and knowingly. "You fancy him then?"

"No."

"I bet you do. We all do Vera. Come on."

Did I fancy him? Do I? Do I even know what that word means? Up until that moment I had been just a child but I'm growing up. I know it and feel almost adult in what I know. Life is changing and life is good.

"Let's run and catch him up," Kathy says, laughing. "Come on!"

She runs a few steps but then realises I am not with her. She stops.

"Come on Vera!"

I give in and run half-heartedly towards Jonny and the school. We catch him as he reaches the gates.

Kathy turns all slushy and says hello.

"Hello Jonny," she says, confidently, with an exaggerated smile and fluttering eyelids.

I stay quiet and just look up and into his rugged face.

"Hello girls," Jonny replies. "Glad to be back at school?"

"Glad to be back here with you," Kathy says, flirting strongly.

Again, I'm quiet and lost for words.

"Hello Vera," he says, softly and looking straight into my eyes. "And how are you?"

"Fine thanks," I reply, quietly.

He smiles a smile that seems to make every one of my butterflies turn into a herd of elephants. I'm excited by his attention but feel almost giddy at the same time.

"She'll be fine when we get in," Kathy tells Jonny. "It's sums first and we all know our Vera is the best at sums."

"Well, perhaps she can tell me the answers then," Jonny laughs. "I'm rubbish."

In class, the room set out with rows of wooden desks and white dusty looking lights hanging from the high ceiling, I eagerly await the start of lessons but it's registration first. Billy Hicks isn't here again. He never seems to be. He comes from a rough family who seem to hold no regard for authority. Billy comes to school when he wants to, which isn't very often. The School Board Man has paid him lots of visits but, in the end, I think they just gave up.

"Mary Atkins!"

"Yes Miss!"

"Charles Bishop!"

"Yes Miss!"

"Jonathan Clitheroe!"

"Yes Miss!"

"Harold Fox!"

"Yes Miss!"

"Billy Hicks!"

No answer.

"Billy Hicks! Is Billy not here again? And on the first day of the new term as well."

She looks to where he usually sits and tuts loudly.

"I suppose he'll make Prime Minister one day," she jokes, feebly.

I don't know about all schools but we start the day off with The Lord's Prayer. I'm not too keen but do say the words, without real conviction, because I want the sums to begin.

"Arithmetic!" Miss says loudly, once we have all said Amen.

I'm excited and feel a slight tap on my back from Jonny.

He says, 'Here goes,' and gets told off for talking.

"Quiet Clitheroe!"

Miss sets out her rules.

"If you know the answer then put up your hand!" she says. "It's as simple as that. Let's see how many have their hands up at the end."

She starts.

"8x2!"

All hands go up and she asks Charles for the answer.

"It's 16 Miss."

She nods.

"8x5!"

Again, all hands go up and this time she asks Harold.

"It's 40 Miss."

She nods again.

This goes on until just a few have their hand up.

"8x16!"

I fluster to work it out and then feel Jonny tap my back again.

"Go on!"

My hand shoots into the air and I realise it is the only one there.

"Vera?"

"128 Miss."

Miss smiles and says, "Thank you Vera." Jonny taps me on the back again.

"Well done V!" He says.

V? He's always called me Vera. Never V. This is a change and the touching is a change as well. I like it.

Sums, or arithmetic, as Miss called them then pass by in something of a blur. I do love the subject so why was I not concentrating? I know why. Jonny was paying me attention and had started to call me V. Was this silly? No.

After school Kathy walks off towards her house instead of her aunt's as her father had called in at the school to say her mother was home from the hospital, and I leave to walk home on my own. I haven't gone far when I hear a call from behind me.

"V! Wait a minute!"

It's Jonny.

"Can I walk with you?"

I blush and nod my head.

"Wish I was good at sums," Jonny says, looking into my eyes again and smiling a huge warm smile on that rugged face of his. "You're the best."

"The best at sums?"

This time it's Jonny's turn to blush a little.

"No," he says quieter. "Just the best."

We walk along together without saying too much more and I leave him at the front door of his cottage which has always had flakes of red paint peeling off. He lays a hand tenderly on my shoulder.

"See you tomorrow V," he says softly.

I look at him and all my butterflies seem to explode. All I can do is nod as I walk away but do risk a small glance over my shoulder. He's waving but I can't seem to lift my arm to do likewise so I just smile.

3.

So that was Jonny, Jonny Clitheroe. He was a month or two older than me in them days and I suppose he still is if you think about it. He must be. It's down to arithmetic and I loved arithmetic. I wonder where he is now. I've wondered that for years. He lived in a small cottage at the bottom of our road. The one with all the red paint peeling off the front door and the roof and chimney that badly needed mending. He was a boy that all the girls liked. Really big and handsome he was. Handsome in every way and all the girls liked him and one or two even said they loved him, but they didn't really did they? They only thought they did. They were just being girls and that's how girls think. We were only young then. Only children still really. We had feelings but didn't understand them properly. I think that's the best way to put it. They were new feelings. Feelings we had to learn to get used to. I soon did.

What's this? Here it comes. It must be time for a drink. I can hear a rattle. I know that rattle. It's Susie with the tea trolley. She's coming up the corridor from the kitchen. Somebody should look at that wheel of hers. Well, not her own wheel of course. She hasn't got wheels. It's her trolley wheel. It's been wobbling and rattling like that for weeks. The other three go forward but that one spins round and round. Not just the wheel either but the whole bit that holds the wheel on. It tries to go in every direction at the same time. I know what she'll say. She always says the same thing. Strange, isn't it? I can't remember what I had for dinner, unless it's sprouts, and yet I can remember the things the staff always say. Susie isn't her real name. She comes from a foreign place. Somewhere hot. There's a lot of them about these days. I would tell you what her real name is but I can't remember. Anyway, it sounds a bit like Susie so we call her Susie. Here she comes. She'll say 'do you want milk in that?'

I always have my coffee black but, "Do you want milk in that Veera?" she'll ask.

No thanks I'll say, smiling. Susie thinks it's our little joke. It was to start with but then it became monotonous but she likes it. She means well. She's coming over.

"My usual black coffee please Susie."

"You want milk in that Veera?"

You see. It's the same every time. Every day and about four times a day. Apart from when she's not on duty that is and then it's young Kenneth, Ken, and he puts the milk in anyway, without asking me. I prefer my coffee black but milk is good for you so I never complain. I know it's good for babies.

"Can I have a couple of biscuits please Susie?"

"You like custard cream?"

I like biscuits. I do. Digestives are nice but sometimes they have them other ones. What are they called? The big sweet ones. That's it, Hobnobs. I love them. They're a bit sweet for me but sugar is good for you as well they say. Well, a little is anyway. Gives you energy but why I need energy I don't know. All I do is sit here all day in this chair, waiting for bedtime and the graveyard.

Susie gives me two custard creams and then, as no one is looking, she gives me a third.

"Thank you dear."

Oh look. Robin's back. He's sitting near Albert while he's eating a bar of chocolate. No, not Robin eating the chocolate. That would be silly. Albert's got a small bar of Dairy Milk and he's sucking it to death. You can see his teeth aren't too strong. Perhaps he should have had milk in his coffee. There's calcium in milk and that's good for teeth.

Jonny. Yes. Was I telling you about Jonny? I was, wasn't I? We were children. Coming up to fourteen I was and Jonny was there already. He was really big and handsome and all the girls liked him, but I think I've told you that bit, haven't I? See, my memory does work sometimes.

I started to get these feelings when I saw him but my friend Kathy just said they were butterflies in our bellies. I didn't know what they were. I just felt them and liked what I felt, although I felt a little nervous of them at first. I know now what those feelings were but then I didn't. I was changing and felt it but nobody told me anything. The facts of life they call them but the fact was that nobody told me what they were. I wish they had. If they had, then I wouldn't be sitting here and telling you my story would I? I'd be a nobody. I was then, after it happened.

Nobody told me a word. Mum was quite good with me and open sometimes but she was too shy to mention such things and dad was… well dad was dad. To put it simply, in his mind if you didn't know everything he knew then you were either dumb or stupid or both. The whole sex thing was disgusting anyway, so why talk about it? With him, even if you thought something that was one degree off what he thought then you were totally wrong in every way. You couldn't question him because he was beyond questioning and you couldn't reason with him because there was no reasoning apart from his. In the end, I almost stopped talking to him but that was fine with him. Children should be seen and not heard was the way in those days and it certainly was his way. I didn't want it to be that way. Kathy's dad really loved her. A gentleman he was. He'd cuddle her and kiss her and tell her he loved her. She loved it and it made her feel wonderful. I would have liked that but it never happened. Not with my dad. Truly, I think he just loved himself and that was that. He only seemed to love mum when things were going particularly well. He was a sad man really. I know that now. I say I would have liked what Kathy and her dad had between them but no. I wouldn't have liked it. I would have loved it. I yearned for it and there would come a time when I was desperate for it. So desperate that it tore me apart so badly that the scars have never really healed.

He did go away to war, my dad, but I can't remember that. I was only three when he went and I was only four when he came back. He'd been shot in the leg. At the top of his right leg and was sent home. He still had a limp years later. Or was it a limp? It was more like a slight leaning over to the right when he put weight on that leg. I suppose that's a limp, isn't it? It must have been painful because he rubbed it a lot but at least it gave him the chance to take over the shop again for himself rather than have old Harry run it for him. Harry was too old to fight and had fought in the first war. He worked for dad and dad put him in charge of the shop when he left for the army. Mum said dad's was a reserved occupation or something but dad was a proud man and said he needed to fight for his country. He did and received a dodgy leg for his troubles though. Still, he came home. He managed that. Many didn't. It was a bad old time. I had a friend whose dad didn't come back. She didn't miss him though because she couldn't even remember him. She was three like I was. Her mum eventually married again. A foreign man. A Polish chap who stayed here after the war. He was a lovely man. He called everybody sweetheart. My dad didn't. He just called in at the bank to put more money in.

See, I remember all this. All this from all those years ago and yet I can't remember what I had for dinner, unless it's sprouts.

I remember the fact that Jonny always used to sit behind me in class. He was there but that was it. He was just a boy sitting behind a girl in class but then things started to change for some reason. It was a reason I didn't know and I didn't understand why. At first it felt lovely but just a little uncomfortable at the same time. Not for long though. I was nervous. Why was this change happening? I wasn't ugly but, then again, I wasn't developed like some of the others. He had been sitting there for a while and had always ignored me but change was in the air. A change that meant just a simple tap on the back meant something. I could feel something coming from him and into me. A sort of electricity. Is that possible? Dear Jonny. My dear Jonny.

4.

Again, as always, a grunt from dad as he leaves the house. It's a lovely day and the sun is wearing a huge smile. Dad's saving his smile again for his customers I see. Can't waste them you know. They're hard to come by unless they're being paid for.

Toast and sweet milky tea again, quickly scoffed down. It's school again today and there's only one thing on my mind. Jonny. Am I being silly? Who knows and who cares?

I put on my shoes and look down at my legs as I do so. Are they filling out? Just a little? Maybe.

"Bye mum!"

"Bye Vera! See you later! I'm going out this afternoon. Remember?"

"Ok."

With the door closed I realise just how much the sun is smiling. It's burning the back of my neck already as I walk but I care not. My eyes and mind are focused down the hill and towards a certain terraced house with red paint peeling off the front door. I stare intently, waiting for Jonny to come out of his gate as I know that, today, he will wait for me.

As I approach, the door opens and my butterflies spring into life again but they soon settle down to only a slight murmur as the figure coming out is not Jonny but his mother. She is a thin lady dressed in her working clothes. I can tell that because they are slightly more shabby than her Sunday ones. Like Jonny, her hair could do with a brush.

"Hello Vera," she says through a gap in her front browned teeth. "Can you tell the teacher Jonny won't be at school today."

My butterflies seem to die inside me and I almost follow them.

"What's wrong?"

She looks at me a little awkwardly.

"He's got a touch of the runs sweetheart," she says, falteringly and looking up to the first floor. "His dad's got a job at the greengrocers now, three days a week, and he came home last night with a whole crate of plums that were a bit overripe. Jonny didn't mind their condition and ate far too many. I did try to tell him but he's a boy and he wouldn't listen."

She relaxes and laughs. We both laugh but in a way, I'm devastated. It means I won't see Jonny all day.

"Ok Mrs Clitheroe," I say. "I'll tell them."

I say this and go to walk away but she holds my arm and smiles warmly.

"You're a lovely girl Vera," she says completely sincerely. "You're pretty and a lovely genuine girl and I know my Jonny likes you."

I blush and she notices.

"Don't blush Vera," she says. "It's true. I know you're only young but if my son could end up with a girl like you one day I'd be so proud I think I'd burst."

She pulls me gently towards her and plants a tender kiss on my cheek.

"Have a good day at school sweetheart," she says. "And enjoy your sums. My Jonny says you're good at sums."

I say goodbye and walk away. So Jonny talks about me at home does he? I'll miss him today but then again, I'm warmed inside by the fact that he does talk about me. What's happening here? I'm not quite fourteen yet. I always said I'd fall in love later. One day. Am I doing it already? But it is only a crush, isn't it? Is it? I don't know. Life is confusing. Confusing but wonderful at the same time. I say goodbye to Jonny's mother and walk to school knowing I'll miss that gentle tap on my back and him calling me V. That's special.

Miss is walking across the playground as I enter and I call her and tell her about Jonny.

"He's got diarrhoea Miss," I tell her with slight smile. "Eaten too many plums."

"Too many plums?"

She too wears a smile and I explain his dad's new job. They have to do whatever they can to earn enough money to survive. We're lucky but they have rent to pay. We're three people who live in a big house that's paid for and they're five people who live in a tiny cottage with the roof hanging off and have to pay to do so. There's Jonny, the youngest, his mum and dad and his two brothers. His mum, dad and brothers do work and work hard but it seems there is never enough to go around properly. His dad isn't too well but does manage to work four days each week. Three at the greengrocers now and one, on Tuesdays, gardening. People say his problems are in his head rather than in his body but, wherever they are, they're still problems.

Miss calls the register but leaves out Jonny's name.

"You didn't call out Jonny's name," Sam Hodges, a fat little boy in a green checked jacket and round glasses, says.

"Well," Miss replies. "He isn't here, is he?"

Sam quickly finds a reply.

"Billy Hicks wasn't here yesterday Miss," he points out. "But you called his name, didn't you?"

Miss is slightly annoyed.

"But Sam," she tells him, trying to be as kind as possible. "I didn't know he wasn't here did I? I know Jonny Clitheroe isn't here because Vera told me. Ok?"

Sam looks at me and then lets out a childish snigger with his face beaming and his hand over his mouth.

"That's because she fancies him Miss," he utters inanely.

"Be quiet and grow up Hodges."

Sam doesn't grow up of course, but he does go quiet.

I'm red with embarrassment.

Lessons, after the Lord's prayer, start with English and we are asked to write a story, or essay as they call them. An essay on any subject we wish. What to write about? Maybe a trip to the seaside, collecting shells. I think and I see myself walking along the beach in the sunshine as the tide goes out. I've got my bucket and am picking up pretty shells of all sorts. Large ones, small ones and colourful ones and plain ones. I like wildlife, all wildlife but especially birds. My favourite is the robin but you don't usually see them at the seaside. Well, not on the beach anyway. The waves are lapping gently as the water recedes and the gulls screech overhead whilst small birds scurry along the sand, finding scraps and morsels to eat. I feel totally happy and free as I'm not with my mum and dad. I'm with Jonny. I must get him out of my head and concentrate.

The essay is written and Jonny is replaced by my parents. I have to give in to imagination though and place both of them on the beach, sitting happily, side by side, holding hands on a blanket. Dad has got his sunhat and sunglasses on and is laughing as he rolls up his trousers in order to get the sun to his legs. He then runs to me and chases me into the water before catching me, throwing me up into the air and kissing me as I drop back into his arms. I melt inside as he tells me he loves me. We are a totally happy and loving family.

Essays are like that. You can bend the truth, can't you? In reality, dad would be there but only under sufferance and duress. He would sit on the blanket but away from mum and he would have his shoes and socks on and his cap on his head rather than a sunhat.

He would wear a white shirt with black elasticated bands around his arms to keep the cuffs off his hands. He started to do this in his shop to keep his cuffs clean. Sunglasses would be far too daring and, as for me, I would play alone, wanting and wishing for him to chase me into the water and catch me and tell me he loved me but that was always a vain hope. A mere pipe dream. In no way would it ever happen. He'd rather have cup of tea from his flask.

Miss walks light-footedly around the room with her hands behind her back. She's a tall slim lady with a long blue skirt and has her long fair hair tied into a bun. She stops at my side and reads my essay intently.

"That's good Vera," she tells me. "I can see you've got a lovely family."

She doesn't sound convincing in her words and I just nod. I can't tell her the truth that everything is just the opposite, can I?

See. You can write anything and people believe you.

At lunchtime Kathy teases me lightly over what Sam Hodges had said earlier about me fancying Jonny and I blush immediately although I try hard not to.

"You do," she says.

I reply by telling her we all do and that seems to satisfy her.

During the afternoon, I keep looking at the big old dark brown cased clock hanging above Miss's desk. Is it still working? I stare intently but the hands don't seem to move. It had a second hand once but it fell off and was removed by the Head Master and was never replaced. It's still on the shelf above the old tortoise stove that we use in the winter. I'm lucky when the fire's lit. I sit three rows back and almost halfway between the front and the back. I keep lovely and warm whereas those at the front get roasted as the bottom of stove glows red and those at the back freeze. They can't see the redness or feel the heat. Annie Turner who sits closest to the fire actually passed out once and they had to take her outside to cool down. Then they sent her home afterwards so she tried it again three days later but Miss took her to the Head Master because she knew she was only acting. She still had colour in her cheeks whereas previously she'd turned a horrible ashen colour and was totally limp.

Time eventually comes to leave but Miss stops me as I walk by her desk. She holds my hand.

"Your essay was lovely Vera," she tells me. "I know life isn't always that rosy but you'll do well. You're a very smart young lady. Keep studying and life will come to you. You'll see. You could be a teacher like me. Or anything if you keep trying."

She smiles and let's go of my hand.

"Thank you Miss."

I smile back at her and walk off. Her comments make me feel good. People do like me and I'm beginning to really like myself.

Kathy gives me a hug at the gate, says her goodbyes and walks off home and I eagerly start pacing towards Jonny's house, wondering how he is. I'm still smiling about his condition and how he came to be like it. It is typical of him. His family don't get much and when they do it is all too easy to overindulge. A huge grin comes to my face as I remember his toilet is still way down at the bottom of his long garden. It's a long way to run when you're in a hurry and in need. It must be a cold place in the winter with its door that doesn't really fit too well and is almost off its hinges. Kathy went round there once and she says they have squares of paper cut up and hanging on a piece of string. Newspaper and even paper bags. She said she used a bag from the cake shop but they can't really afford cakes. They can't even afford proper toilet paper. We can. My dad buys it in bulk from the wholesalers. Mind you, it is only that slippery stuff. Seems almost like tracing paper. We either get Izal or Bronco Brand. They're both the same really. Slippery and horrible. And they block the toilet. Dad complains when that happens but he still keeps bringing it home but only because it's cheap. He makes money easily enough but he finds it harder to spend it than make it. We do have a lovely big house for just us three and we do have our car but spending on trivial things seems against the law. The law according to dad that is. It's frowned upon just the same as smiling is. Mind you, mum does smile when he's not around. We do have some good times sometimes, mum and me, when we're alone.

I come out of my thinking and catch a glimpse of Jonny peering out of a bedroom window. It's him but all I can really see is a mop of thick, springy brown hair. He hasn't combed it at all today. That's obvious. He disappears and meets me at the door and I mention it straight away.

"Look at the state of your hair Jonny Clitheroe," I say, automatically reaching up to run my fingers through it as if they were a comb.

"I haven't combed it today V."

That letter again.

He laughs and bends forward.

"That's nice."

I'm innocent of what I'm doing and don't realise just how much he's enjoying it. I stop eventually.

"You better?"

"Better now I've seen you V."

I blush again.

"I like it when you blush," Jonny says. "You look really cute."

I blush some more. He does really like me.

"I like you V," he tells me, with a face that could melt a whole series of icebergs. "Do you want to come in for a while?"

Quickly my brain is naturally on guard. I want to. Of course I want to. I want to but I'm nervous. Not nervous of Jonny at all but nervous of what I should and should not be doing. At that stage I knew I should not be doing anything. I was only thirteen, nearly fourteen.

"I…I can't Jonny. Got to get home. Mum's waiting."

Mum's not waiting. She's out and I know I'll be going home to an empty house with the key hidden on a ledge at the side of the porch. She's out three days in the week. Once on a Tuesday, visiting her mother, my nan, once on a Thursday when it's 'her day' and she goes out with a friend or two or three and the other day is Fridays when she helps dad in the shop because it's a busy day. I don't mind. I quite love the house to myself for an hour or so. I have freedom. Freedom to do what I want without my parents interrupting and asking why.

Jonny doesn't know when mum is out though and just suggests I go into his another time and I readily agree. I want to now but I'm nervous. I look at his handsome and rugged face and want to kiss it but I'm far too nervous for that. I do really really want to though.

I look into his eyes and melt once more before turning for home. He calls me.

"See you tomorrow V! I think I'll have stopped running down the garden by then! I do hope so. We're getting short of newspaper."

I look back at him and laugh. I'd bring him a roll of Izal but I know dad would miss it. He counts everything.

As I walk I feel so happy that I feel like skipping but I'm too old for that, aren't I? I almost float along the pavement though and hold my head high as if I was a lady. I do feel like one. Again, life is changing and life is great.

Being taller now, I can quite easily reach the ledge on the side of the porch where the front door key is kept. It's not really a ledge but just where a brick has somehow gone missing. How that happened I don't know. Dad could put it back but he says it's the ideal place to hide a key. I think we could actually leave it in the door round here though. I've never heard of a burglary taking place. Old Mr Roberts next door did say once he had a pint of milk stolen but that was in 1943 when there was a war on and they were short of everything. He said he knew people were short but that day he was short, short of milk.

The lock of the door is a bit stiff but it turns with a grind of metal against metal and a snap as it frees and the door opens to a tiled floor of creams and reds and browns. The inner door is closed but I can still smell the freshness of polish from inside the house. Mum is always proud of her home. She says you never know who's going to call and you always want them to feel welcome when they do. She's right course. Not even King George would feel uncomfortable in our house.

My shoes are left in the hall and I go straight up to my room, dropping my bag on the floor just inside the door by my chest of drawers. The sun is shining brightly through my window and I lay in its rays on my bed. This is my time. My time to be on my own. My time to think and my time to let my mind wander and what do I let it wander to? It has to be Jonny, doesn't it? I look up at my light and the ceiling and the crack in the ceiling and tell myself off. I'm at home on my own when I could be with Jonny. He'd invited me in. All his family were out as they all have to work and my family are out as well. We are both alone when we could be together. I realise though that I am only thirteen, nearly fourteen, and if anyone found me alone with Jonny all hell would break loose and I would be in trouble. In no way would my father stomach that kind of thing. Maybe children shouldn't be seen and not heard but they certainly should never be seen with a boy. Especially with a boy such as Jonny. He is lovely, kind, handsome and everything else but dad wouldn't see it that way. All he would see would be a boy from 'the terrace'. One whose family had no money and were, therefore, much lower than him both in status and altitude. We live up the hill and, according to my father, the further down the hill you live, the lower class you are. He's wrong of course but you try telling him that.

I'm comfortable on my bed with my thick eiderdown almost wrapping itself around me and cuddling me. I lay and think and then drift off into another world. A world of sleep. Then later, quite a bit later.

"Vera! You up there?"

"Y...Yes mum."

I eventually wake up properly to see mum has climbed the stairs and is standing at my bedroom door.

"It's an early night for you tonight Vera," she says, smiling. "Come here."

She holds out a hand but it drops as I go to take it. She's smiling broadly. Obviously dad's not home yet and obviously she has something for me. She seems excited. We go down the wide wooden stairs that are adorned with a heavy, mainly blue patterned carpet which is held in place by heavy and shiny brass stair rods.

At the bottom are two brown paper carrier bags with string handles.

"One's for you and one's for me," mum tells me. "I've been out with Beryl and Dottie and I thought I'd give us a treat but don't tell your father, will you?"

I shake my head and she hands me my bag which I start to take to the living room.

"No," mum says. "Upstairs. Let's go upstairs and look at them in case your dad comes in early."

We sit on mum's bed and I take out a flattish cardboard box which is tied loosely with a thin pink ribbon. Mum's obviously in a very good mood and I love it. I also love the dress I take from the box. It's light brown in colour with a darker hoop of brown around the arms and the bottom. The quality of it is plain to see and I fall in love with it immediately.

Without thinking I lean over to mum and throw my arms around her in a sincere, loving and thankful embrace. I kiss her on the cheek but she pushes me away. Not because she doesn't like the attention but because she feels somehow unsettled by it.

"I do love you mum."

"I know."

Instead of cuddling her, I get up and remove my dress to try on my new prized possession.

"You're growing up Vera," mum says. "You're actually starting to fill out a bit."

I look down at myself. I thought I was and hoped I was and now mum has confirmed it. I'm growing up at last. Was I still a child or was I a woman? In truth, I had to be somewhere in between.

5.

I didn't go into Jonny's then and he seemed a little sad at the fact. He didn't say so but I could see the disappointment on his face. I was young and nervous and didn't really know what going into his meant. What would have happened? I think Jonny knew. Were we going in as school friends or were we going in as boyfriend and girlfriend? We did like each other. That was plain to see but nothing else had happened then. I was only thirteen years old but I did want to be his girlfriend. It would have been something we'd have to keep secret but yes, I did want to. Two weeks would go by before anything more happened. I began to think he'd lost interest but the odd tap on my back again and him calling me V relayed the fact there was still hope. Did I need to hurry things? I felt I did. Or was I just being a girl with a crush? See, I remember all that. Remember it as plain as it was yesterday. But it wasn't yesterday was it? It was all them years ago. Back in a time when innocence mattered and a life and freedom were great resources.

Anyway, what would my dad have said? Me from up on the hill and Jonny from the terrace below? He would have been livid even if I was eighteen or nineteen, but I wasn't was I? I was thirteen, almost fourteen and had no right to any feelings whatsoever.

He did make me angry, my dad. He was so 'set in his ways' as they used to say. Dogmatic is the right word these days I think. If you were 'up the hill' you naturally looked down on those at the bottom of the hill. That was his way. I did try to ask him one day about those that lived further up the hill than we did. Were they better than us? He didn't answer, did he? He just told me to shut up. You see, I had no right to an opinion. Not about hills or about Jonny.

Oh it was funny, my Jonny and the plums. I still laugh when I think about it. Even now. He did love food. Especially fruit and just didn't know when to stop. He didn't know when to stop at anything and that would prove to be my downfall later.

My feet are totally numb today. It's the diabetes they say. That's why I can't walk now. Can't feel them. They know all about sugar levels these days but back in my day we just ate what we had and had plenty of it. I hope I'm not dying from the toes up. Today they say eat, drink and exercise but back in my day we just said eat, drink and be merry. We did but look at me now. A crippled old battle-axe.

"You're not," Norma says.

"Not what?"

"You're not an old battle-axe."

"Sorry love," I tell her. "Did I just say that last bit out loud?"

A nurse appears. The short tubby one with the brown skin and the mop of black hair. She comes over to me will her hands full of bits and bobs.

"Are you new?"

"I'm from Trinidad and Tobago Vera," she tells me. "I've been here for two weeks now haven't I?"

"Oh. You here on holiday then?" I ask her.

I know different of course but thought I'd make a joke. She doesn't get it. She doesn't even laugh when I say Trinidad and 'Lumbago'. She just wants to change my bandage. The one on my leg that I can't feel. The right one. Well, the right one as I look down. I suppose it's the left one as she looks at it. I can't feel either of them too much today, can I?

"You've got a nasty ulcer Vera," Norma says. "And Rosetta is going to clean it and put a new bandage on for you."

I know I've got an ulcer but it doesn't really bother me, does it? As I've said, I can't feel my legs too much anyway. It gets a bit uncomfortable sometimes but it never bothers me.

Rosetta is a nice name. Especially for someone from a foreign place. It wouldn't suit an English girl so well but for someone from foreign it's quite lovely.

Rosetta manoeuvres her uniform ready to squat down. Hers has a dark blue top and she wears a white upside down watch pinned to her chest and has a matching white pen in her pocket. Her teeth are lovely and white as well. They almost dazzle me every time she smiles. And she does smile a lot.

With her uniform arranged she squats down ready to change my bandage and I'm sure I hear a slight rip as a seam lets go somewhere. She sits on a small footstool which almost seems to get lost and enveloped by her larger frame. See, I said larger frame. I can be nice sometimes. I didn't say fat. I have to be nice really. They're all nice in here and they do everything for me. You can't really mock someone who wipes your bottom for you can you?

I can smell a bit of a smell as the bandage is taken off and I turn my head to my left and look out of the window. I'm glad I do because just outside it, sitting at the bottom of a big plant pot is my Robin. He's come to see me again.

"Hello sweetheart."

"Who are you talking to Vera," Rosetta the nurse asks in her Mediterranean accent. Or was it Caribbean? It's foreign anyway.

I point to the robin.

"I was talking to my Robin," I tell her.

"You like robins?"

"I do. I really do. Especially that one. He's my Robin come down to see me. He knows it wasn't my fault."

Rosetta just looks at me and shakes her head slightly. She smiles and then carries on bathing and re-bandaging my numb and ulcerated leg.

It's funny really, and the doctors say so but most people have eye trouble as well as leg trouble when they get diabetes. I've been lucky. I can't walk now but I can still see, through my glasses. Not as good as

I used to but I can see good enough for an old lady. I can see old Mrs Winthrop over there. The other side of the room. She's a really old lady. Must be a hundred and ten nearly. I'm only on numb legs but she's on her last legs. She used to be a customer in my dad's shop. Used to buy candles. Three a week to save on the electricity. She's got one of them button things you press when you need help. A buzzer. She never presses it though. Too weak you see. She hardly moves a muscle. What a life when you can't even press your own buzzer thingy. Staff have to do it for her but then it's too late. They're there to help by then anyway aren't they? Something should be done. If she was a dog you'd get done for keeping her alive. Poor old love, bless her.

What was I telling you? See my memory's gone again. Was I talking about Jonny? No. I wasn't was I? Was I? Was I talking about up and down the hill? I think that was it. Dad had his shop and was making money. He smiled when he was making money and, one day, he actually smiled indoors. Indoors! I was shocked. He'd been to see the bank manager who'd given him some advice. Dad never listened to advice normally but he did to this.

6.

Again, the sun is shining brightly as I walk home from school. We've been lucky lately with the weather. I'm wearing a short sleeve dress and a slight breeze is cooling my face and arms. Jonny is by my side. His dad is indoors. It's not his day to work so I say goodbye to Jonny at his gate and start to leave for home. Jonny has been quite quiet since I declined his offer to go in with him that day although I try hard to tell him not to worry. I still want to. I want to be alone with him.

"I will come in with you Jonny," I tell him as I begin to walk away. "I haven't upset you have I?"

Jonny smiles and lays a large hand gently on my little shoulder as I step back to him.

"I don't think you could ever upset me V," he utters, honestly and sincerely.

He looks into my eyes as he says it and I immediately melt and forget myself and stretch up slightly to kiss him on the cheek.

"Love you," I say without thinking.

Suddenly Jonny's not thinking either. Either that or he is only thinking and no longer in a real world. He's touching the cheek that I've kissed and is staring vacantly into thin air.

"B…B…Bye V," he says.

I laugh as I realise just what an effect that small peck of a kiss has had and then I blush and go quiet as well when it hits me what I've just told him. Did I actually say 'Love you'? I know I did. I'm not quite fourteen and have fallen in love. In love? Yes? It does feel real.

We just look again at each other and I leave him to go home knowing it is half day closing and both mum and dad should be at home.

As I climb the hill and reach our house, dad is getting out of the car and is carrying some papers.

"Hello Vera," he says, loudly and happily. Blimey! He's smiling! Something's happened. Has he won the football pools?

I'm stunned and even more so as he hands me the papers from his right hand and takes my left one. What's happened? My dad is smiling and is actually holding my hand. It's the first time he's done that since I was a toddler and he only did it then to stop me running away from him. It's wonderful but my head tells me straight away that there must be money involved. I'm not wrong.

Indoors he calls mum to come down and we go into the front room. Not the living room but actually into the front room; the best room of the house. These rooms are sometimes kept for visitors or Sundays and ours is as well to a certain extent but it is also where dad has his desk and keeps everything to do with his money matters. I knew that smile of his had been brought about by money. I'm only surprised that I'm invited to be in on his plans.

"I've been to see the bank manager," he tells us as we are sat down on our best sofa, an old but quality one from the nineteen thirties. It was bought new but it's years old now and is still like new as it is hardly ever used.

He repeats himself again and smiles the biggest smile I've ever seen him produce.

"I've been to see the bank manager," he continues. "And guess what? He says we've got too much money. What do you think of that?"

He looks at us both and his face is actually beaming.

"How can you have too much money?" mum asks him. "Is that possible?"

Dad smiles again.

"You can," he points out. "Mr Franklin at the bank said I've got too much money laying around that isn't doing anything for me so we've come up with a plan. A big plan."

He hesitates and mum has to ask him what the plan is. That's what he wanted. I'm still thinking about what I said to Jonny.

"What we are going to do, me and Mr Franklin," dad explains, "is we are going to, with his guidance, convert the garage at the back of the shop into a store and put a set of outside steps up to the first floor which will then become a flat that we can rent out. We'll remove the stairs inside the shop which will give us more room and put a door from inside the shop into the old garage. We'll have a bigger shop without the stairs. We'll still have a store and we'll also have a two bedroom flat above to rent out."

Mum looks very pleased with the idea and dad says he didn't know why he hadn't thought of it before. He would lose nothing but would gain everything.

"And there's more," he explains, excitedly. "There's a pair of cottages for sale in Quarry Street and I'm buying them both."

"What?" mum gasps.

"We're moving up in the world Connie," dad boasts. "I'll soon be the owner of the shop, the flat, two rented houses and this one and all paid for. Mr Franklin says house prices are set to rocket. We'll have the rents coming in and the values going up. We'll be the talk of the town and nothing could go wrong. We can all hold our heads on high and be proud."

He looks down at me and smiles again. This property thing must be good. He's smiled at least ten times in the last twenty minutes.

"And you my girl," he shocks me. "You're almost fourteen and you're going to have a party. You can have some friends around here and mum will look after you."

He wouldn't would he? He would make sure he was out. One child at a time is enough for him to handle and that one child is usually his own daughter. He always said one child. I think more would take the limelight away from him.

"Now," he says, continuing with his eleventh smile that afternoon. "You two go and let me study my figures."

Unusually, he puts an arm round mum and pulls her close to him. Then me and mum leave the room and a short while later I'm asked to go down to the shops. Mum gives me the money and tells me I can have a shilling for myself. I'm not usually asked to go shopping and find it odd but I go anyway. It's good to be out in the sunshine again. I know there's a reason I've been sent out but my mind cannot fathom what that reason is. Maybe I'll work it out one day.

I go to the shops and fill mum's basket and then, after about an hour or so, I take it back home.

"What do you think of all that Vera?" mum asks as I eventually put the basket down on the scrubbed top of our pine kitchen table. She looks rather flushed and her hair is dishevelled. The collar of her blouse is all twisted.

"You alright mum?"

She doesn't answer and, instead, carries on talking about dad and his plans.

"As dad says Vera," she points out again, "we'll be the talk of the town. What with owning this house, the two cottages and the shop with the flat above. And you having a birthday party as well? Who are you going to invite?"

I hesitate and can only think of Jonny.

"Not thinking of having boys, are you?" mum asks, reading my face and thoughts.

"Can I mum?"

"Your dad would go mad," she answers with a smile.

I can read her as well.

"But he won't be here will he?"

Mum smiles again and readily gives in with a stipulation.

"As many girls as you like but only two boys. I'll do sandwiches, cakes and jellies."

My heart races. Two boys and she thinks she's laying down the rules and the law. I'm exploding with the thought of just the one. I'm told to do a list. Mum has said as many girls as I like but then she changes her tone slightly.

"Keep it down to about a dozen Vera. We don't know what the weather will do and we can't have too many indoors all the time. And if they do we'll have to keep dad's door locked."

Dad's door is what we call the door to the best room. I'm not even normally let in there. Only when there's momentous news afoot.

I'm soon up in my room and sitting on my bed with a pencil and paper. I start my list with a J but then rub it out with the other end of my pencil and put Kathy at the top and then another nine girl friends before I put Jonny and his friend Freddie at the bottom. Freddie, Freddie Hoskins, is a year younger than us but he's lovely and Jonny really likes him. He's a smallish boy with leg problems and Jonny protects him in the playground. One of his legs is normal and the other is quite thin and weak. Most of the others like him but one or two boys do pick on him. Jonny sorts them out because he's one of the biggest boys there. I write them down but then I screw up the list. If dad saw it he too would screw it up. Screw it up and then get angry and cancel the party. Instead, I write another and leave out the boys' names. They will be coming though. Mum won't go back on her word. I can't let her.

The party is Saturday and I leave school Friday afternoon with Jonny by my side. Well, not exactly by my side as we go out of the gates but he goes first and waits just up the road for me. Little is said and I can tell he's thinking. Thinking what? That's the trouble. I can sometimes read what mum's thinking but not Jonny. Perhaps I just don't know him well enough yet. He walks just a step ahead of me and then he stops and looks all around. I follow his actions. No one is around so he takes my little hand in his huge one and suddenly, with that one small token of a notion, we are boyfriend and girlfriend. No one is watching and, to tell you the truth, I want someone to be watching. I want everyone to see. Though, in reality, I would be in trouble if anyone should see. Everyone knows my family and everyone knows me. I'm the daughter of Reginald (Reg) Hobbs the shopkeeper. The man who had always owned the hardware shop and was about to own much more.

We say nothing, me and Jonny, but walk on, clasping hands and getting closer together until a familiar rattle is heard from further up the hill. Jonny lets my hand go.

"Ernie," he says, with a grin.

Ernie is the coal man. He's in his old dark brown lorry that has seen seriously better days and it chugs around the corner and into view. He's only half loaded and is coming down hill but it seems the lorry is still gasping for oxygen. On the side, in gold, is written 'Ernie Elsethwaite, Cool Merchant'. The word 'Coal' had been spelled wrong and all Ernie had ever done was use chalk to try and turn the second o into an a. It washed off. Why hadn't he thought to paint it? Why hadn't he taken it back to the sign writers? Jonny explained that the old sign writer had died before Ernie had noticed. The best thing was it had been spelled correctly on the other side.

With Ernie chugging past and gradually trundling out of sight but not earshot, we reach Jonny's house. No one is in but the door is unlocked. They never locked it because, as Jonny's mum would say, 'they had nothing worth stealing'.

Jonny opens the door with his free hand and keeps hold of mine with the other. This time I'm not asked if I want to go in. I'm led in and the door is closed. I'm nervous but excited at the same time. He eases me backwards so that my back is against the wall and my head taps gently against a black framed dull picture of an old lady dressed in Victorian clothes. I look up and feel she is watching me. Let her watch. Jonny smiles.

"The other day," he smiles again.

"Yes?"

He colours up slightly.

"What did you say?"

I know what I said and when I said it but, as a tease, I make him squirm.

"I said a lot of things Jonny."

He knows I'm teasing so I reach up and plant my arms around his neck and pull him down to me. It's quite a long way.

I pull his lips to my lips and we kiss passionately. It's my first ever real and passionate kiss and I feel a crescendo of fireworks going off in my head. He puts his hands on my waist and pulls me close to him.

"I said I love you," I tell him, in answer to his question as our lips finally part.

"Love you too V," he replies with a bit of a struggle.

He then pulls me to him again and I almost feel he's going to crush me but I'll suffer it. I can feel my body tightly against his and… and, bloody hell! I can feel my chest against him and that's not all. I can feel something else. I've got breasts!

We eventually part and just stare into each other's eyes before the moment overwhelms us. A great milestone has been passed and our emotions turn into laughter but where do we go next? What do we do next. I fluster.

"I'd better get home," I say, without thinking. "Mum's…"

"Mum's not in," Jonny replies. "Not today. It's Friday and she's in the shop with your dad."

I've been found out and look to the floor but Jonny lifts up my chin.

"You go," he says, as gently as only Jonny could. "I'll see you at the party tomorrow."

I nod and kiss him again.

"Just make sure you don't come in if my dad's car is there."

"I won't."

I tap my head on the old lady's picture again as I turn to open the door. In no way do I want to leave but I feel I should. We've just taken a huge step and Jonny realises that he mustn't be too hasty in overstepping that mark. He truly is a gentleman, even at the age of fourteen. He's a gentleman that all the girls like or love. He's a gentleman and yet now, he's my gentleman. I give in to my desires and, this time, skip towards the hill and home but am stopped by a sudden and almost deathly thud ahead and to my right. We have a run-down and now abandoned shop just past the terrace and a bird has flown into the window. It's laying helpless and almost motionless on the ground. I hurry to it and pick it up. It looks at me and is rapidly gasping for breath the poor little thing. It's a robin that just didn't see the glass in the window. It looks at me and seems to know I'm not going to harm it. Or am I reading too much into its feelings? My cradling does seem to be helping though and it gradually settles and its breathing becomes slower and more relaxed and steady. I wonder what it's thinking as I raise it to my lips and kiss it gently before opening my hand expecting it to fly away. It does but not straight away. It lays there, still composing itself and then it turns over slightly and manages to stand giddily on its feet before looking at me and giving its whole body a shake. It then looks at me again before fluttering off gently into a nearby bush. I'd held a robin and saved its life, probably.

The next morning, Dad's smile has all but gone but he is still talking about his plans. Mum comes down for breakfast and looks flushed again. Perhaps she's not too well. She's been in the bath and has done her hair but she doesn't look right. Dad does. He's strutting proudly around like a cockerel in a farmyard with his head held high. The world seems right enough with him. He's like a cat that's found three pots of cream. Well, that's what my nan says when someone's as happy as him. He's happy but he's not going out of his way to be happy with me. I did love it when he held my hand the other day but that was only because he had some really good news. He did it because he was overjoyed with the world at that moment. He didn't do it for me, did he? I do wish he did. Then I suddenly realise he shouldn't be there.

"Shouldn't you be at the shop dad?"

"Harry's opening up," he tells me. "I'm going to the builder's yard to see their boss about converting the upstairs. Need to get some prices in and see which is best. It's all exciting Vera. Got to get plumbing up there somehow."

I'm hugely excited as well but for a different reason. He's thinking about pipes and grips while I'm only thinking about Jonny and his lips. The party is this afternoon.

Then dad surprises me. He actually kisses mum goodbye. Don't get me wrong. It's lovely to see but it happens so rarely that it comes as a shock. Money must be in the air still.

"See you later," he tells her. "I won't be home until seven. I'm having a drink, down at The Grapes with Arthur and Henry Miller.

This, I suppose, is to serve two purposes. One, the Miller brothers own the bakery and dad could tell them all about his plans and two, it means he won't have to come home until my party is finished. My birthday isn't until Monday really but that's a school day and we are taking nan out tomorrow so today is the best day for a party.

"You wearing your new brown dress?" mum asks as dad leaves.

I nod because I'm eating a piece of toast again, with jam this time, and don't want to speak with my mouth full.

"Yes mum," I eventually say as a crumb drops onto the table and my mouth is finally empty.

Mum looks at the green and black clock on the windowsill above the sink. It's an alarm clock really but has been sitting there for quite a few years. Not to wake us up but to time mum's baking. She's good at baking.

"Is that the time? We'd better hurry Vera. We need to get down to the shops to get everything. I thought I'd do cheese in the sandwiches and cucumber and ham."

"And jam?"

I smile.

"No. Vera, you may like jam sandwiches but you are not having them for your birthday party. What would people think?"

I think. I'm only thirteen still, until Monday. What would people think about jam sandwiches at a party? Whatever would they think if they knew how I felt about Jonny?

"What about a birthday cake mum?"

She smiles.

"Made it in the week. And I've made a blancmange and two jellies."

I smile too.

"Jonny likes jelly."

"Jonny?"

"Yeah. You said I could invite two boys mum so I've invited Jonny and Freddie."

"Jonny Clitheroe?"

"Yes."

"But he's…"

"I know. He's from the terrace but he's a friend mum. He sits behind me in class."

"And who's Freddie?"

"You know him. Little Freddie. Freddie with the bad leg. He's alright. He lives in St Mary's Lane. That's quite posh. His father works at the hospital. Something clerical."

"Oh, that Freddie. Freddie Hoskins. His father runs the hospital's records department. He's alright but be careful with this Jonny Clitheroe boy. That family have got a reputation."

"I know mum," I tell her in quite an adult way and surprising myself. "His family have got a reputation.

Everyone knows that. They've got a reputation for being poor but that's not a crime, is it? He's a friend mum and he's lovely, honestly."

She looks at me sincerely.

"Just keep him as a friend Vera," she lectures. "And don't let your father know even that. You're a teenager and I know how teenagers think. I used to be one a long time ago."

"Yes mum."

"We'll go to the Millers," she suggests, softening her tone. "And we'll get a selection of cakes. I'm sure Jonny Clitheroe likes cakes as well."

"He does mum. He loves food."

After a walk around town and carrying a basket each we quickly visit dad's shop. Harry is busy and mum helps out for a few minutes until the queue disappears. Dad walks in as we walk out. He's full of smiles now that he's in his money-making emporium. Those smiles are the genuine ones with him. They're the ones that are being paid for.

Twelve o'clock comes and then one and then two, followed by two thirty. The party starts at three so mum tells me to go and get changed. Soon I'm standing in front of the long mirror on my wardrobe door and am admiring myself in my new dress. The light brown one with the darker hoops round the sleeves and bottom. How could I be changing so rapidly? I'm still not fat by any means and I don't wish to be but I have filled out over the last few weeks. My hips seem bigger, or wider, and the fact that my chest has developed a little thrills me immensely. I brush my hair and am well satisfied with my appearance.

"My word girl," mum says, cheerily as soon as I see her. "It's only a couple of weeks since I bought you that dress but look at you. You're a little woman."

She changes her tone slightly and it harshens just a little.

"It's now you have to be careful of boys like that Jonny Clitheroe," she warns.

"Yes mum," I say again, with a shrug.

Three o'clock comes, party starting time, and there is a knock at the door. It's Kathy. She's first to arrive but not far behind her, coming up the hill with little Freddie sitting on his shoulders is Jonny. Freddie is loving it but Jonny is glad to get to ours and let his rider dismount.

"I've bought you these V," he tells me, puffing slightly but trying hard to seem manly by not letting it show.

I shake my head in his direction.

"Jonny. It's Vera today. Remember?"

"I've bought you these Vera."

He hands me a brown paper bag which, when I open it, is full of big yellow plums. Jonny laughs.

"I was going to bring you red ones," he jokes. "But they make you run down the bottom of the garden."

Freddie hands me a small and very neatly wrapped parcel. It's covered in brown paper and is written on with a fine hand and pen.

"Thanks for inviting me Vera," he says, in his little and quite articulate voice. "I've bought you this. It's a book of poems by mixed authors. I hope you like them. I know you like poetry. I do. I've read it already."

I do love poetry and immediately bend down and give Freddie a quick peck on the cheek.

"Thanks Freddie."

Jonny looks a little downcast.

"Doesn't he get a kiss as well?" Kathy asks.

"What for? Plums?"

Jonny bends forward and I try to kiss him on the cheek but just as I do he cheekily turns his head and I catch him on the lips instead. He stands up proudly.

"Thanks V… uh Vera," he says, laughing.

Kathy and Freddie laugh too but I just worry in case my mother saw us. She hasn't though. She's busy making sure the house is perfect.

Poor old Jonny only has a small kitchen or scullery and the one sitting room. This is the first time he's been in our house and I can see that he's amazed as we walk from room to room. Firstly, the kitchen and then the main sitting room and then I point out where dad's room is before his face almost explodes as we enter our large dining room which has in it a large table that is almost completely covered in food of all kinds. Around the table are eight chairs and mum has fitted in two foldable card tables and each have two more chairs set at them.

I look at Jonny.

"I'm sitting at the head of the table," I say, pointing at name cards that mum has set out. "And you're sitting at that table there."

He looks disappointed but understands.

"You and Freddie."

"But you can eat all you want."

His face cheers again.

Everyone else seem to turn up at the same time and soon the house is thronging with teenage voices and laughter. We go out into the large back garden where mum has set out blankets on the lawn, the corners of which have been turned in by the gentle breeze. The sun is strong but it is tempered by the leaves of dad's treasured trees and bushes which provide dappled shade. Jonny peers into dad's shed through the window.

"Your dad's got an Ariel square four!" he exclaims, excitedly. "Does he like motorbikes?"

"It's been in there for years," I tell him. "Dad doesn't ride it now but he can't bear to sell it. He likes them but doesn't ride them anymore."

I always knew it was a motorbike but had no idea or interest in what make or model it was. Jonny seemed to know immediately.

"I'm going to have a motorbike when I get bigger," he tells me.

"Don't get too much bigger, will you?" I reply. "You're big enough already."

He steps closer to me and looks around the garden but everyone is watching us so he steps away again. We then walk over to the others, put the blankets together and all sit, talking and joking. Jonny is quick to find his spot and sits with his leg gently and, seemingly nonchalantly, touching mine although I do my best to ignore it. I try, but can't. Do I even really try?

Eventually mum calls.

"Come in everyone! Time to eat!"

We all go into the dining room to take our positions. We go through the door almost all at the same time and in something of a crush. I feel a large hand on my waist and don't have to guess who it belongs to but he quickly takes his seat before getting up swiftly as mum tells everyone to 'tuck in'.

With a huge plate of sandwiches, Jonny sits down at the small table he is sharing with Freddie and does exactly what mum has told us. He 'tucks in' alright but does slow down when he sees me glaring at him.

Mum leaves us to our own devices but does pop in from time to time, judging the optimum time to enter with a lit birthday cake of fourteen candles and everyone begins to sing in unison.

As we had already found in school, Jonny's voice is loud. Loud and getting deeper and, to start with, he doesn't hold back. It's almost as if everyone else is whispering but, again, I give him a glare and he quietens. He's a lump and, maybe, even something of an oaf but he's gorgeous, handsome, funny, a gentleman and he's mine.

Mum had suggested we should play games like 'pinning the tale on the donkey' or 'pass the parcel' but I'd said no. I'm growing up and don't want to play games. I'm happy with everyone being here with me so I blow out my candles, make a wish and open the presents bought for me by my friends and then we all go back out into the garden just to sit, talk and laugh until mum eventually sees me from the back door and points at her watch. She wants to make sure everyone has gone home long before dad gets here so that there is no chance of him seeing boys in his garden. We are treated to cartwheels from Kathy, Jonny standing on his head and then Freddie doing a poetry recital before I manage to usher everyone through the front door at six thirty. Even as the last person leaves, mum's already tidying away the last of the dishes. She's already tidied everything in the dining room and washed all the crockery. All she has to do is put items away in their rightful places and then the house is perfect again. Dad will never know that anything had taken place. I sit with mum in the kitchen. It had been my birthday party and everything had been just right. What wouldn't I have given for a few minutes alone with Jonny though?

Mum surprises me.

"He's quite funny that Jonny Clitheroe," she says.

"That's why he's a friend mum."

She turns stern and serious.

"I can see you like him but you just make sure he stays just a friend my girl," she warns again.

My party is over and life returns to normal. I know mum does mean well. She is concerned for me but she is mainly worried about what dad would say. She has always been mum and dad has always been dad but I'm changing. I'm growing up and can see that she would live a far more light-hearted and free lifestyle if she wasn't with him. Her life revolves around him and she is always subject to his dogma and direction. I'm only a teenager but I can see that.

7.

He held my hand that day on the way home from school and then we were together. It was that simple. I was only young. Nearly fourteen was no real age to have a boyfriend. Not in those days anyway. It just wasn't done, was it? I know they do these days but these are different times. Times were harsh then. There'd been a war on you know. Anything goes today. Nobody seems to judge anything now and it all happens, anything happens, but back in the days of me and Jonny, everybody judged everybody, every time and for everything. Or was it judging as such? It wasn't really judging. Not totally. I think a lot of it was worrying about what other people thought. My parents certainly wouldn't have understood. My father never understood anything. As I think I've said already, if it was just one degree off what he thought then it was wrong. Wrong and that was that. He wouldn't or even couldn't contemplate anyone having even slightly different thoughts to him. He did understand money though. He was good at understanding money.

He had done well for himself. I have to admit that. What with owning and running the hardware shop in town. He was quite well respected for that. And even more so with his new money making ideas of the flat and the houses. We were to be the 'talk of the town' he said. That's what he said anyway. And we were soon to be the talk of the town for a long while but not for reasons he relished.

We lived in a large Edwardian house in a posh street and Jonny lived further down, towards the school. He lived in a small cottage with his mum and dad and two brothers. It's strange really. I never had any brothers or sisters and yet we lived in a big house with four bedrooms and yet poor old Jonny lived in a little cottage with his big family. He had to share his bedroom with his two brothers. One in bed with him and another in a single bed up the corner by the piece of wallpaper that was always hanging off and flapping. Why they never stuck it back on again I don't know but there it was, always hanging and flapping in the wind when the window was open. There was always quite a draught even when the windows were closed because, really, the houses were falling down.

You see, I know all about Jonny's bedroom. It was the bedroom for all the brothers, Jimmy, Jonny and Joe, but we did find times when we could be in there, alone. They all worked, you see.

Hang on, he's tapping on the window again. He's going now and he's saying goodbye. I can't hear what he's saying but he's waving as well.

"Goodbye Albert. See you tomorrow."

Robin is staying. He's still looking for food. Titbits that Albert has left lying around. He's found a caterpillar or something. I think it's a caterpillar or maybe it's a grub that lives in the ground. There it goes. He's swallowed it now. Down it slid. He enjoyed that. You need all the goodness you can get when you're a Robin. Enjoy my little man.

Jonny and his bedroom. That's it. That's what I was talking about wasn't I? His brothers were older and both had jobs. He was the youngest by five years. They said he was a mistake but I didn't understand that until much later. How could such a lovely boy be a mistake? I did ask my mother about it but she just told me to be quiet and not talk about such things. I didn't understand then. I do now. I found out. I found out, didn't I?

In school I used to sit at the other side of the classroom to Jonny because they had boys on the left side and girls on the right in those days but Miss, our teacher, came in and she had different ideas. One day she said we could sit where we liked so Jonny sat behind me. He couldn't sit with me because that was always Kathy's place. Do boys sit with boys and girls with girls these days? I don't know. Everything's changed. The whole world has changed. Some say for the worse but I don't know. At least children are taught these days to understand. Are they loved like they should be today?

I used to sit and sometimes turn round to look at Jonny and then he'd look back and sometimes he'd blow me a quick kiss. He was a boy, a big and handsome boy, and yet he'd sit in class and blow me a kiss. It felt wonderful and, one day he did it and I mouthed the words 'I love you' back to him. He just smiled a huge and beautiful smile, directed into my eyes. Little Sam Hodges stuck up his hand enthusiastically and shouted to Miss again that me and Jonny fancied each other. She just told him to be quiet and I looked at her and smiled in appreciation.

There's this girl who comes in here now. Young girl she is. Young, slim and quite pretty. Long straight blonde hair tied at the back with a black elastic thing. Always wears tight black trousers. Nice figure. She says she wants to be an actor and comes in to entertain us. I suppose she's using us old codgers to practice on. Anyway, how can she want to be an actor? Surely girls become actresses, not actors? I suppose that's changed as well now. Everything's changed. Even old Cuthbert Grimwade, him from what they call the East Wing. That's the posh part with the bigger rooms and their own showers. He's changed. He's changed his wig. I'm sure he has. The one he had on yesterday was more ginger.

My arm is aching. Oh! Let me move it a bit.

Sorry. Forgot what I was talking about. It was the girl who wanted to become an actor instead of an actress wasn't it? She comes here to entertain us. Yesterday she stood there in her tight trousers and hair tied back and said we were going to do memory games. I told her she was lucky I'd remembered to turn up. I hadn't remembered had I? I'd been stuck in this chair all day.

"I'm going to give you a subject," the girl started. "And I'm going to give you a letter and then you've got to give me something that begins with that letter.

Like if I was to say town and the letter B you might say?"

No reply.

"You might say Birmingham or Bristol."

"But you said town," someone piped up. "Birmingham's a city."

"And so is Bristol," someone else pointed out.

I think she underestimated old peoples' intelligence.

She thought again.

"Plants," she said. "What about plants that begin with B?"

This started them off alright and we soon had Begonias, Bluebells, Buttercups and Bananas.

"And L?"

"Lupins, Lettuces, Leeks and Lemons."

"And P?"

"Primoroses, Pears, Potatoes and Petunias."

"And Q?"

She thought she was being clever and had stumped us with that one. She'd had it planned you see. Nobody could think of an answer and everything went quiet. I had an answer but it wasn't the one she was expecting. I let them all think and then I told her.

"Q-cumber!" I suddenly said, loudly.

The girl didn't know whether to laugh or not but old Mrs Williams over there did. She was about to take a drink of tea and laughed so much that her top set of teeth fell out and splashed into her cup and the tea went everywhere. It wasn't hot. It was cold because it always takes her an hour to drink it. They had to get the girls to come and clean her up. You have to have a laugh in here otherwise we'd all go mad.

And that wasn't all. Old Tom finished it off when the girl asked us to name a flower beginning with S. Oh he was quick.

"How about self raising Miss!" he shouted.

And poor old Mrs Williams had only just got her teeth back in as well.

I didn't think the girl would be coming back in again but she did take it well and actually came back the next day. This time though, we played bingo. This was a lot better for the girl but old Tom did insist that number 82 was one fat lady and a duck.

I don't want to be in here but I know I have to be. I couldn't manage at home, could I? Not with my legs and aches and pains and my… you know. That thing I forget with. My memory.

My party was on a Saturday but my birthday wasn't until the following Monday. I remember that. I opened my presents with mum. Dad was at work in the shop and he wouldn't have been interested anyway. He certainly would have been embarrassed if he saw what was inside one of the parcels. I had opened one which had a nice dark wooden jewellery box in it. I later kept a picture of Jonny in the bottom of that. It was a school one. Then there was a lovely pen and pencil set and Mum gave me a five pound note but my best present was a small parcel that had clothing in it. It was special clothing. There were two of them. Two bras! One white and one pink. I was amazed. I loved those times but those times would change all too soon. We would all change and life would change too. Things would never be the same again.

Everyone else would say I was too young to fall in love and they would all say I was being stupid but I really did love him and that love naturally moved on. My Jonny was a gentleman, even at his age. And when I say things moved on I must say they only moved on at my pace. Not once did Jonny rush me or push me into anything. To tell you the truth I didn't know what there was for him to push me into. He was a darling, bless him.

Yes. Jonny's bedroom. It took time but I did get there. Or did he get me there? I don't know. As I've already said, he never rushed me but, on the other hand, I had no objections anyway. I was so naive though. It all made perfect and simple sense after a while but, honestly, I had no idea then. No idea of what we were doing and no idea whatsoever what the consequences of our actions would be.

8.

On a Saturday I usually go out with Kathy and one or two of our friends but today I'm staying indoors. Dad's going to the shop but mum is in bed. Dad has asked me to look after her as she has a chest infection and has spent the last two days in bed really ill. She's there now but says she will try and get up later. It's been very showery outside but the sun is shining again and perhaps I can put a chair outside for her and a blanket for her knees. It will do her good.

"Bye dad!"

He doesn't answer because he's in a terrible mood. Everything is ok with the flat above the shop and the buying of the cottages is going through but it's all taking time and he's getting frustrated. Last night he hardly said a word apart from a grunt of, 'look after your mother tomorrow' and he just quickly gulped his food down and then disappeared into his room. It was food that I'd cooked for him. Some appreciation would have been nice.

I was hoping to 'accidentally' bump into Jonny in town but not today. Not now. I'll try and see him tomorrow, although contacting him isn't easy. It's alright with Kathy as she has a telephone but no one in Jonny's position has one. The only way I can talk to him is by knocking on his door but even that raises suspicions. I thought to ring Kathy and tell her to tell Jonny why I wasn't there but then that would give the game away. She knows me and Jonny like each other but anything above that has to be kept between the two of us. I can't let anything get back to my mum and dad. Especially dad. He's in a bad enough mood as it is.

"Vera love!"

A call followed by a loud and rasping cough.

"Coming mum!"

She is lying in bed but with the covers half pulled back from her. The fan light window is open but the room seems terribly stuffy. Maybe it's me but I can almost smell illness. She looks washed out, bless her. Her face is almost as pale as her bedsheets and pillowcases and her hair is moistened with sweat. She looks a sad figure as she tries to speak to me but has to raise a handkerchief to her mouth and give out another large but painful cough instead.

"Can I open the big window for you mum? You look like you need some fresh air."

"No thanks Vera."

"You need something. You look…"

"Dreadful?"

"Well, yes."

"What I need is to get up. I need a bath and I need to get dressed and I do need to get some fresh air. Outside."

"Are you sure?"

She nods.

"Do me a bath love."

She isn't well but she is doing her best to fight it so I immediately do as she says. I'm almost lost in my own world with the hot tap running and gurgling as she walks in the bathroom behind me and makes me jump. I laugh.

"You made me jump mum."

Mum laughs as well but it makes her cough a little again.

"You nearly jumped out of your skin," she says, coughing yet again. "There's only you and me in the house. Who else did you think it was?"

I turn off the hot tap, test the temperature of the water with my hand, run a little more cold and then get up to leave. Then I ask mum if she will be alright on her own but, of course, the answer is yes, she will be. In no way would she have me in there with her when she took off her nightie. Nudity is a strict taboo. Wouldn't it have been a treat for her to have had her back scrubbed?

Outside the closed door I hear her sink into the welcoming water and sigh a huge sigh as it takes away some of her symptoms. The steamy atmosphere in the room is doing her good as well. I leave her and go downstairs.

"Call me if you need anything mum!"

"Thanks love."

Another slight cough.

I skip down the stairs and just as I reach the front door there is a knock. A deep thud from the well-polished brass door knocker. I go to it. It's the coal man, Ernie Elsethwaite.

"Mornin' Vera," he says, automatically holding out his blackened hand for money. "I've put it round the back as usual. Five bags. Stocking up for the winter?"

Dad has left the exact money on the table by the coat hooks so I give it to Mr Elsethwaite and for the first time I really look at him. He's in his fifties and is only slightly larger than me and yet he carries hundredweight bags of coal around all day. There's not an ounce of fat on him, bless him.

"Thanks Vera. I hear your dad is branching out. Good luck to him I say. A lovely man. You're lucky to have a father like him."

He doesn't know dad too well. Or perhaps he does. He just doesn't have to live with him. He walks off to the road and to his old brown truck with 'cool man' written on the side. He's tried to change it with chalk again. Why doesn't he just have it repainted? Perhaps he just does it like that because he knows everyone likes it and has a laugh about it. I don't know.

The truck is started with a louder cough than even mum can muster and it grinds and groans as it moves away. Then, as it disappears from view, I see a figure. It's Jonny. He's been standing just around the corner, waiting for Ernie to leave.

"V!"

He tries to shout to me but doesn't want to shout too loud in case someone hears him. I want to talk to him but I'm not alone. Then I remember mum is in the bath so I look up the stairs and then go outside, beckoning for Jonny to come down the drive. He thinks I'm going to him but, instead, I go round the corner of the house on the path which leads to the back garden and I wait for him beneath one of dad's favourite trees. He's with me within a few seconds and I'm taken into his large arms without a word being spoken. Our lips meet but not in the tender way we are used to. There seems a frantic urgency in Jonny's actions and I love it. With one swift and easy movement, he lifts me off my feet and kisses me so passionately that I seem to almost lose the ability to breath.

"I needed that V," he says, panting as he eventually puts me down.

I look into his eyes and laugh.

"I think you did," I reply, straightening my dress and getting my own breath back.

We both laugh.

"Tomorrow," Jonny says. "I'm on my own. They're all going out. Mum and dad are going on a church outing and the others are going swimming down the river. Will you come round? Half past two? They'll all be gone by then."

Again, I look up to where mum is and I think. She is getting better and dad will be home. Surely I can go out?

I nod.

"I'll be there Jonny."

A faint voice comes from upstairs.

"Vera!"

Mum's calling.

"Got to go Jonny," I tell him. "I'm looking after mum. She hasn't been well."

"I know. Kathy just told me."

He holds me again and again he plants his lips against mine. Far more tenderly this time.

"See you tomorrow sweetheart," he says as he turns to leave.

"Am I?"

"Are you what?"

"Your sweetheart? Am I really?"

He shakes his head and turns back to me. Another slight kiss.

"Of course you are V," he says. "You are now and you always will be. See you tomorrow, sweetheart."

"Tomorrow."

At the gate, he hesitates and looks around as if he's a fugitive on the loose, avoiding being captured by the police. A wave and then he disappears to freedom.

"Vera love!"

Mum is at the top of the stairs, wearing her dressing gown.

"Can you put me a chair in the garden love? And a blanket for my knees. I do need some fresh air."

"It's a lovely day mum. It will do you the world of good."

"One of the best ones from dad's shed."

"Yes mum."

She turns for the bedroom to get dressed but then asks who was at the door.

"The coal man, mum. Ernie."

"Mr Elsethwaite to you. Did you give him his money?"

"Yes mum."

"Thanks."

She goes to the bedroom and I look at myself in the hall mirror. I'm shocked at just how flushed I look and then I think back. This is just what mum looked like that day when dad told us about his new plans and after they'd sent me down town. Had they been kissing? My mum and dad?

At suppertime mum looks better and isn't coughing half as much. The evening has turned quite cool considering the hotness of the day and I go and make us each a mug of hot chocolate which mum takes with relish. She holds it to her face and breathes in its steam and fragrance.

"This is what I need Vera," she says with gratitude in her voice.

Dad's in his room. It's Saturday evening and he's like 'the king in the counting house. Counting out his money'. He is calmer tonight but certainly is not cheerful. I think to Kathy's dad again. He would be in their sitting room with the family, doing his best to entertain everyone with a laugh and a joke. I do wish my dad was like that. He's stubborn, dogmatic and downright moody but I do love him in my way. Every girl needs a dad and I'm lucky. Some lost their dads in the war but I still have mine. It's just a shame he's not more loving. I would really like that.

"You do make good chocolate Vera," mum says as she nears the bottom of her mug and swills it around gently to make sure she mixes all the bottom dregs in with her drink so as not to miss anything.

"Can I get you anything else mum?"

"You're alright."

"But you would like something else, wouldn't you? I can see it written all over your face."

"You've been brilliant with me today love," she says. "And I don't want you to be my slave."

"But?"

She smiles a big smile that would not have been possible yesterday.

"Have we got any crumpets?"

"Of course we have. Plenty of butter and a little jam?"

Mum nods again sweetly.

"You look so much better mum."

"Thanks love."

I don't like it when dad disappears into his own room and deserts us but, then again, that's the time when mum is mum and we seem to become close. When dad is around, mum becomes seemingly automatically distanced from me. All her attentions have to be towards him and she feels she has to share his attitude towards me and take his side. It's self-preservation I suppose. She doesn't mean to and probably doesn't even realise she's doing it but I do like our times together, when there is just the two of us.

Bedtime comes without seeing my dad at all. I walk past his door and think to knock and go in to say goodnight but then change my mind. He hasn't bothered to come out so why should I bother to go in? Neither mum or me have seen him all evening so let him stay there and be miserable.

Sleep seems hard to find and I'm not surprised as my head is only filled with the thought of being with Jonny tomorrow. We'll be alone. I'll tell mum and dad I'm just popping out with my friends after dinner. They won't mind. It's what I do most weekends.

Sunday comes and I'm so excited. Too excited to have any kind of appetite.

"Eat up Vera," mum says as she sees me picking at my food with little enthusiasm. "You're not coming down with what I've had are you?"

I'm not ill but can't eat. It's excitement mixed with a little nervousness but I can't tell mum that. She seems so much better today and has managed, with a lot of help from me, to cook roast beef, roast potatoes and vegetables. Dad's not in his room today. He does like his Sunday roast and sometimes, just sometimes, he even wears a smile when he's eating it.

"Why don't we all go for a walk this afternoon?" he says, quite cheerfully.

My heart sinks but then, without realising it, mum comes to the rescue.

"Vera's meeting her friends Reg," she tells him.

I expect him to say I can't go and must go with them but then he surprises me. He can occasionally. Just occasionally.

"Then it's just you and me mother," he says. "We'll go up church lane. I'll drive us to the bottom of it so you don't have to walk too far. The fresh air will do you good."

He looks at me, smiling almost naturally. Should I pay him for that smile? Most people have to.

"That's where your mother and me did our courting," he says. "Plenty of haystacks up there."

Mum looks at him with a false stern look on her face.

"Reg! Not in front of Vera."

He's unusually cheery. 'Chipper' my nan would call it. But, then again, he is eating his Sunday roast and drinking beer. At least that makes him happy. It's good to see something can, other than money.

They leave at just after two o'clock.

"Put the key on the ledge Vera!"

"I will."

I want to run down to Jonny's house but we did say two thirty. If I go now, then someone might still be at home. Got to wait so I finish putting away the dinner things that mum has washed up and then stand and take a good look in my bedroom mirror. I am changing and, once again, I do like what I see. It isn't a child that looks back at me anymore. It's a proper teenager. A teenager that is going to see the boy that calls her 'V', his sweetheart. He had been a little rough the day before with his passionate kissing and I can only hope for more of the same today. I did like it. People get together, people marry and people talk but nobody seems to demonstrate any passion. I've never seen it apart from in the cinema when the characters kiss and cuddle, but I always thought that only happened in the films. They're not real life, are they?

It's twenty seven minutes past two and I can wait no longer. The door locks with a grind and a clunk and I reach up slightly to place the key on the ledge. Last night was quite cool and it is still cool today. Clouds cover much of the sky with light ones above and wispy darker ones skimming by beneath. It looks like we are about to have showers. The blossom on the cherry trees has long since disappeared and the trees are now adorned with fruits that are not quite full sized yet but are already showing a blush of colour which indicates they will soon be ready to eat. Ready to be eaten by Jonny and his brothers that is. It's their street and they are always first there. I see a face at the upstairs window. Jonny's waving. It's ok. Everyone must be out.

The door is opened as I approach and is quickly closed behind me as I enter.

"They've all gone," Jonny assures me.

The old lady in the picture in his hallway is still looking at me somewhat disapprovingly but we ignore her and head for the stairs.

"Mind the bannister," Jonny warns me. "It's a bit loose."

I hold it gently as we climb, me behind Jonny, and find out it isn't 'a bit loose'. It's virtually falling off.

"Mum and dad have the bedroom at the back," Jonny tells me. "Me and my brothers have the front one because it's bigger. We can get the two beds in there. We're a bit cramped for space."

At the top of the stairs we turn right and Jonny holds my hand to lead me into his room.

"Me and Joe sleep in the big bed," he explains, pointing. "And Jimmy sleeps in that bed there."

The room is shared by three big brothers and is not as big as the one I have on my own. We even have two spare rooms when Jonny doesn't even have a bathroom.

I look around and, although the furnishings are sparse and old, everything is clean. Impeccably clean. There are the two beds, one large wardrobe and an old Edwardian style dressing table which has a mirror that's somehow crazed and it is difficult to see anything in it. Perhaps that's why Jonny's hair is always a mess. On the dressing table is a large white jug and bowl set.

The floor is just bare boards and they are only slightly covered by a rag rug which is made out of pieces of old cloths and rags. It's handmade and homemade but the colours are bright and vibrant and, like everything else, it is spotless.

The curtains are a cream colour but have been thinned with age and wear and, although partially drawn, they don't block out too much light. It is a simple room but seems to draw me in with its comfort and warmth and welcome. I smile as I notice a flap of wallpaper that has come off by the window and is hanging and moving with the breeze from outside. Judging by the colour of it, it has been hanging doggedly there for some time when fixing it would have been so simple. Still, you can see Jonny's mum looks after her side of the chores even if the man's work isn't so well maintained.

"You need to get that wallpaper fixed," I tell him. "How long has it been like that?"

Jonny has shown me which bed is his so I naturally go over to it and sit on it before removing my shoes and laying down. Jonny stands quietly for a few seconds and then speaks.

"I love you V," he says again, openly and totally unashamedly.

I pat the heavy dark green quilted bedspread beside me as an indication that he should join me. He does so readily and takes me in his arms.

"I love you too Jonny Clitheroe," I tell him back as he draws me to him.

We kiss. Not a passionate or rough kiss, the kind we had yesterday, but gentle, long and loving. One that ends in quietness as we just lay in each other's arms, happy and totally contented as the sun begins to shine brightly through the small window. As it does so, Jonny sits up.

"I'm hot," he says, unbuttoning his shirt and taking it off before letting it drop onto the floor.

I'd seen many men on the beach without shirts on so why is it so different seeing Jonny in the same state? I've looked at men on the beach and nothing has happened but as I look at Jonny my whole insides seem to quake and I want to touch him. He lays back down with me and I do touch him. We hold each other again and my hands are on his bare flesh. It's wonderful. I feel I want to undress as well but something in my head blocks it. Would it be so wrong? I don't know if it would be wrong or right but Jonny doesn't push the issue. We just lay together, kissing, touching and enjoying each other's company and the love that was developed between us.

I tell him about dad's plans and he tells me about his dad's illnesses. I tell him about dad's car and he tells me about his dad's bicycle. I also tell him about my birthday presents but omit telling him about my first bras that mum bought for me. We talk and talk. We talk about everything and we talk about nothing.

"Mum and dad have gone for a walk up church lane," I tell him. "It's where they used to do their courting. Dad says there's haystacks up there."

Jonny smiles broadly and tickles my belly.

"Then that's where we should go," he says, grinning cheekily and running his finger through my brown hair. "We'll go the next time your mum's out when we come out of school. Then she won't know, will she?"

"But what if people see us?"

"I'll go first and then you follow. We'll meet on the haystack by the second barn. The one on the corner."

I smile back.

"I'd like that."

In tickling me, Jonny has made my dress rise up and he looks at my legs which are almost totally exposed.

"I like your legs V," he says.

"They're skinny."

"Not they're not. They're lovely."

"You're easily pleased you are, Jonny Clitheroe."

"Oh no I'm not."

He looks again at my legs and I slide my dress even higher. He lays a hand on my leg but goes no further.

"I do love you," he tells me again, kissing me tenderly on the neck. "I really do."

"I know."

9.

"You need to get that piece of wallpaper fixed," I told him. "How long has it been like that?"

He didn't answer, did he? He wasn't interested in a scrap of wallpaper, was he? He was interested in me. Being with me. Me, Vera Hobbs, who was just fourteen years old but who already loved him dearly. I still do. Even today, wherever he is.

I know I've said it before but he was such a gentleman. I remember saying that. I knew nothing then but he did. Well I think he did. He must have done. There I was, laying on his bed, on that green quilt, with my legs all uncovered and my knickers showing and all he did was put his hand on my leg. I knew nothing then about going any further but if he had I wouldn't have stopped him. No way would I have stopped him. And that chest of his when he took his shirt off. My word. I felt all funny inside and didn't understand it. I do now. Oh he was a handsome lad. He was handsome, he had no top on and he was all mine. Do you know, I'm eighty now and can't ever remember what I had for dinner, unless it's sprouts, but I can remember every bit of what we did together all those years ago. I was fourteen then so it had to be around 1950. 1952? Good days they were. I loved it then and I certainly loved Jonny. My Jonny. Jonny Clitheroe from the terrace.

The other morning. I remember this. My doctor came to see me.

"He's not your doctor Vera," old Mabel who always sat over there said, in her poshest voice. "He's your GP."

"I don't care what he's called," I told her. "As long as he's got warm hands this time. He examined me the last time he was here and I nearly died of frostbite."

He came to see me to see if I was over the flu. I was, so why did he have to know? What difference did it make to him? He got his stithy… his stethy… that thing he listens with and said he was going to warm it up and then examine my chest.

I was in a very naughty mood for some reason and I told him he wouldn't be able to examine all of my chest because a lot of it was tucked into my knickers. I laughed but he didn't. He had one of them turban things on and I don't think it appealed to his particular sense of humour. People are different to each other and we all laugh at different things. He didn't laugh at me. Not him.

"That wasn't funny Vera," old Mabel said, harshly.

I had to admit she was right but I couldn't just leave it at that. Not me and not on that day. I told her it may not have been funny but it was true. I told her she wouldn't know what it's like as she was so skinny and flat-chested she looked like a zip when she turned sideways. I was like that once, skinny, but it really did surprise me how quickly things changed, growing up was a wonderful time.

Jonny laid on his bed, the one he shared with his brother, and he held me. Gentle he was. Always gentle. He never pushed me.

Do you know? I was naughty with old Mabel wasn't I? I shouldn't have been, should I? It wasn't really like me. I was unusually moody that day. Sometimes my naughty sense of humour does get out of hand. It does that to you in here. One day's the same as the next and Sunday might be Tuesday for all we know. She died the next day, Mabel. It wasn't my fault, was it? Poor little Robin wasn't my fault either but I do still worry about it even after all these years. He would probably have been retired now had he lived. Fancy that.

A lot of people die in here. I suppose that's why we come in. We don't seem to get released again. It's a one-way ticket when you come through that big front door. Not the gates of hell or anything like that but it is the last stop on the line of life. 'Line of life'. That's a good one from the mind of an old lady, isn't it? We die from all sorts here but it's mostly old age. I'm not ready to go yet.

"God will take us when he's ready," the vicar that comes in here on a Sunday said. "He has his plan."

"Well tell him there's no hurry," Old Tom told him, gruffly. "I'd rather go when I'm ready. Not when he's ready."

The vicar did try to laugh but he didn't really manage it either. People are so serious these days. We can't be too serious about life, can we? If I was serious about everything that's happened to me then I'd be depressed forever. I thought I had it all when I was fourteen but it didn't last. No. Hang on. I'm wrong. I didn't think I had it all. I did have it all. I was turning into an adult, I was reasonably intelligent, I was quite pretty and to top it all I had my Jonny. We had each other. I do seem to always think of myself as being the lucky one but we were both lucky, weren't we? We had each other.

I remember my mum and dad saying they went up church lane to do their courting on the haystacks. They were straw stacks really but we always called them haystacks. There is a difference. I told Jonny and he suggested we should go there as well. We did, but not the first day we'd arranged it.

10.

The end of August has brought cooler mornings. Cool enough to wear a cardigan over my school dress. The cherries growing on the hill are not quite ready to eat but the blackbirds don't seem too fussy. There are at least four of them in the trees and discarded pips and stalks littler the ground. It looks like Jonny will have to hurry if he is to get some. He usually does and there should be plenty to go around if he does hurry.

Jonny's bedroom window is open but there's no sign of him. He's usually there these days, waiting for me, but not today. Perhaps he's gone to school early. Kathy did ring me and say there had been some trouble. She didn't know what the trouble was but it seems the policeman was called early in the morning. My pace quickens a little as I realise I will be walking on my own and I'm eager to find out what the trouble is.

A wooden ladder is leaning up against the biggest of the windows of our classroom and a man is standing halfway up it. He's measuring a gap that, yesterday, was filled with a pane of glass. As I approach, the light changes and I can see not just the one missing pane but four more. Miss comes out from inside and is carrying a brush and a dustpan full of broken pieces. She doesn't look happy. My school friends are all standing, looking and talking, discussing what has happened.

"I think it was robbers," Sam Hodges says loudly and childishly.

"Robbers? Why Robbers?"

"They robbed the post office once."

I just look at him and scowl. What's the point of even trying to explain anything different?

"It's all cleaned up inside now," Miss shouts loudly as she comes back from the rubbish bin. "We can go inside and let these men get on with their work."

We go inside and all the girls watch the young man up the ladder. We had only seen him from behind when we were outside and they are all pleasantly surprised to see his face now. Kathy blows him a kiss and he responds in the same manner.

"Sit down girls!" Miss commands, sharply. "Sit down and leave the man to get on with his work."

As I sit down I suddenly realise there is no one sitting behind me. Where's Jonny? Surely, if he wasn't coming to school either him or his mother would have told me. We say the Lord's prayer and Miss starts the register.

"Mary Atkins!"

"Yes Miss."

"Charles Bishop!"

"Yes Miss."

"Jonny Clitheroe! Jonny Clitheroe?"

A totally out of breath voice suddenly fills the air from the doorway.

"Yes Miss. I'm here Miss. I didn't wake up."

Everyone laughs as Jonny almost stumbles through the door. He's still doing up his shirt, his shoes are undone and his hair looks even worse than normal. Even Miss laughs at the dishevelled sight before her.

"Nice of you to join us at last Jonny," she says, smiling.

"Sorry Miss."

He comes to his desk, doing up the last shirt button as he does so. He reaches me, smiles a sweet smile and lays a hand briefly on my shoulder before noisily taking his seat. Miss carries on with the register. Billy Hicks is not here again.

"Same as always," she says. "I don't know why I even bother to call his name."

Just as she finishes, the classroom door to the right of me opens and the Headmaster, Mr Conway, enters the room. He has a stern look on his face and a cane in his hands and is flexing it back and forth. His anger is all too plain to see. Showing etiquette, Miss steps quietly back from her desk and he takes her place. He is not a large man but does seem to find it very easy to take control of any situation and to assert his authority.

"Last night," he booms, pointing his stick towards the broken window panes and then placing his hands on the edges of the desk. "Last night, or early this morning, somebody or 'some bodies' thought it would be a good idea to throw stones through our window. Why, I don't know."

He scans his eyes across the room from right to left, letting them pause briefly upon every boy in attendance.

"And why would anyone want to do that Charles Bishop?"

"Don't know sir."

"You don't know. And what about you Jonny Clitheroe?"

"Don't know sir."

He scans again.

"And what about you Sam Hodges?"

"I think they were robbers, sir!"

"Robbers?"

"Well, they robbed the post office once sir."

Everyone laughs but Mr Conway doesn't. He looks around at us all.

"So Sam Hodges thinks it was robbers does he?" He almost smiles. "And what do you think they tried to rob, Hodges? Three pencils and a sheet of blotting paper? And were they going to climb in using a ladder? Don't you think they would have broken windows lower down if they were trying to rob us? You're an idiot Hodges. What are you?"

"An idiot," comes a very mumbled reply.

"Sorry Hodges. I never heard that," Mr Conway says loudly and holding his left ear so that he can hear better. He's enjoying showing Hodges up. "I never heard that at all. Speak up boy! Let the whole class know what you are."

Hodges mumbles again and this angers Mr Conway. His cane is smashed down upon Miss's desk with an almighty crack.

"Stand up boy!"

Hodges stands, frightened and embarrassed. His head is down.

"Now lift your head up and tell everyone what you are boy!"

"I'm an idiot," Hodges announces, louder, before sitting back down again, a tear in his eye.

Mr Conway continues.

"Now, we all know Hodges is an idiot," he says, loudly. "But we don't know which other idiot, or idiots, broke our window do we? Not yet but I shall find out and when I do, if they are at this school, they will receive a visit from the police, six of the best from me and, hopefully, a good thrashing from their fathers as well. Not only will they wish they hadn't broken the windows but they'll also wish they hadn't been born at all. Now get on with your work!"

He marches off and Miss steps back into her place. She watches Mr Conway leave and waits until the door is noisily closed.

"Nouns, Verbs and Adjectives," she announces.

We start work but it is difficult to concentrate with all the hammering behind us as pieces of board are tacked into place to temporarily cover where the panes have been broken. One of the workers knocks and comes in to explain that they will be back tomorrow with new panes of glass. He tells Miss that he has a busy day ahead and will cut them for us first thing in the morning. The ladder is taken away and all goes quiet at last.

Miss starts telling us all about Nouns and Proper Nouns and the fact that a Verb is a 'doing word' and then she asks us to write down a list of ten Verbs. I start and then I feel a tap on my back. Miss is not looking so I turn around and Jonny smiles and hands me a note. I hold it on my lap and read. It says, 'Haystack this afternoon?'

I write yes under the message and wait for the right time to hand it back. Sam Hodges sees me but I just stick my tongue out at him. I think he's had enough embarrassment for today. He says no more.

The thought of me and Jonny laying on a haystack fills my mind and it seems my heart wants to skip a beat or two. I write my Verbs but have little interest in what I'm doing. For all I know they may be Verbs, Nouns, Adjectives or even just made up words. The only words that matter to me are Jonny and haystack. It was a cool start to the day but it is warming up and the sun should shine this afternoon.

It doesn't though. After our dinner break the sky seems to gradually darken and become menacing until the sun is obscured and Miss turns on the classroom lights. A crack of thunder is heard in the distance and rain eventually starts to fall. The room is lit up briefly by a vivid flash of lightening and the rain intensifies to such a downpour that water starts to run down the inside of the window, having found its way between the window frame and the newly installed pieces of board that are covering for the lost glass. Jonny passes me the same note again. He has written another word. It now reads, 'Not Haystack this afternoon.'

I add something to it.

'Not Haystack this afternoon. Jonny's bedroom.'

It comes back to me again and, in big letters underneath everything else, it reads, 'YES PLEASE.'

My heart skips another beat.

Time comes to leave and we walk out of the class with Jonny tightly behind me. We are off to his house. Off to his bedroom and off to a place where we can be alone. Alone in a place where nothing else matters. Just us two. That's what I think but, as I reach Miss's desk, she stops me.

"Can I have a little word please Vera?"

I stand still as everyone else leaves. Jonny points outside and I take it he means he will be waiting for me there.

"Are you alright Vera?" Miss asks, kindly concerned.

"Yes Miss."

"It's just that you don't seem quite right to me at the minute."

"I'm fine Miss."

"Everything alright at home?"

"Yes Miss."

I can't tell her about me and Jonny, can I?

"Everything's lovely," I tell her, and then I think. "I think I'm just growing up Miss."

She lays a tender hand on my wrist and smiles broadly.

"I understand Vera. I was at that stage once but it was thirty years ago now. We all go through it and, thankfully, we all get over it."

I start to walk away but she stops me again. She stops me by speaking and stops me in my tracks with what she has to say.

"Jonny really likes you Vera," she says, kindly. "And I bet he's waiting for you somewhere. Enjoy your life Vera but do be good. You've got a bright future ahead of you. Remember that, won't you?"

At first I'm shocked at what she says but then it dawns on me that she isn't stupid. She stands at the front of the class and watches everything. She's not stupid and she's a lovely and caring lady.

"Yes Miss," I answer, not understanding just what she meant by saying the words 'do be good'.

Outside, Jonny is nowhere to be seen. My eyes scour the playground.

"If it's Jonny you're looking for," someone says, "he's gone home."

He could have waited. I'm just a little annoyed with him but decide he must have gone home without me for some reason but is it a good reason or a bad one? Perhaps he's changed his mind. Perhaps he doesn't want to see me this afternoon after all. That's a little irrational. I'm still a little annoyed when I reach his house. The front door is open so I go in and sneer at the old lady in the picture. I'm not in a good mood. Jonny comes to the top of the stairs. He has no shirt on and his trousers are half undone. He's holding a towel that has seen far better days.

"You could have waited for me."

I'm moody and reluctant to climb the stairs.

"I slept late this morning V," Jonny explains. "I didn't have time to even wash. I've felt dirty all day so I thought I'd run home and make myself smell good for you. You're not too annoyed with me, are you?"

I smile, shake my head, realise I'm being an idiot like Sam Hodges and start to climb the stairs to him. I'm not annoyed any more. He did it for me, bless him.

As I reach him he throws the towel into his bedroom and takes me in his big strong arms. I melt and almost get lost in them as he pulls me to him and envelops me. When I manage to free my arms, I reach up and place them around his neck, pulling his head down towards mine until our lips meet.

"I love you Jonny Clitheroe," I tell him, truly and passionately.

"And I love you more," he replies, before loosening his grip and leading me into his room and onto his bed where I lay, just looking at him in all his beauty and majesty.

He looks back and then reaches down and undoes the last of the buttons on his trousers before letting them drop to the floor.

"Do you want to take your dress off?"

I do want to and don't hesitate. Somewhere in the back of my mind there is a nagging voice telling me that no, I should not be taking my dress off, but I ignore it and do so. My Jonny just has underpants on and I want to hold him without having too much clothing between us.

We lay together on his thick dark green quilted bed cover and hold each other. I feel like I'm in heaven, a heaven that I never want to leave. I notice the errant piece of wallpaper moving in the breeze but ignore it. My focus is just on Jonny.

"What did Miss want?" he asks, caressing my back gently through my thin petticoat.

"She warned me to be good with you."

"What?"

"She knows Jonny. She's not stupid. She sees everything. She thinks it's nice but said I should be good."

Jonny's face is showing confusion.

"But Jonny, you mouth the words 'I love you', you blow me kisses, you tap me on the back and you pass me notes. She notices, doesn't she?"

"Bloody hell. I'd better stop."

I hit him playfully on the back.

"Don't you dare stop Clitheroe!"

He just smiles and holds me closer. Maybe to show his love or maybe so that he doesn't get another slap. He then, without ceremony at all, stands up and I'm more than a little shocked when this action is explained. He removes his last piece of clothing. I've never seen a male with no clothes on before and I gulp, seeing what is before me. I never expected it to happen and I never knew what to expect if it did happen but, there he is, in all his bare glory, and I can only think he looks magnificent. The sun is now shining again through his small bedroom window and it lights his body with a clear and almost yellow light and I'm sure my heart doesn't skip a beat this time. I'm sure it stops.

"I love you," I say, almost panting for no known reason.

Jonny joins me again on the bed but, this time, he doesn't lay beside me. He lays on top of me.

11.

"Take your dress off V," he said.

Perhaps I should have been shocked but I wasn't. Perhaps I should have been ashamed but I wasn't.

I didn't think it was just childish infatuation. I did really love him. I was sure of that, even then. He was lovely and he'd said he loved me so many times so I would have done anything for him. So, with only just the tiniest bit of self-conscious hesitation, I did. I took my dress off and then he gently laid on top of me. Me with just my petticoat on and him totally naked. I know now that it was wrong at my age but then it felt so right. Oh, it did feel right, bless him. I looked at him, standing there with no clothes on before he laid on top of me and I was amazed. I'd never seen a man, or boy, naked before and I'd certainly never seen one of those things. I was shocked a bit but it seemed so natural, standing there looking so upright and proud. I know my sense of humour is naughty so even then and at that serious and life-changing moment in my life I couldn't help but laugh to myself.

'You could hang your hat on that,' I thought.

I thought it but didn't say it. I couldn't say it, could I? It would have spoilt everything. That was my first time and it did feel so right. I couldn't say anything and go and spoil it, could I? Jonny badly wanted me and, although I didn't know what it was I was doing, I now know that I badly wanted him as well. It hurt a little at first but then he was so gentle that I cried. I didn't cry because I was upset but because I was so blissfully happy. I had Jonny, I had youth, I had love and life and I had it all.

And so this was the way it was to be. We'd go to his room or we'd go to the haystack. Yes, we did make it to the haystack once or twice before autumn set in and the weather changed. We'd go there and, each time, we'd do what we had being doing that first time in his bedroom. It was beautiful. We were showing our love for each other. We were making love. Why the hell didn't I work out exactly what it was we were doing? Was I stupid? No, I wasn't stupid. I was innocent. An innocent and maybe naive girl who had not been told anything and had to work it out for herself. I did work it out eventually. It would all soon dawn on me but, by then, it would be too late.

The struggle of thinking so long and deeply takes a toll on Vera's spirit and she drops her head slowly and drifts off into a deep sleep. A smile is still on her face as she thinks about her and her Jonny. Half a cup of cold coffee and a biscuit are on the table beside her and the robin looks in through the window as if to keep a watchful eye upon her.

Eventually she stirs.

"I'm not dead yet!" I say out loud, waking and looking at a man beside me wearing a dark suit and thinking he's the undertaker. "I'm not ready for my coffin yet."

"I know you're not," the man says with a smile. "I'm doctor Sharpe. You remember me, don't you?"

Of course I remember him. He was the one who gave me the suppositories a while ago. I think to tell him they were useless and for all the good they did I may as well have stuck them up my bum but I think again and think perhaps that would be going just a little too far.

"You've had a touch of the flu Vera and I'm just checking up on you."

I think to say I hadn't touched Flo but I don't think he would see that joke either. The one with the turban didn't see jokes. I've just woken up and don't feel like cracking one anyway. Another doctor checking up on me? What's going on?

"I have," I said. "I've had the flu but I'm better now. I told that to the turban doctor."

"He said you are still not well Vera, and he asked me to come and listen to your chest again."

I think again but say nothing about it being tucked into my knickers.

He takes my hand gently and it reminds me of Jonny.

"I'm going to take your pulse first."

He looks at the bruise on my head and I say that looks better as well.

"You'll have to slow down with that frame of yours," he says, smiling. "I've seen you. You go round the corners far too fast."

He's trying to be funny and isn't really but I've just woken up and am not in the best of moods.

"Keep her in for a couple more days," he tells the nurse lady who is looking after us today. "Perhaps she can go out and get some fresh air on Sunday."

"I will," I say. "I'll go out on Sunday. I'll look forward to that."

He gently squeezes my hand again and again I think of Jonny. My lovely Jonny.

"You be good Vera," he says.

I remember my teacher telling me that.

He always calls us by our first names, Doctor Sharpe. He likes to be informal. Either that or his memory is as bad as mine and he can't remember surnames. He doesn't know that I can't use my frame any more. He doesn't know I have to be pushed around in a wheelchair all the time now when I'm out of my room.

"Goodbye doctor."

"There's the robin out there," the young nurse lady says.

"Yes," I tell her. "He's always out there. That's my Robin."

That time, with Jonny, in his bedroom, I was so innocent and had no idea what he did to me, what we did together. I had no idea at all but all I know is it was lovely. He was such a gentle boy and he looked almost beautiful when he took his clothes off. Perhaps I shouldn't have thought that but I did. We did what we did and he told me he loved me and that was that. He was beautiful and it was all beautiful and we spent a lot of time in that room after school or up on the haystack. I was in love and so was Jonny and we could see nothing wrong in that or what we were doing and yet we knew others would see it as being totally wrong. How come I could see others judging me badly if they knew and yet I had no idea at all just what it was we were doing? All I could see was the fact that I had feelings and I wanted to do what we were doing. I loved it so much and so did he.

Do you know, this went on for quite a while, months and months, and nothing happened? We weren't found out and all I ever told anybody that bothered to ask was that we were friends. I told my mum this but my dad was always at work. He wouldn't have understood. Understanding was never his forte, was it?

'You can't have a friend who is a boy. He'd want others things beyond a friendship.'

Why didn't he tell me what the other things were, meant and would lead to?

That time he was right in his words of course. He'd bought the cottages and changed the shop upstairs into a flat and money was rolling in. It didn't stop there as he still had plans to do more. Another two houses.

He was a busy and excited man and, really, he had little time to think or worry about what I was doing. I was only his daughter after all. It was a strange situation. I was totally in love with Jonny and wanted everyone to know but, then again, no one could know. I was bursting with joy and pride and yet I had to keep it all inside. We were happy in our own little world but we so did want everyone else to know.

That night at the fair we nearly let everyone know. In fact, some of our friends saw us and word did get around but it never got back to our parents. Well, not mine anyway. Kathy knew. Mum had given me some money to go out and enjoy myself but she told me to behave. It was a travelling fairground that came to our market place every year, in the summer, and I loved the dodgems and the waltzers and all the music they played. You are probably too young to remember but they played songs by people like Perry Como, Guy Mitchell and Frankie Laine. See, I remember all them. I could even sing their songs for you if you like. Perhaps not though. They all think I'm mad enough as it is.

We'd just left school so this year at the fair was special. It was a kind of celebration of freedom in a way. In my mind, I had left school and that meant I was an adult. I was still only fourteen but did feel grown up. My body told me I was grown up. I really had changed. I wasn't fat but had put on a few pounds in the right places and my chest had filled out. I remember it so well. I wore a red and white flowing dress to the fair and had let my hair grow a bit longer. I really did feel good. I popped in to see my nan on the way there and she said I looked a 'right bobby dazzler'. That was kind of her. She was my mum's mum, not my dad's.

I remember leaving her house and meeting Kathy just around the corner, where we had arranged. She looked good too and we walked arm-in-arm to the fair without a worry in the world. A ten shilling note mum had given me. That would be fifty pence in today's money. In those days it was almost a fortune and you could have the whole day at the fair, buy food to eat and still take half of it home again. You would struggle to spend ten shillings, fifty pence. They were good times.

12.

"Kathy!"

"Vera! You look lovely!"

"And so do you!"

I hold out my arm and Kathy links hers in it. She is wearing the same styled dress as I am but hers is blue and white whereas mine is red and white. They both look fantastic, especially as I catch our reflection in the window of Woolworths.

"Have you seen the new boy in town?" Kathy asks me.

"No. Who?"

"He's sixteen and has moved into Church Street. The old house with the tall chimneys."

She giggles.

"He's gorgeous. You'll love him."

She looks at me seriously and I look at her.

"You won't love him as much as you do Jonny Clitheroe though, will you?" she says.

I blush. It's the first blush I've had for ages.

"Jonny?"

Kathy stops and keeps hold of my arm and makes me stop too.

"I haven't said anything Vera, but it is obvious isn't it? How long has it been going on?"

I have to be honest with her.

"Months," I answer. "I didn't think anyone knew."

Again, I'm being naive and innocent and stupid probably.

"I know," Kathy says. "And even Sam Hodges knows. I think it was him who put it about. Why do you keep it a secret? We've left school now."

"Dad."

That one word says everything and Kathy understands. We walk on again.

"My dad wouldn't mind me having a boyfriend," she says. "Not now I'm working. He sees me as a grown up."

"Yes, but my dad's not your dad, is he?"

"No."

She understands alright.

We walk on again and soon see the fair ahead of us. We've heard it for some time but as we see it our pace quickens as excitement takes over. We approach the base of the Helter Skelter as a young lad comes noisily down on his mat. His parents wait as he looks at them and then quickly gets up and runs back up the steps to the top for another go. Ahead of us are the

Hurricane Jets and my favourites, the Dodgems. We walk over to them and then Kathy grabs my hand and squeezes it.

"Look."

"What am I looking at?"

"That's him."

"Who?"

"The new boy. I think he's called Isaac something."

We look ahead to a tall figure who is leaning against the rail of the dodgems circuit. He has longish dark hair under a cap and is wearing a blue chequered shirt and quite baggy brown trousers and boots that are just a slightly darker shade. He has his back to us. Kathy leads me towards him.

"Are you Isaac?" she asks, cheerfully.

He turns around and looks at Kathy. He has looks similar to Jonny and is about the same height and build but his hair is far better kept. It has to be. Jonny wouldn't even get a cap on his head with his hair the way it is.

"Yes, I'm Isaac," he answers, smoothly. "And you are?"

"I'm Kathy. And this is my best friend Vera. I was wondering if you'd take me on the Dodgems?"

She points to the cars being driven around roughly.

He smiles and moves his head down slightly, towards Kathy's.

"I'd take you anywhere Kathy," he says, smoothly again, touching her chin. "How about the seaside? I've got a motorbike."

This time it is Kathy who blushes.

"Tomorrow?"

Kathy flusters a little.

"W...Well. O...Ok."

The power to the Dodgems is cut and the cars come to a halt. Then it's one mad rush as everyone gets out and others jump in. Kathy runs off towards a green car with Isaac and I'm suddenly left on my own and sitting in a white one. The man comes over for the money and I have my ten shilling note ready but suddenly there is a jolt and a voice.

"No. I'm paying for this one," says a familiar voice as a body eases me over and across the seat and lumbers in beside me at the wheel. It's Jonny and soon I'm squashed in beside him. Just where I want to be. He takes the wheel with one hand and puts his free arm around my shoulders, pulling me gently to him. I look at him and he kisses me briefly as the power is restored and we set off, in chase of Kathy and Isaac.

"I'm going to get him!" Jonny says loudly and pointing at Isaac. "He's got a motorbike and I haven't! It's not fair!"

Soon we are scurrying along and are hot on the tail of the green car and its passenger but Isaac sees us coming and spins around through 360 degrees and is then behind us. He's obviously done this before and Jonny is a little slow in realising it. We are soon shunted in the side as we turn and I'm banged against Jonny's body. I don't mind. It's such fun.

In no time at all, Isaac's arm is around Kathy and this takes his mind off his driving and the tables are soon turned as we ram them and spin them around. Kathy is laughing. She's happy alright. She came out with me and is now with a handsome boy. She is, and so am I. It's great fun so, as the power is switched off, we pay more money and go again. This time, Isaac keeps his mind on his driving and his hands on the wheel and we are in trouble.

I'm a little apprehensive but, next we go on the Hurricane Jets which is a ride that goes round and round but you can pull a lever and go up and down as you wish. It's fast and exhilarating and I soon become relaxed and enjoy myself, especially as Jonny lets me take control. He does have an ulterior motive though. My hand is on the lever and his hand is on my thigh. I don't complain. I go up and down but his hand stays where it is.

At the top of the Helter Skelter, I put my mat down and sit on it.

"Don't go yet," Jonny says.

I hesitate and he puts down his mat and sits behind he with his legs around mine and his arms around my waist. He shouts, "One, two, three, PUSH!"

We both do and are soon speeding down, with both of us shouting loudly.

Kathy is waiting at the bottom, on her own. I'm concerned.

"Lost your new boyfriend already?"

Kathy smiles and shakes her head. She doesn't look like she has lost her new boyfriend. She looks like the cat with all the cream. Isaac approaches with two huge sticks of candy floss and hands one to her. She takes it and kisses him in gratitude.

"Want one?" Jonny asks.

I hand him some money and he takes it reluctantly.

"You've paid for most things so far," I say. "I'm paying for this."

"Yes boss," he answers, taking the money.

I love candy floss.

We walk over and sit on the steps of the dodgems to eat our treat. Me and Kathy both in the arms of big and handsome lads. Kathy and Isaac seemed to get together so quickly and I have no idea what will come of it but they're happy and that's the main thing isn't it? Bless them. Kathy is now wearing Isaac's cap. We chat and laugh and eat our candy floss to the sound of Nat King Cole singing the song *'Too Young'*. Are we? I don't think so. It certainly feels right.

The time passes and the atmosphere only increases as we enjoy the rides and sideshows and each other's company. We pay to go on the air rifles. Jonny wins a goldfish and pretends he's going to eat it when he gets home. I know he won't but also know he'd eat anything else. Kathy's certainly enjoying herself as she finishes her candy floss and gives Isaac a kiss for buying it for her. The kiss is on the lips and is quite long and lingering and it's in public so even I feel a little uncomfortable with it. Mind you, it's nothing to what me and Jonny have been doing in private.

Once again, it's a lovely warm evening and, eventually, we say goodbye to Kathy and Isaac and make our way home. Not by the direct route though. Without a word being said me and Jonny make our way up church lane and to the haystack on the corner by the second barn. Jonny helps me up to the top. A rain cloud is in the distance but it doesn't seem to be heading our way. We hope not.

Once again, Jonny is in no hurry. He lays with me and we talk, watching white fluffy clouds travel across the sky above us, with swifts flying and screaming beneath them. The straw smells good and we can feel the sun of the day has warmed it well. It feels good against our backs.

"I love you V."

Jonny always says this. Especially as he is about to make love to me.

13.

I was only just fifteen when it happened. I still loved Jonny and he still loved me and we still went to his bedroom and the wallpaper was still the same, flapping, but I became ill. We'd left school and he worked in the builder's yard, Stebbings, and I worked in a local food shop on the corner but we did manage to be alone sometimes. Sometimes in his bedroom and sometimes up on the haystack. Sometimes we did it in other places but it was always good. On and on we went, doing what we were doing, with little thought of any consequences, but then I became ill. Every morning and sometimes all day. I was as sick as sick could be. As I say, every morning I was sick and sometimes I couldn't go to work. Looking back, I'm amazed now that it took that long. We'd been making love for over a year. Well, what had happened was obvious. It never happened again. In all my years, it never happened again.

Do you know? When I talk to you like this, things seem much clearer; and better. I like talking like this and I think I need to. I do need to talk about it and I hope you don't mind listening. I didn't have anyone to talk to back then. Not even Jonny. I've had no one to talk to since either. Well, apart from my aunt Gloria later. They split us up eventually, me and Jonny. They seemed to think they were clever, working it all out and what to do but why clever? Me and Jonny had been together for ages and it was obvious, wasn't it? It should have been obvious to everyone else but it wasn't even slightly obvious to the very person who mattered the most, me. Me and Jonny had been together for all that time and we had been doing things which were frowned upon by others but I still had no idea what it was we had been doing and why I was being so violently sick. Two and two made four but I couldn't work that one out, even though I was very good at sums.

It'll be teatime soon and I wonder what's in store today. We had beans on toast yesterday. Well, I say beans and it was beans. It had to have been 'beans' because there was more than one bean. I think I had six nearly. And the bread wasn't really toasted either. I think they showed it to the toaster and then switched it off. If you're going to serve toast then you should, at least, toast it. If it's still all cold and floppy, then it's still called bread isn't it? What I had was six beans on bread and margarine. I could tell it was margarine. I'm not stupid. Well not these days. Even the sauce in the beans couldn't disguise the taste. It was margarine alright. Although there was plenty of sauce, about a pint of sauce for every bean, it still tasted like margarine. Someone said we're having coppers for tea tonight.

"Coppers?" I said to them. "You can't eat coppers. The truncheons would get stuck in your throat."

It was my hearing again.

"It's not coppers Vera," the nice girl with the long hair said. "It's kippers. Do you want some?"

"Oh no," I said. "I can't eat kippers in the evening. I'll have them repeating on me all night. Perhaps I'll have one for my breakfast then I've got all day to get rid of the effects."

So that's what I'm having for breakfast, kippers. They say they're oily and they do you good. Good things keep you alive.

When I started being sick I thought I'd eaten something that hadn't done me good but it went on and on for weeks and I got worried. Eventually my mother noticed and she thought I must be quite ill. Even she couldn't work out why. Those were the olden days. Days when innocence seemed to reign over everything. Obviously, you all know what had happened because you live today and you all know and talk about those things openly now but we didn't. Things were different then so my mother innocently took me to the doctors. Did she not realise? Did she not think her daughter capable of such things? Did she think it couldn't happen to her? Did she not want to know? Did she think at all? The doctor thought though. He thought for just a couple of seconds and he saw the problem straight away. That was Doctor Greenwood, not Doctor Sharpe, the one in here today who gave me the suppositories that time. Doctor Greenwood was our doctor, our family doctor, or GP as old Mabel would have asserted.

14.

It's almost twelve o'clock and I've been sitting in the small dark doctors' surgery for twenty five minutes. We've been told the doctor is running a little late. I've been sick again this morning and still don't feel too great. I'm afraid something is seriously wrong and it is playing badly on my mind. I haven't been to work for a few days and I haven't even seen Jonny. The last time we were together I was feeling quite ill and did snap at him over nothing and then I walked away. I know it hurt him, bless him. He didn't deserve that. I must make an effort to see him later today.

"Vera Hobbs!" the doctor's receptionist calls, finally.

I pick up my coat from the chair beside me and stand up. Mum stands up too and we walk towards doctor Greenwood's door. There is a small plaque on the door which denotes it is his room. The door is slightly open so we enter. Doctor Greenwood is sitting at his large wooden desk and is writing up notes and beckons us to sit. I sit, relaxed slightly. I now feel I'm in good hands. Doctor Greenwood has been my doctor all my life and is always good, kind and calm. He talks deeply but calmly and does everything with a nice smile. That alone makes you feels better.

"What's the problem Vera?" he asks, putting his pen and papers to one side. "Why have you come to see me today?"

I begin to speak but mum butts in.

"She seems to have a terrible sickness doctor," she explains. "It's been going on for nearly three weeks."

I'm naive and stupid and so is mum it seems, but doctor Greenwood isn't. He diagnoses my symptoms straight away, without hesitation.

"Have you missed your period Vera?" he asks, bluntly and yet as calmly as always.

I'm shocked. What's that got to do with being sick? I think to myself. I have missed my period. Two in fact. I never really thought about it.

"I have," I tell him. "Twice."

Well, suddenly my mother looks at me and her face turns ashen and she looks sick herself. Far more sick than me. Completely and utterly sick.

"Why do you ask?" I say naively. To the doctor, I must sound stupid. And to mum.

I look at him and then I look at my mother. Her face is distraught and she can't speak. Suddenly she can't even look at me. She looks at the doctor and then just stares blankly at the wall with her hand partially covering her face, trying hard to disguise her tears and anger.

"What is it?"

I'm sitting in a room with two people and neither of them seem to want to speak to me.

"I think you are pregnant," Doctor Greenwood says at last. "I can check but really there is little need."

"I'm what?"

I say that but don't really mean it in the way I say it. I said 'I'm what?' but then I knew. Suddenly it all hit home like a huge avalanche just what it was that me and Jonny had been doing all those months. We were making babies. I have always been good at sums and they suddenly add up. I've been thoroughly stupid but at last the penny has dropped and two and two do make four, although I wish I'd got my sums wrong for once this time. I've a baby inside me and it was Jonny who'd put it there. It's mine and his. We made it. We made it together. It is mine and his but we love each other, so does it matter? I'm only fifteen and yes, it does matter. Of course it matters. It matters to everyone. Suddenly it matters to everyone far more than it does to me and I know I will suddenly be hated for it. Hated for falling in love.

Doctor Greenwood examines me behind a white screen and asks for a urine sample whilst mum sits in a shocked silence but, as he has already said, the examination is not really necessary. I'm pregnant and that's that.

"When did you do it Vera?" he asks me, calmly but coldly as we sit down again.

I can't really tell him can I? So I tell him the truth.

"We've been doing it for months," I say. "A year or more maybe."

Maybe I'm too pragmatic about the situation and mum looks at me with hate oozing from every pore. In my mind, I'm having a baby when I could have had cancer or something. Isn't that something to be glad of? At least I'm not dying. But that's only my way of thinking but I'm not thinking in a real world. I think in my world but I live in a real world. A world where I have suddenly been branded as a sinner and a harlot. An altogether bad person. Mum tries to look at me but can't and I do feel sorry for her because she is suddenly lost, lost completely. In one short visit to the doctors her life has suddenly been turned on its head with absolutely no way of ever turning it back again.

"Who has?" she asks, looking straight ahead.

"Who has what?"

I'm being stupid again. Doctor Greenwood is looking at me in a cold way and my mother is distraught to the point she has lost all rational feeling and yet I answer her question in a stupid way. She finds it hard but she asks again.

"Who have you been laying with?"

"Jonny."

"Jonny?"

"My Jonny."

"J… Jonny Clitheroe? That boy from the terrace at the bottom of the hill?"

"Yes mum. Jonny. We love each other."

Mum then says something without thinking and her statement suddenly puts a hideous twist on proceedings.

"Just wait 'til your father gets hold of him!"

She then almost looks at me, then at the doctor and then into thin air. She looks up at the ceiling and her face turns even more ashen as she has just realised and told herself that her husband will have to be informed. She leans forward with her head in both her hands and sobs and sobs. I want to cuddle her to make her feel better but she never accepted that when I wasn't a bad person. She certainly isn't going to accept it now, is she?

"Are you alright?" the doctor asks.

Mum shakes her head.

"No."

She lifts her head as best she can and it's plain to see that she is almost in a faint situation. Her face has no colour at all and her skin is clammy. She looks around without actually taking anything in.

Doctor Greenwood looks at her and then at me.

"There's a glass over there," he utters, almost fiercely for him. "Go and get your mother some water."

I get up with the consequences of my actions gradually sinking into my young and foolish mind. I'm pregnant and I've got my Jonny. Things could be alright. I can see that, but no. Who am I kidding? Things could be alright but in no way will anyone let them be that way. I let the tap run for a few seconds to cool the water and then fill the glass and take it over to mum. She looks at me in a horrible way and refuses to take it from me so doctor Greenwood takes it instead and then she takes it off him. This action seems stupid, and almost childish to me but it is a taste of things to come.

She manages to drink half of the water and then explains to the doctor that she will have to tell her husband and she knows he will go completely bananas. Mad, she says, and then she looks at me. For the first time in that room, since my examination, she does look at me. She had even talked to me before without looking at me but when she does look it is no pleasant look. She just glares and hate and worry and panic are all too plain to see.

"I didn't know," I try to tell her, now sobbing my heart out as well but she won't listen. She's beyond listening. I seriously and genuinely feel that our relationship is over as if a switch has been turned off. Just like the dodgems.

I try to explain to her that I had never been told about babies and how they are made and had only just realised. I tell her what me and Jonny had been doing was beautiful but that only angers her more.

"How can sex be beautiful, you stupid girl?"

She stands up and tries to grab me by the hair but then she realises she is in the presence of the doctor so she doesn't. She calls me filthy and shameful names. Why had nobody told me? Yesterday I was Vera Hobbs, the cheerful and likeable daughter of Reginald Hobbs, the ironmonger and property owner. Yesterday I had it all but today I have nothing and am only a wanton harlot who deserves nothing but scorn, hate and ridicule. In one single doctor's appointment, I've lost his respect and that of my mother. What I'll lose when my father gets to know is anyone's guess. I had been stupid in not working out what me and Jonny were doing but I'm bright enough to know that there is a chance that I could be losing my head later. I've already ruined mum's life and I can plainly see that mine has to go the same way. Dad has always wanted to be the talk of the town. He will be now. How do you keep your fifteen year old daughter's pregnancy a secret?

"It does seem obvious," doctor Greenwood tells us. "But I will check a sample to be sure. I'll be in touch. We will also have to inform the midwife."

I get up to leave but mum seems wholly reluctant. It seems that whilst she is in the surgery she is safe and this sorry matter doesn't have to go any further. Once she leaves she has to face the real world with her new found problem and that problem, to her, seems insurmountable. That problem is me.

"Mum?"

She doesn't look at me but takes another sip of the water I fetched for her and then she stands on wobbly legs. A faint voice.

"Thank you doctor."

I want to hold her hand and help her along the short corridor to the surgery door but I know she would hate it. She hates me now, already.

In the reception I see a familiar face. It's a man who is a regular customer at dad's shop.

"Morning Mrs Hobbs. Vera."

I say hello but mum just stares faintly ahead.

"You alright Mrs Hobbs?"

What do I say?

I say nothing but just keep walking. Mum needs some fresh air. In fact, mum needs a miracle.

Our journey home normally takes a walk past Jonny's house but not today. Mum doesn't utter a word but just trudges along through back streets with me following and her with her head down and her body hunched forward.

"I'm sorry mum. I didn't know."

I say it with a plead in my voice but know that pleading will do nothing. Mum has always loved me but that love has always been tarnished by her devotion to dad's needs and his life. That love has now vanished so I walk on, slightly behind, and with silence filling the air in abundance.

Another familiar face as we walk up towards home.

"You alright Mrs Hobbs?"

I speak without thinking.

"She's had some bad news."

Bad news is the understatement of the year. The person walks on and so do we. I try to walk close to mum but she will not have it so I leave the gap between us, an icy gap.

Back at home, mum still stands hunched over as I reach for the key on the ledge and undo the front door. It opens with its grind and click and she nudges me to go inside.

"Room," is all she can say but I know what she means and climb the stairs.

My room is my haven and I find solace there. I'm in a terrible situation but, being on my own, I have time to think. I have a baby growing inside me and, although wrong to everyone else, it feels so right for me. Alright, so I'm only fifteen years old and this should not have happened but it has happened. If the world outside my window could possibly accept it, I'm sure we could work something out. I love Jonny and he loves me. I'm sure we could both dearly love our baby.

My head is filled with positives but those are highly overshadowed by one big negative. The fact is no one will accept it and I have no idea what is going to happen to me. I'm worried but curious and almost happy at the same time. One side of me does like the idea. Me and Jonny together with our own son or daughter. I think of this and then pull my blouse from my skirt and feel my bare belly. There is actually a baby in there!

15.

Vera is crying but takes a used tissue from her sleeve, straightens it out and then wipes her eyes and nose after lifting her glasses. She is looking down but slowly lifts her head.

Sorry for blubbing but do you know, it all happened sixty or so years ago but it still hurts you know. Not the thought that I was having a baby but the thought that my own dear and loving mother had so quickly and cruelly turned against me and hated me. She didn't have to do that. I needed her then like I had never needed her or anyone else before, but I was never to have her again. Not really. Not totally. In doing what I did I lost all the love and respect she had ever showered me with and, just like that, I had become a thing to hate and to throw scorn at. I was her daughter but I was just filth and an outcast. Something to be tolerated but only just. Tolerated? Why did I say tolerated? I wasn't tolerated was I? I was hated. Hated for what? For falling in love and being innocent of life? She would come to speak to me again as the years went by but our relationship, which I always took as quite special, had gone. It was gone and was never to come back. She took me home and sent me to my room to wait for my father to shut the shop and come home. She could have rung him because we were quite well off and did have that telephone but she didn't want him to have to shut up early. He would have to explain to everyone why.

It was four hours before shutting up time so I had four hours to think. I was a young girl. Young and pretty I'll tell you. I never thought so at first but my Jonny made me realise that with all the compliments he gave me. Bless him. I was young and pretty and had a good life but, in everybody's eyes I was then and suddenly a good for nothing piece of trash who had debased herself and her family by committing this terrible sin. Why was it such a sin? Why was it a sin at all? In my mind, all I had done was fall in love with Jonny and had shown him how much. It did seem so natural and if we did love each other then what was so bad about having a child together? And if it was such a bad thing then why didn't anyone tell me all about it? Why didn't they say what happened and how it all worked? Why didn't they tell me? Why did I have to find out when it was too late? Was it my fault though? Why did the whole penny have to drop there in the doctor's surgery before my brain could fathom it out? Why? Why? Why?

"Vera! Vera! Vera!"

Hang on a minute. Sorry. Somebody's talking to me.

"Yes?"

"Where were you Vera? You certainly weren't with us, were you?"

It's the nice young nurse lady. The one whose brother was in the navy. She's quite new. She's come with my pills. Whole load of them I have to swallow and four times a day every day. Even on Sundays. They have pills to stop you having babies these days. I never had them. I have so many now. I used to remember what they all were and what they were for but that didn't really matter because I had to swallow them whether I remembered what they were or not.

"This one's for..."

"Oh never mind," I say. "Just give them to me as usual nurse."

She does and I swallow them.

"It'll soon be teatime, won't it?" I say to her.

"It will Vera. Are you having the kippers?"

"No," I say. "I'm having them for breakfast. If I have them now they'll only repeat on me all night and make my breath smell."

"It doesn't matter if your breath smells," she says, smiling. "You won't be kissing anybody tonight, will you?"

"No," I say. "But I used to. I used to kiss my Jonny... And my little Robin."

Once again Vera wipes her eyes and nose on the used tissue.

"Here," the nurse lady says, taking some tissues from a box on top of her medicines trolley. "Have these Vera."

"Thanks."

"Are you alright Vera? You seem sad."

"No love," I say. "I'm not sad really. I'm just talking to the ladies and gentlemen, telling them about me and my little Robin."

The nurse looks around but can't see who Vera could possibly be talking to so she just closes the door to her medicine trolley and walks away.

"Here comes Susie with your tea," she says. "Would you like a nice plate of sandwiches and a cup of tea?"

"Yes," I say. "That'll do nicely."

"Vera seems a little sad," she says to Susie with the wonky wheel. "She'd like a nice plate of sandwiches and a cup of black tea."

"Do you want milk in that?"

I smile.

"Two sugars today," I say. "Sugar's good for you. Well a little is anyway. I need my energy in this place."

I don't really.

Susie takes a sandwich from each plate and gives them to me.

"Would you like a piece of Madeira, Vera?" she asks.

"That rhymes," I say.

"What does?"

"Madeira and Vera."

"Does it?"

She isn't from this country. I've told you that, haven't I? My memory's good at the minute.

I end up with an egg sandwich in brown bread and a ham sandwich in white bread. The other one I'm not too sure about. I'm not knocking it though. It does taste lovely. I never had tea that night. The night after the doctor's surgery visit. I was just left in my room and was ignored. Ignored that is until my father came home. I heard his car pull up and the door close and then he came in whistling and loudly asked my mother what was for tea. He was happy and had obviously made good money that day. There was nothing for tea and once he was told about me, for some reason, he lost his appetite anyway. It was quiet for some time downstairs and I couldn't hear a thing that was being said but I did suddenly hear a huge smash as something large was thrown and then crashed to the floor. Doors slammed and his feet then thumped unevenly on the stairs due to his bullet wound problem. My door was almost smashed off its hinges as he opened it forcefully. Mother's face had turned ashen earlier but his was red. Red as a beetroot it was and seemed about to explode. He came in and just stood there, fuming. I tried to tell him I was sorry but no words could possibly sink in. Nothing would go in but everything was to come out. 'Nobody told me dad' I tried to say but he just came over and he did grab my hair. There was no doctor around to worry about like there had been with mother wanting to do it in the surgery. I was looking down at the floor but he made me look up and at him. Into his red and fuming face.

16.

It's been quiet downstairs for quite a long while but a huge smash has just filled the air making me jump out of my skin, letting my semi-pleasant thoughts evaporate. It sounded like glass being thrown. Maybe a jug or a bowl. My peace has been smashed too as a door slams and dad's feet come to slam unevenly onto the stairs, making each one groan as he climbs to face me. I knew and fully expected he would be angry. It would have been silly to expect anything else, but I now know I've grossly underestimated his reaction. Especially as my door is smashed open and it crashes back against my chest of drawers, making everything on it rattle and quake. A perfume bottle falls over. He stands before me with a face that is as red as a beetroot. It looks like every blood vessel in it is throbbing and about to burst. I know I'm in serious trouble as he turns and closes the door behind him. I'm his daughter and I need love and support but that's definitely not what I'm going to get. He is always in control and this is not going to be a cosy two-way chat. I shy away from him.

"Nobody told me dad," I say, scared and leaning away from him but looking at him. "I... I didn't know."

"Shut up bitch!"

"Dad?"

He raises his hand and I know if I utter another word he is going to hit me with it. I'm quiet and the hand lowers. Instead, he takes out a handkerchief from his pocket and wipes his fuming and perspiring face.

I utter more words.

"Sorry dad."

He fumes again and comes over to me. Mum had thought of grabbing my hair but stopped because of doctor Greenwood being there. Dad has no doctor to stop him so he grabs a handful of hair and lifts me to my feet with it. I whimper in pain.

"It hurts dad."

"Hurts? Hurts? How do you think I feel, you stupid little bitch?"

He has control of my head and turns it so that I have to look into his face. I try to avoid his eyes.

"Hurts?" he says again, pulling harder. "I'm the one who's hurt you little slut! I'm a respected man in this town. I own the shop, the flat and the other houses. I'm a successful man who's spawned a bitch who can't keep her knickers on. You're hurt? That's what hurt is! Where did I go wrong?"

"But..."

"Don't 'but' me, girl!"

"Dad."

"I'm not your dad, girl. I'm not your dad and you're not my daughter. You're just a cheap little slut and I want you out of my life."

"But dad. I…"

My head is still being held in his left hand and his right suddenly flies through the air and connects with my cheek. It hurts badly so I raise my hand and hold it. It brings little comfort. Tears flood from my eyes and I begin to see the huge magnitude of my situation. My position is hopeless and I feel bruised. Bruised by the hand of my own father. He's hurt me but still I need him. I stop crying and speak again, looking now into his angered and bloodshot eyes.

"But I need you dad. I need your help to get through this."

Then I say something which is true but which is only going to enrage him further. In normal circumstances, he would have been so proud but these are not normal circumstances in any way so why do I say it?

"You are going to be a granddad, dad."

It really is the wrong thing to say. He looks even more angry than before and my head is pulled towards him and then is violently pushed away. My body moves with it and I fall over the corner of the bed and land on the floor under the window. He stands over me with his right foot raised slightly behind him. I'm sure he is going to kick me right where my baby lays but he hesitates and then his foot goes begrudgingly back to the floor. I jump as it moves again and connects with the bed instead, rattling it against the wall.

"I didn't know what we were doing dad," I plead. "Honestly."

"Didn't know? Didn't know? You were laying with a boy and you didn't know what you were doing? Don't give me that girl! You're just a filthy little whore who's let some boy do whatever he wanted with you. And you probably encouraged it. You even probably enjoyed it, you slut!"

"I did dad. I did. I love him."

He now has his hands on his hips and stares down at me as I lean against the woodwork below the window. He has not calmed at all but is still at least. I still cower away from him but don't feel the threat of violence. It seems to have subsided.

"Love him? Love him? What do you know about love girl? You're just a child. You know nothing about love."

"I do dad."

I'm still sitting on the floor and look up at him seriously.

"I do dad. I do love him and he loves me. And I wish you could love me as well. I'm in a bad place and I need you. You're my dad and you should be helping me, shouldn't you? You've never told me you love me. I wish you could now."

I've easily managed to anger him once more and he moves forward and grabs my hair again. He then lifts me to my feet. It hurts really badly but he shows no temperance, remorse or sympathy and firmly holds his grip. He lifts until I am on the tips of my toes and my body is held, quite tightly, against his. The top of my head still only reaches his chin, even in this position.

He's hurting me badly but my body is against his and I want to put my arms around him and hold him. Maybe if I do he would relent a little and we could work things out. I hesitate and, trying not to think about the pain too much, my arms slide slowly, tentatively and nervously around his waist.

"I do need you dad."

I gently squeeze his waist and his grip loosens enough for me to lay my head against his chest. I'm still on tiptoes but only because I want to be now. I'm holding my dad and he does seem to be responding. All seems still and calm.

"I really do love you dad."

I nestle my head into his chest more but it is slowly, but gently, moved away. I look up and into his eyes. He's looking into mine and I see what I think is warmth radiating from him. Are things becoming better?

"If you loved anything about me girl," he snarls, "then you would have kept your knickers on wouldn't you? You are a disgrace! A disgrace to me, your mother and the world. You're filth!"

Things are not better. Not better at all. I'm just being innocent and naive again.

He's let go of my hair and it's a relief but his hand then quickly goes for my throat. He squeezes and with that one almighty hand he almost lifts me off my feet. I'm struggling for breath.

"Who did it girl?"

His face is blood-red again and his grip tightens even further. I move my hands to try and free myself enough to breathe but my efforts are futile.

"Who did it?"

Obviously mum hasn't told him.

I don't want to tell him but he is really hurting my neck and I can't breathe at all now.

"Jonny," I somehow manage somehow to utter

"Jonny?"

"Jonny Clitheroe? I love him."

I'm struggling even to talk as there is little breath to do it with.

He suddenly lets go. It's as if he feels disgusted to be touching something that Jonny has touched. He looks at his hand as if it has been tainted by some terrible spell.

"Not only have you let somebody violate you but that somebody has to be Jonny Clitheroe. Jonny bloody Clitheroe! That boy from that family who live in the terrace down the bottom of the hill. I'll be going to see him girl and I don't think he'll be too pleased to see me. He might just get to live if he's very lucky."

He says this in anger but, although I'm upset and hurting, I know he'll do no such thing. He would have every right to go and see Jonny and he would have every right to be just as angry with him as he is with me. but he won't go. I know he won't. And why? The answer is obvious. I'm pregnant. I'm expecting Jonny's child. If he went after Jonny, all he would be doing would be advertising my pregnancy. It would be spread around the town in no time. No. He has to keep this to himself. My Jonny is as guilty as me but he'll get away with it, bless him. I'll go and see him when things calm down and I'll explain. I said some horrible things to him the last time we were together but we can sort things out. I wasn't well then. He'll understand that things can't be perfect all the time.

Dad has let go of my throat and I can breathe again but it still hurts to do so. He thinks hard and then pushes me backwards onto the bed. He has hurt me and perhaps I should feel angry towards him but I can't. I still need him.

"Dad?"

"Shut up girl."

"But dad?"

He raises his hand as a threat and I go quiet.

He looks towards the window and then towards the door, thinking long and hard as he does so.

"You will stay here," he says, formulating a plan in his mind. "You will stay here and I will sort things out. No one must know. I don't quite know what to do but I'll think of something. No one must ever know that Reg Hobb's daughter is a slut who has got herself pregnant. I've got a reputation to keep. Got to keep this quiet."

"But what about me, dad?"

"What about you? Have you got a reputation? Oh yes, you have, haven't you? You've got a reputation for being a little whore, haven't you? Why should we worry and you? Why should anyone worry about you? I never will again. You're nothing to worry about any more. I'm free from you. Or I will be soon."

He shrugs his shoulders.

"You're not even my daughter now, are you?"

"What's going to happen?"

"I don't know," he answers, looking towards the window and thinking again. "But what is going to happen for now is you are going to stay here in this room. You can use the bathroom but you are not coming down the stairs. I don't know how long it will take to organise things but you are up here until things are arranged. Clear? Clear?"

I have no power to argue so I just nod. Dad has been thinking and it seems he has already thought of something.

"You'll stay here, in this room, and you'll not talk to anyone. Got it girl?"

I nod again, reluctantly.

"I'm not coming near you and neither is your mother."

Another nod.

"Your food will be left on a tray outside the door and, when you've finished it you can put the tray back again. Your door stays shut and you speak to no one. If I see you even trying to come downstairs, then I'll not be responsible for my actions. Don't even try to talk to your mother either. I've told her she's not allowed."

I do not answer. What's the point when he's in charge fully and not one tiny aspect of it all is up for any slight amount of negotiation?

He raises his voice again.

"You got all that?"

I nod again.

"I said, have you got all that girl?" he repeats.

"Y…Yes dad."

He turns away from me and then looks back as he is about to leave the room. I then hear a word coming from his lips that I have never heard him utter before. It sums up his disgust of me.

"Fucking stupid little bitch! You've fucked your life up but, believe me, you're not taking me down with you."

He repeats the word several times and then leaves the room, still doing so and pulling at the door and slamming it into place.

I'm alone and all goes quiet. I lay on my bed with a sore face, neck and scalp, trying to relax and thinking hard but, seemingly from nowhere, a huge despair suddenly rattles through me and a sadness all of its own wells up from the pit of my stomach and erupts into a huge inner sob that I have no control whatsoever over. It takes over my very being and huge tears run down my face and dampen the bed covers until I'm lying in something of a puddle. I need my dad. I need my mum. I need Jonny. Even Kathy could be of great help and comfort, but no.

I've got nobody. At a time of great crisis, I am all alone. I have to face things on my own and I don't even have any real idea just what it is I'm going to have to face.

I take a small handkerchief from my sleeve, straighten it out and wipe my eyes, nose and mouth. It helps but does little really to alleviate my suffering.

17.

Do you know? You might never believe me but I've never uttered a serious swear word in my entire life so I can't say aloud exactly what he said because just about every other word began with that letter, f. I was a...bitch, a... slut, a... idiot and I was... ignorant. Yes, I was ignorant. I admit that. I wholeheartedly admit that. I was ignorant of how things worked. I was ignorant of the process of reproduction and I was ignorant of the effects of everything me and my Jonny had been doing all that time. I was ignorant but I needed help, dad. I needed it badly. I needed support, dad. Not violence. I didn't need that!

She looks at the tissues that the nice nurse has given her and looks thankful for them. She wipes her eyes again.

He hit me, you know. I never expected anything else. You can't be that enraged without lashing out, can you? His hand smacked my face and it really hurt. He shouldn't have done it but I was expecting more, much more, but it never came. He lifted his foot and

I thought he was going to kick me but for some reason he just kicked the bed and it rattled into the wall. Then he left, telling me to stay where I was. To tell you the truth, I was glad to. That bedroom was my sanctuary just as Jonny's room had been for the both of us. I needed to see Jonny but knew I couldn't. I needed help but knew there would be none. My bedroom would become my home, my sanctuary and even my prison for the next three days. My mother did bring me food but there was no idle chit chat. She just left food outside the door as she had been ordered. There was no talking at all until the third day when she told me, through a closed door, that my father was sorting things out. He'd been to see Mrs Bloomfield who owned the shop where I'd worked and he'd told her I didn't want my job any more. I did want it. I loved that job but couldn't argue. I couldn't argue with anyone as there was no one there to argue with. Dad had taken charge of everything and my life was no longer mine to decide anything.

Once again Vera's head drops and she sleeps.

"Let's get you into bed Vera," she hears someone say. "You look tired today. You've had the flu you know and it's taken its toll."

"Yes," I reply. "I have haven't I and I think it's taken its toll. Bed would be nice."

I'll talk to you again in the morning.

Two carers attend to Vera and she is helped into a wheelchair and is taken to bed. We find her, the next morning, in her same chair again, looking out of the window. She turns to us, smiling.

Oh hello. Another day. I went to bed early last night, didn't I? Had a good night's sleep though. All I remember hearing was an owl out in the trees. There's a lot of trees outside. Well, I suppose they wouldn't be inside, would they? That'd be daft. I sit in a wheelchair under the trees sometimes when it's warm. When it's not raining and when I haven't had the flu. There's a lot of owls out there too. And robins.

Albert's not here today.

"Why isn't Albert here today?" I ask Norma. She's on again.

"It's Saturday Vera," she says. "And he doesn't work on Saturdays, does he?"

How am I supposed to know what day it is? Every day seems the same in here. It could be April Fools day for all I know. I was the fool once, wasn't I? They get me up, sit me in this chair and that's it. It could be Saturday, Tuesday or even Easter Sunday for all I know. Still, I tell myself I'm lucky to be alive. Some don't live this long do they? Some don't even really live at all. Can't see little Robin today.

She burps and puts her hand to her mouth and then smiles again.

Sorry about that. It's the kippers. Had them for breakfast this morning and they're repeating already. They tasted nice but the problem is I'll be tasting them all day. Susie's not here today so it's the young lad. Can't remember his name but I had milk in my coffee earlier. Ken. That's it. Ken. He always does that. Black coffee with milk in. He doesn't understand, does he?

I see old Joyce has got visitors already. It's her daughter and granddaughter. They're always here first thing on a Saturday morning, bringing her flowers and sweets. No one ever brings me flowers. I don't even get visitors let alone flowers. But hang on though. That's wrong, isn't it? I'm telling you a lie. My granddaughter does come sometimes doesn't she? She's the one who had the baby, 'out of wedlock' as we used to say. She doesn't come very often but she does come to see me sometimes, when she's got time. When you think about it, we do have that something big in common me and her, don't we? Why did I wonder what day it was when old Joyce has visitors first thing every Saturday morning? See. Memory again.

'Out of wedlock'. Yes. I was telling you yesterday about my doings with Jonny and my visit to doctor Sharpe, no, doctor Greenwood, wasn't I? What was I telling you? I had been to see doctor Greenwood and I had gone home again but I hadn't been sent away had I? I don't think I told you that bit. I'll start from there and forgive me if I repeat myself, not just with the kippers.

Was I in my bedroom for four days? Maybe it was only three but it doesn't matter. It was a long time ago and I can't remember everything. I only remember what I've had for dinner when it's sprouts.

I was in my bedroom all that time and spoke to nobody and nobody spoke to me. At first I needed that peace and quiet but after a while it started to hurt. I wanted to tell Jonny all about our baby that was growing inside me. I desperately needed him and wanted him to hold me and reassure me everything would be ok, but no. I had been horrible to him when I saw him the last time and perhaps he thought I didn't want to see him anymore. I know now I was cross because of being pregnant and my hormones were all mixed up but I didn't know that then and neither did he. Surely he couldn't think I'd had enough of him after everything we'd said and done together? I didn't know what he thought, and still don't come to that. I don't suppose I'll ever find out. It's too late now.

There had been knocks at the front door and muffled voices downstairs but did one of those knocks come from Jonny? I don't know. I did try to look once but my mum saw me creeping out of my room to see and glared hatefully in my direction. Her message was put across without the need to say a word. No one was there with her, in the house. It had just been the postman that time and she had a small parcel in her hand. Certainly not a present for me that day.

I must say I do like my own company but only for an hour or two. On the second day, my thinking had been done and loneliness set in. There are only a few things a girl can do in her bedroom, on her own. Especially in those days anyway. They have computers and phones and televisions in bedrooms these days, but not then. All I had were dolls from my childhood, a limited make-up collection and some pens, pencils and paper. I even tried snakes and ladders on my own but that was boring. I think I lost anyway.

On the third day, a huge depression and total boredom set in. I honestly thought I was going mad. The same thoughts had run through my mind so many times that I definitely didn't want to think of them again. I'd made up stories and I'd cried so many tears but, in the end, little was left. My baby was inside me but there was nothing else. I was empty of most emotions and honestly thought some amount of insanity was creeping in. So much, in fact, that I sat at my dressing table, looked in the mirror and used lipstick and powder to draw a clown's face on me. A clown was what I felt like so why not look like one? Was I becoming insane or was I just fed up? I pressed hard with the lipstick. Was that insanity or was it through frustration? I had white around my eyes and a red nose and cheeks. Mum saw me as I crept to the bathroom to wash it off and she was stunned by my mad appearance. She burst out crying and ran to the kitchen and slammed the door behind her. Boredom or insanity? I don't know but I must admit, it wasn't the most sensible thing I have ever done.

Anyway, later the following day, my father came up the stairs and into my bedroom with a big suitcase. The one we used when we went to stay anywhere. It was plenty big enough for his and my mum's clothes for two days. We only ever went away for two days because he had to get back to the shop. He threw the case on my bedroom floor and told me, in no uncertain terms, to put all my clothes in it and to take my boots. He returned a couple of minutes later with a cardboard box and a piece of string.

He said I was going away. I asked him where and for how long but he didn't answer. The boots should have been a clue to where. He was doing the talking and I was just doing the listening. I needed him but he couldn't see that. All he could see was hatred for the daughter who had so badly let him down.

I'm being interrupted again. It's a different girl in a white top.

"I'm Rachel," she says, with a cute smile. "I only started today and I need to change your bag."

"I'm not an old bag," I say to her, smiling.

She knows I'm joking. Sweet girl she is. Short dark hair and a slim and slight feminine figure.

My hair's grey now and has been for years but it used to be a lovely colour. Not short though. I grew it quite long and my Jonny used to love it. I grew it for him. He used to run his fingers through it and kiss it. Bless him. He was a sweetheart.

"Get the screen round Vera," Norma tells her. "It's over there in the corner by the rubber plant."

"Yes," I say, pointing. "Over there in the corner by the rubber plant that no one ever bothers to water."

"I'll water it later," Ra...Ra...Ra...the new girl said.

She will later as well. I know. Such a sweet girl, bless her.

She takes my bag off my leg and tells me it looks like I need to drink more.

"It looks like you haven't been well," she says.

"I haven't," I tell her. "I've had a touch of the flu."

"You've touched who?" she asks, smiling a wide smile.

It's her turn to make a joke.

"I've been touching Flo," I say.

She laughs and changes my bag and then she puts her hand on my shoulder and squeezes it gently.

"Must go Vera love," she says. "Got things to do, but I'll come and have a chat later."

She is a lovely girl. We need a few more like her around here. Don't get me wrong. They're quite a good bunch really but people like her are special. I needed that little bit of tenderness. I haven't ever seen much of that, other than from my Jonny.

Oh yes, Jonny. I'm getting away from the story again aren't I? I will tell you about Jonny but I was sent away wasn't I? I'd committed a terrible sin against my family, against the world in fact, and I could not be tolerated in any normal society so I had to go. Fifteen I was and I was cast out, just like that.

18.

My bedroom door opens at last and a large case is almost thrown into my room. It lands the right way up and then falls over. Then I hear the first clear voice I've heard in three days.

"Fill that with clothes girl! You're leaving. And take your boots as well."

"Where am I going?"

"Just fill the bloody case and stop asking questions. You don't get to ask questions. Whores just do as they are told, not as they want."

I didn't deserve that.

"But dad, I'm not a whore. I'm your daughter; Vera. I need you dad."

"You need me alright. You need me to drive you as far out of my life as possible. Will the edge of the world do? With a bit of luck, you just might fall off."

"But dad?"

"Shut up bitch and fill the case."

He leaves and returns with a cardboard box and a piece of string.

"Fill this as well."

There is to be no real conversation, no pleading and certainly no help but I need help. Am I to face all this alone, not knowing the first thing about what will happen? Yes. I answer my own question. I think I am.

The door is slammed again and, once more, I'm alone. I'm leaving. What to take? It suddenly dawns on me just how much my life is about to change. I've got a large suitcase and a cardboard box. I'm not going away for a week, fortnight or even a month, am I? I may be leaving for good. Even naive me knows that a pregnancy lasts for nine months. I had no idea how they came about but I do know how long they last. Am I going away for that amount of time or am I going away forever? I'm not stupid enough to think I can have my baby and then come home as if nothing has happened. Where do we say the baby came from? We can't say we just found it under a bush, can we?

It's October. Soon be winter. I won't be at home this Christmas but where will I be? The seasons are changing and I'll need warm clothes and plenty of them. Better pack trousers, woollies, coats and hats. My scarf. Better find my gloves and socks. Long warm socks to wear inside my wellingtons.

But then I stop and think. Why am I planning all this so simply and stoically? I'm being sent away from my home for goodness sake. Sent away from my bedroom. Sent away from my Jonny and sent away from the life that I love and yet, here I am, planning it with such ease, stoicism and calmness. I'm planning as if the suitcase is for me to get ready to go on a holiday. This is to be no holiday. It's going to be hell and, underneath my calmness is a knowing that all is not to be rosy. It's going to be horrible and it is all too plain to see. But what choice do I have? Dad's not going to suddenly run up the stairs again, throw his arms around me and tell me he loves me and cannot live without me, is he? He hates me and that's that. I could easily be the downfall of everything for him and it isn't hard to see that his reputation is of far more value than the love of just a daughter. And that's what I am, or was, 'just a daughter'. Kathy isn't just a daughter. She's a girl who is loved dearly by her mother and father. I'm nothing at all. Especially now.

No. I've got to go and I've got to pack. I'm only fifteen for God's sake! Should I be doing this? I look around my room. It's been my sanctuary and my life but it has also been my prison. My feelings are totally mixed. I realise I'm becoming screwed up. I do need to get out but I don't need to be out for months or years. Perhaps it wouldn't be so bad if I even knew where I was headed. I need my mum and, despite all of his all too apparent faults, I do even need my dad. Have I got one now? He doesn't seem to think he has a daughter. I don't need punishment or banishment. I need help!

I go over to my wardrobe and start to open the door but stop as I catch sight of myself in its mirror.

"What's happened to you Vera Hobbs?" I say aloud and in shock. "What's happened to you?"

I look tired, pale and drawn and the sight of my own reflection actually frightens me. Where has that lovely, lively, happy and vibrant girl that used to be

Vera Hobbs disappeared to? She certainly isn't at home any more. I cover my face with my hands. I used to love my face and my smiles but, suddenly, I hate them. My hands cover my features but they also suddenly cover huge tears that well up from the very pit of my stomach and take over my soul. They seem to come directly from the very place that my baby is lying. None of this is dad's fault though is it? Or mum's. This is all my doing, but I did it through a beautiful love and through complete innocence.

My tears become utterly uncontrollable as I look at myself again and break down.

"I'm only fifteen!" I shout, through immense emotional torture. "I can't go through this!"

So, without being able to get fully to my feet through the torture of my feelings, I stumble out of the door and onto the landing.

"Mum! Mum! Mum! I need you! Please!"

At the top of the stairs I sink to my knees, almost as if to get in a prayer position.

"Mum! I need you!"

My top is absolutely drenched with tears and I can't stop them. It is as if a dam has burst or flood gates have been crashed open.

I plead pitifully again.

"Mum! Please Mum! Please!!"

Eventually a door opens and she comes out of the kitchen. She speaks without really looking at me. Her voice is cold, heartless and hurtful. It rips through me like a knife and rents my very being apart.

"Go and pack Vera," she orders, totally without emotion. "You're leaving."

"But mum. I…"

My sentence is cut short by the opening and closing of the back door and mum disappears back into the kitchen, closing the door between us.

"I'm fifteen and pregnant! I need support mum! Not this!"

I sob and sob. Not a silly little girlie cry but a sob from inside. A sob that is rocking the very foundation of my body. I'm lost. Utterly and wholly lost.

It was dad who came in through the back door and suddenly he is there at the bottom of the stairs.

"Packed girl?"

I shake my head and tears fly to the left and the right. I wipe my nose on my sleeve. Dad looks at his watch sternly and then points to it.

"Fifteen minutes girl! We leave in fifteen minutes and what you haven't packed by then will stay here and be burned."

"What?"

"You heard. I'm having nothing left of you in this house."

"But I don't want to go dad. I want to stay here. This is my home."

Dad smiles, or even smirks. A horrible smirk. He actually seems to be enjoying it. He's in total control and he loves it. Is that possible?

"Want to stay here? This is your home? It's a bit late for that girl. You should have thought of that before you let that boy come near you, shouldn't you? You act like a whore girl and you'll get treated like one. The trouble is, you didn't think and now you're going to pay the price. You're leaving."

"Where am I going?"

"That's for me to know and for you to find out."

He looks at his watch again and again he smirks. He looks evil.

"And now you've only got thirteen and a half minutes girl. Pack!"

I'm desperate and in a complete mess. My body has been quaking with tears and is still almost uncontrollable. I try to stand but my frame will not hold me. My legs are jelly.

"Move girl!"

I try again but it seems impossible. I'm not defying his orders but it must seem that way.

"You move or I'll bloody well move you!"

He starts to climb the stairs with his hand raised. I know I have to move, but can I? I must or violence will be the consequence. He has a heart of stone and a voice like thunder.

I'm just to my feet as he reaches me and his hand connects with the back of my head. I'm too numbed to feel anything. He then pushes me into my bedroom before looking at his watch again.

"Twelve minutes girl! Pack!"

I have to pull myself together and do manage it. I could say I do well in doing so, but no. I have no choice but to concentrate my mind on the task in hand. I open my wardrobe fully, take things off the hanging rail and place them in the case before doing the same thing with my chest of drawers. Must take my dressing gown and slippers. Will I need them? I don't even know where I'm going. It's not going to be a hotel in Brighton, is it?

Within a few minutes things are packed, clothes in the case and shoes and other bits and pieces are in the box which is tied tightly with the string that was oh so generously given to me. I'm exhausted and empty and just sit on the edge of my bed. My life isn't over but my old one certainly is. Things can never be the same again and I have to start anew. I have no wish to though. My only tiny hope is that I can see Jonny as I pass by his house. That is if I pass by his house. I don't know.

Dad enters the room with the door smashing against my chest of drawers again. The scent bottle doesn't fall over this time because it's in the box. He grabs my case.

"Bring the box!"

I get to my feet and pick up the box, trying not to look back as I leave. Will I ever see my bedroom again? I somehow doubt the fact. I'm still not fully in control of my legs or body and sniff to hold back more tears as I go down the stairs for the first time in three days, trying to force my legs to hold the weight of my body and my box.

I look at the door to the kitchen which is slightly open but it is slowly pulled to.

"Mum!"

No answer.

Will I ever see her again?

"I need my wellingtons."

"They're in the car."

"And my coat, hat and scarf."

"They're in the car as well."

Dad opens the front door.

"Stay there."

He looks around to see no one is looking. It's as if he's smuggling a fugitive into hiding. It reminds me of when my Jonny did the same thing some time ago.

I stand in the hallway as he puts the case and box into the boot. He then opens the back door of the car and beckons for me to get in. It's a wonder he doesn't put a blanket over my head or something.

I sit on the back seat next to my wellingtons, coat, hat and scarf as he gets in and starts the engine.

"Lay down girl."

"Why?"

"I said bloody lay down!"

I do so as we set off. I'm not to be seen. Then again, why should I be seen? I'm a nobody aren't I? Who wants to see me?

All I can see are the cherry trees flashing by as we drive beneath them. Their leaves are brown and are falling. I hope Jonny and his brothers had plenty of cherries this year. The trees stop and I know we are passing the terrace. I'd love to see Jonny but am terrified of the consequences should I try to look.

A right turn and then a left and then another slight hill. This time upwards. I know where I am and I suddenly know where I'm headed. Why am I always so stupid? We are passing the water tower and that can only mean one destination. I'm being taken to aunt Gloria's farm. Of course. I'm pathetic. What better place to hold me? It's over thirty miles from home, it's out in the middle of the woods and no one ever visits. I'm sad about my realisation but comforted a little as well. At least I know the place, I think to myself. I know aunt Gloria as well though. Can I survive living with her for months, or years? I have always enjoyed a visit but then I've always known I would be going home later. I've been banished from that home now and have no idea if I'll ever see it again.

As we head out of town and into a forested area, I dare to venture into a sitting position. Dad says nothing.

"I didn't mean to dad. You know that, don't you?"

No reply and no emotion.

"I know it's been a shock to your dad but it was a shock to me as well."

Still no reply. He just turns on the windscreen wipers as it's started to rain.

"I didn't mean to. It just happened. Nobody told me anything about it, did they?"

"Be quiet girl."

I can't. I'm devastated at this drastic turn in my life and need to talk to what has now become a captive audience of one.

"I need you dad. I need you and mum. I'm pregnant and don't know what's going to happen. I need you two to see me through it. You're my parents."

He just shakes his head and concentrates on his driving as the rain increases.

"Me and Jonny love each other dad. We love each other and everything seemed so natural. When we took our clothes off and laid on his bed it didn't seem wrong. It seemed so right. It all did. I know we're only young but we really do love each other."

I can see dad is getting a little irate. His colour has changed and he's running his finger between his shirt collar and his neck in order to release any built-up heat. It's plain to see I'm annoying him but I need to talk and talk I do.

"It could all work out dad. Would it be the end of the world if me and Jonny were together? Not just yet I know but we could be together one day and you could be so proud to be a granddad. Can't you imagine holding a baby and knowing it is your own grandchild? Can't you..."

Suddenly the brakes of the car are sharply applied and the whole thing judders as it comes to a sudden and vicious halt. A puff of acrid smoke from the tyres fills the air. Dad turns his head and glares at me before we set off again, this time slowly. He looks in his mirrors and then takes a sharp left down a track into the trees before driving a few yards and stopping again. He gets out and comes around to my door. He pulls it open sharply and grabs my arm.

"Get out slut!" he orders, fiercely.

I have little choice but to move and am soon on my feet. The rain is quite heavy and constant and I'm getting wet. Dad goes round to the boot of the car and takes out my things. He unceremoniously throws them on the grass beside me before throwing my boots, coat, hat and scarf with them from the back seat and then he climbs back into the car, starts it and heads off down the forest track where he finds a spot to turn around. It's now raining even harder and I'm not dressed for it. He returns and I think he's going straight past but he does stop and his window is wound down.

"You walking to Gloria's girl?"

I shake my head and, this time, it's raindrops that fly instead of tears, although there are a few of those as well.

"But dad, I…"

He starts to drive off again.

"Dad!"

The car stops.

"Put your things in the boot girl. I'm not getting wet for you."

I undo the heavy boot lid and put in the case, my now soaking cardboard box and other things before shutting the lid again and getting back into my seat, soaked to the skin.

"I'm taking you girl," I'm told. "But another fucking word out of you and you're walking. Alright?"

I nod again.

"I said alright!"

"Yes dad."

We leave the forest track and he increases his speed. His driving doesn't seem safe but he just wants to get to the farm and dump me. We arrive thirty minutes later and the car lumps and bumps down Gloria's muddy and unkempt long lane. The rain has stopped and we arrive at the house with Gloria standing, arms crossed, at the front door. For some reason, she doesn't seem too pleased to see me.

"Stay there."

I do and watch as my things are dumped at Gloria's feet and dad gets out his wallet. He takes out some money and hands it to Gloria. She immediately puts it in the pocket of her dark blue apron. I say pocket but there should be two of them. One is hanging down and is in dire need of repair. They talk but I cannot hear a word of what they're saying. I can only see lips moving and gestures being made. They're not talking about the weather, are they? They have to be talking about me, the fallen woman who is still a child.

As they talk I look at Gloria. She's a tall plump woman with straggly hair that's tied back. She's wearing a short sleeved dress under her apron and that only accentuates the fullness of her arms. They're flabby and flesh seems to rock from side to side when she gestures as she talks. She is wearing wellingtons that have seen far better days and I can see the need for mine. I'm being paid for by dad but I'll be cheap labour for her. I'm not going to have months of rest. I'm going to be a cheap workhorse. They finish talking and dad comes over. He opens my door again.

"Get out girl."

I do so and we walk over to aunt Gloria.

"Got yourself in the club have you girl?" she sneers. "Well, now you have, you can't stay at home, can you? Your dad is a respected man in your town. He can't have a little tramp like you living with him, can he? You've let the family down girl so now you've got to come and live with your auntie Gloria."

She looks at dad and sneers. Their faces share the same, almost smug and sick, expressions.

"Don't you worry Reg. Gloria will make good use of her. There's plenty to do around here. She'll not be sitting around getting fat."

She then sniggers.

"Mind you Reg," she says, almost laughing, "she's not going to stay little, is she? Not in her state."

Dad turns to me and points his finger in my face.

"Give Gloria any trouble girl and I'll be after you. Got it?"

I nod again. Perhaps I should have learned by now.

"Got it tramp?"

"Yes dad."

He turns to get in the car and, automatically I fall to my knees again as if to offer him a prayer.

"Dad!"

I'm surprised that he stops and turns around.

"I do need you dad. I know I keep saying it but I really really do."

Huge tears well up again from where my baby lays and the floodgates open once more.

"Please don't do this dad. Take me home to mum. Please!"

I'm shocked as he comes over to me and takes my hand to help me to my feet. He smiles and, for a second or two I take it as coming from genuine care and concern.

"I love you dad."

He smiles again and then squeezes my hand. Gently at first, just as Jonny would have done, but then viciously until it really hurts. It feels as if my bones are grinding together. His face changes and he seems to rejoice in using all his effort to crush me. I want to fall to my knees again in pain but he holds me firm before looking at Gloria.

"See what I've bred Gloria," he says, still squeezing hard and almost grinding his teeth. "Where did I go wrong? I've bred an imbecile."

I'm now back on my knees and crying in pain, torment, anguish, despair and any other horrible emotions anyone can think of. He lets go of my hand and almost chuckles.

"The bitch is yours now sis," he tells Gloria. "Make sure she behaves. At least there'll be no boys around here to take her knickers off for her."

He's hit me and he's hurt me. He's abused me dreadfully both physically and emotionally but then he adds a final insult as if to crown his abuse. He aims a large amount of spit down upon me. It lands in my hair.

"Don't give the bitch an easy time Gloria."

"Don't worry. I won't."

Another heavy shower starts and dad gets into his car and drives off. I watch him go, now glad to see the back of him. He's gone a step too far this time. Gloria walks indoors.

"Come on girl!"

I start to go in but she stops me.

"Get your stuff girl. It's all getting wet. You don't think I'm going to get it for you, do you? I'm being paid to look after you, not be your servant. You're nothing special just because you're an idiot and have got yourself pregnant you know."

I look into her eyes. She is actually enjoying all this.

My cardboard box is wet, torn and ruined and my things fall out of it as I lift. This makes Gloria laugh.

"Hurry up girl!" she shouts, looking skywards from the dryness of being just inside the door. "It's going to rain soon!"

I'm eventually indoors with all my things. I'm wet, devastated and heartbroken. I'm at the bottom of a huge pit of despair but am suddenly so annoyed with the world around me that I'm determined to face up to it, hit it square in the face and beat it.

"Back bedroom," Gloria utters.

I go there via the back stairs and am glad to.

19.

Vera has been crying but wipes her eyes on another tissue. She sits more upright than she has been and seems positive.

So the next thing you know we were in the car. Him in the front, me in the back and the suitcase and box in the boot and we were off somewhere. My mother didn't come with us and she never even said goodbye. She hid in the kitchen. I saw her close the door. When we headed out of town and up by the water tower, I realised we were headed for my aunt Gloria's place. Then it all made sense. They were going to hide me away. Aunt Gloria lived miles and miles out of town and down a rough lane that went into the woods. There was no one else about anywhere. She lived down there on her own with just her chickens and ducks and dogs and cats and pigs and loved it, but was I going to love it so much this time? I used to. This time I'd sinned and sinned badly. I was a disgrace to my parents and had to be shut away. Hidden from the sight of everybody who was still decent. Not like me. I was tainted. What better place to put me? It would have been nice if my parents were the kind sort who could visit at weekends but they wouldn't come would they? I knew they wouldn't. I didn't want to see dad any more anyway. Not after what he'd done. I had months to go. I knew that. I also knew it was only going to be me and aunt Gloria and she was never exactly a bundle of laughs even before I turned into that 'tramp', as she called me.

Dad, I prefer now to just call him my father, stopped the car and got out. Without a word to me he went round the back and took the old suitcase and box and my boots from the boot and walked to the door of the house with them. Gloria was there. I couldn't call her 'aunt Gloria' any more after that day. Not for some time anyway. I couldn't hear what they were saying because I was still sitting in the car. I knew I had to get out but realised that decisions weren't mine to make any more and I think I was sitting there waiting for permission. I saw him take his wallet out and give Gloria some money. It was obviously for my board and lodgings. He then came around to me and told me to get out of the car. They were the first words he'd spoken since he nearly left me in the forest. I got out of the car and walked towards the door to join them but as I did they both turned nasty and both seemed to revel in my misfortune. And then he… That man actually spat on me. I was so disgusting that he actually spat on me. Could a real father ever do that to his daughter; his child? His child who had always desperately sought his love? Maybe I was pregnant but I was still his daughter and even a simple goodbye would have healed some pain, but no. He spat on me instead. He hated me so much that I just sat on my knees in the rain and watched as he got into the car and drove off.

"I did need you dad!" I screamed, loudly. "I did really need you! But not now! You've lost everything from me now. You can't do that and still be respected. But please tell mum that I still love her!"

He had been so vile to me but I still did love my mum, despite her fully taking his side in the matter. She was a weak woman though. Weak willed.

Vera wipes her eyes again.

Gloria's house was old, dark and dingy and it always reminded me of Cold Comfort Farm which was one of my favourite books. I'd read it at least five times before I grew up and spent all my time with Jonny instead. Maybe if I'd read it a few more times instead of playing games that I didn't understand I wouldn't have to be here telling you my story, but it did happen and at least I had my little Robin for a while. I was never to see Jonny again and never will but I had Robin and he still comes to see me. Haven't seen him yet today though but it's not nice outside and Albert's not here to find him food is he?

I started to walk into Gloria's house but she stopped me and asked me if I was leaving my things outside. I'd tried to go in without them and she told me just because I'd been an idiot and got myself pregnant it didn't mean I was any sort of special case. She said she wasn't my servant. She told me I would be with her for months and I would do as I was told and I could also carry my own bloody stuff in as well. My mother and father had turned hostile towards me so quickly and it seemed that Gloria was all too willing to follow suit. She seemed to be loving it as if it was some kind of perverse entertainment. It was to her.

She told me that my room was at the back of the house. It was up the second flight of stairs, the back stairs. She said I could come down when she said and I would do what she said. 'You'll work hard my girl,' she told me. "There's plenty to do round here to keep you out of trouble." Then she laughed a horrible laugh and said I was in enough trouble as it was.

She was against me and she was the only person I had. It didn't take too much working out that I was in for a lonely few months, or year, or whatever, stuck in the middle of nowhere on a run-down small holding or farm in an even more run-down house.

Somehow though, through it all, I was adamant that I was going to win. I had to for myself and what was inside me, my little baby. My little Robin.

These days I suppose anyone in my position would have just taken out their mobile telephone thingies and would have spoken to a friend. I had friends, lots of them, but them mobile things were never even dreamed of then were they? All I had was me. Me and a baby inside me and the sickness which did soon pass.

Gloria had been on her own for years. Ever since her husband Fred died of a heart attack in the pigsty. She lost him and she never looked for anybody else. She'd spent so long on her own that I think she'd almost forgotten how to speak to anybody, apart from my father. She certainly didn't make too much of an effort with me anyway. She…

"Your tablets Vera."

It's a different nurse today. It's that big one, the one with the mole on the back of her hand. Huge it is. Old Ted in room 11 upstairs, he says it's too brown for a mole. He says it must be a rat instead. I haven't seen him lately. Funny old soul he is, or was. He hasn't been well. I've had the flu but they say he's got pneumonia.

"What about Ted in room 11 upstairs?"

"He's not well," the nurse says. "You've had the flu but he's got pneumonia."

"I know."

"To tell you the truth Vera," she tells me, concerned, "we don't think he'll get over it. They wanted to take him to hospital but he said no. He said this is his home now and this is where he wants to end his days."

I tell her I can understand that. I tell her to give him plenty of good things to keep his strength up. Some sugar perhaps. Just a little.

She gives me my tablets and I swallow them the same as I do every day. Every day, two or three times a day, and at night. It seems half my life these days is spent swallowing tablets. It's a drudge but they do keep me alive. My little Robin didn't have tablets did he?

"We're having a man in this afternoon playing the guitar and singing songs Vera," the nurse says. "You'll like that won't you?"

"I will," I tell her. "Is he doing country and western?"

"I think so," she says. "But I'm not sure. I'm more into Adele myself."

Who he is, I don't know.

Then the new girl comes back to me.

"Alright Vera sweetheart?"

"I'm alright...?"

"It's Rachel."

She holds my hand and kneels down beside me. It's lovely and I look at her. Her eyes are level with mine instead of me having to look up at her. That's the trouble with life. You always seem to have to look up to people. Especially when you're in a chair or if you've been bad.

"You look sad Vera," she says.

"No sweetheart," I tell her. "I'm just telling my story."

"Who to?"

I laugh.

"Anyone who'll bloody listen sweetheart," I say.

"I'm busy," she says. "But I will listen one day. I will."

I hold her one hand with both of mine. She does have two hands.

"Have you got a husband?"

"A boyfriend."

"Well," I say, "you tell him that old Vera says he's a lucky chap."

"And I'm lucky as well," she replies. "He's a cracker. I bet you had lots of boyfriends when you were younger."

"I had a husband," I tell her. "I did have a husband but only one real boyfriend. Only the one and he wasn't my husband. He was my Jonny, but I lost him."

"Can you please go and see to Mrs Graham, Rachel?" one of the other girls orders her, a little abruptly. "Her buzzer is ringing and we haven't got time to talk at the minute."

"Got to go," Rachel says, standing up. "Sorry. We are busy."

She stands up and is about to walk away.

"Look," she says, "there's a robin by the window."

"Yes," I answer, smiling a knowing smile. "That's my little Robin that is and he's come to say hello."

"See you later Vera."

"Bye love."

She's a lovely girl. All smiles. I used to be like that before I went to see doctor Greenwood. How life changed.

20.

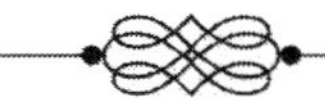

I've spent the night in a strange house, in a strange bed that felt damp and I'm also in a condition that worries me immensely but, for some reason, I've slept. I came to bed last night in a mood that I certainly didn't expect. In my mind I'd taken stock and, because I realised my situation was hopeless, I seemed to accept it. As I thought when I saw doctor Greenwood and he told me I was pregnant, I'm not dying of cancer am I? I'm in a mess but I'm still young, I'm still fit and healthy, I've still got a life ahead of me and, most importantly, I'm still Vera Hobbs. I must get to love her again. I vow to myself that this is my goal and I will achieve it. So, with a slight pain in my belly but the same sized smile on my face, I get out of bed and go to the window to open the curtains. As I do so, I smile again.

It looks like the curtains used to be white many years ago but they are now a dirty shade or orangey brown where rain has easily forced itself through the ill-fitting window frames and stained them. There are still one or two patches of white to be seen but only in the top corners. They have also thinned through the years and don't stop too much light coming through. The funniest thing is, they are held up with a piece of string. The sort farmers use to tie their straw bales together.

I need the toilet but that's not just a few steps across the landing any more is it? It was at home but isn't now. It's across the yard so I go down, out of the back door, past the dog kennel and head there. It's quite a warm day and the smell of it seems to come out to greet me. I hold my breath and think of Jonny as I sit down on the wooden seat and notice the squares of paper that are hung up on a nail in the wall to my left. They are held there with the same kind of string that hold my curtains up. I do miss my Jonny. My father has lost my respect and my mother will probably never have anything to do with me again but I do wish my Jonny could see me and hold me. A tear comes to my eye again but I banish it just as I have been banished. I'm in a fight and tears are never going to win even a single round for me. I do love Jonny but I have to be realistic. He's no idea where I am and I've got to do this on my own. Then I think to myself and smile. Why am I pulling off a piece of paper from the string when I did manage to bring two of Dad's Izal toilet rolls with me? They're in what's left of my cardboard box. Perhaps I can give Gloria the string that tied it up. Looks like it could come in handy. She obviously uses it for everything. I'd stolen the toilet rolls and had hid them in a drawer in my bedroom. I was going to give them to Jonny as a present.

Back in the kitchen, a fire has been lit in the cast iron cooking range. The door of the fire is open and sparks crackle and fly across the red pamment tiled floor. A small rug shows quite severe signs of burning. The room is slightly smoky and nothing is quite clean but it does smell good. There is no electricity or gas on the farm and everything runs just as it would have done when the farm was built all those years ago. When it was, I don't know but all the beams and cobwebs tell me it is hundreds of years old. Gloria enters the room, still wearing the same apron over the same dress. Her boots are by the back door and her feet are bare.

"It's Sunday my girl," she tells me.

Her mood seems to have brightened. If only a little.

"It's Sunday and I've let you have a bit of a lay in. It's seven o'clock already and tomorrow you'll have done an hour's work by now. We've got to get things sorted. Get into a routine. You can't stay in bed on a farm. There's work to do. We'll have breakfast and then I'll spend the day showing you what to do. Show the ins and outs of everything. I'm only showing you the once and tomorrow you are on your own so watch and listen good and then there'll be no mistakes. Right?"

"Yes."

She turns away from me and takes a huge frying pan down from a large iron hook in one of the heavy oak beams. It rattles against an equally large saucepan as she does so. Then she spits onto the hotplate and it sizzles. I've seen it before. This is her way of testing that the fire beneath is doing its job. Then she takes out a huge piece of lard from her meat safe and throws it in the pan before letting it melt and then dropping in five rashers of bacon.

The room has smelled good but it immediately fills with the aroma of bacon and the smell turns from good to delicious. Mind you, the spitting did remind me of my father and it has saddened me a little but, again, I fight it and look forward to breakfast. The bacon is soon set aside and three eggs are dropped in the pan instead, each half submerged in fat. No wonder Gloria isn't the skinniest of women with the best of complexions.

"Get the bread and butter girl."

A half loaf of homemade bread is sitting on the breadboard with the bread knife embedded into it and she tells me the butter is in the meat safe. It isn't meat but the safe does keep flies off. I place both the bread and the butter on the breakfast table.

"Cut it."

I do. I cut it thick as I've seen Gloria do before. She looks at me and nods in approval. I then spread lashings of butter on it as she comes over with two plates of steaming egg and bacon. One egg and two rashers for me and two eggs and three rashers for her. Mine is smaller than hers but I don't argue. It's more than I normally eat at home and I'm grateful. We eat egg, bacon and doorstop sized bread in silence under the large three branched oil lamp that hangs above us. I've only ever seen it fully lit when her and my parents play cards.

"Right girl," Gloria says, as she wipes a crust of bread around her plate to mop up all the excess fat so as not to waste anything. "Let's get you familiar with the farm."

"Can you call me Vera?"

The atmosphere had been quite convivial but I've pushed things too far. Her mood changes.

"You used to be called Vera, girl. But that was before you took your knickers off for every Tom, Dick or Harry in your town. I'll call you what I like from now on. Would you prefer Girl, Tramp, Slut, or Whore?"

I shake my head.

"You choose, girl. What's it to be?"

I just look down. She seemed in such an almost cheerful mood and I've spoiled it.

"I only did it with my Jonny."

"I don't care if you did it with Jonny and Tom, Dick and Harry girl. You're a tramp and that's how you'll be treated if you don't behave. Do as I say and things will be alright. Cross me or question me and they won't be. Got that?"

I nod.

"I said got that?"

"Yes."

"Good."

No one could fail to see her and my father are brother and sister.

"Go and finish getting dressed."

"I haven't washed yet."

"Wash? Wash? What, first thing in the morning? Don't be stupid girl. We wash at night. No good washing now when you're going to get dirty out there.

What sense would that make? You can have a jug of hot water this evening."

We are soon out in the farmyard with the sights and sounds filling the air. The cockerel is almost constantly crowing, chickens are clucking and ducks are quacking as they swim across the small pit that takes up part of the farmyard, under the trees. Sounds come from the cow shed. The cock crows yet again and Gloria picks up a stone and hurls it in its direction. It lands a foot or so from it and it quickly runs for cover.

"Bloody thing," Gloria laughs. "I have to do that every morning. I'll hit the bugger one day and then it can go in the pot."

"But then you won't get any baby chickens."

She looks at me and smirks.

"So you're learning at last then? Shame you didn't learn a few months ago isn't it?"

We move on to the pigs who are shut in their sties.

"Have to get them out in the mornings and clean all the shit out. We give them fresh straw. But not too much. Only replace what we take out. Straw costs money you know. Have to make it last. The string comes in handy though."

I'd noticed.

"Eggs."

Gloria has picked up a bucket from a shed next to the pigs and throws corn from it into the chicken run and then we go over to the back of the chicken house where there are compartments jutting out with liftable roofs on them. Gloria lifts the first one and shoos out a hen. A couple of feathers fly and she clucks fiercely. Gloria lifts out two eggs.

"Don't miss any."

"I won't."

A bark is heard from next to the house. Bruno, the golden retriever, has been quiet in his kennel but has stirred. Gloria told us he was named after her late husband's favourite brand of pipe tobacco.

"Go and let him off."

I do so. He's on a chain and relishes his freedom. He jumps up at me playfully as a thank you and then runs over to the pond where all the ducks flee immediately to the middle to escape any hostility. They look at him and quack loudly in triumph.

"Come here dog!"

He's 'dog' and I'm 'girl'. Don't we both have names?

Bruno comes to me and sits obediently beside me, looking up at me. At least he still loves me. He's not judgemental.

Next stop is the vegetable garden. Potato tops are dying off and lay limp and colourless on the ground while runner bean plants are also changing colour. A few runner beans are still on the plants but they are drying out fast and look inedible.

"I'm saving them for next year," Gloria tells me. "When they're dry, you'll pick them, take out the seeds and store them indoors in a paper bag. Got to keep them somewhere where the mice won't get at them. The meat safe is the best place."

She points to the potatoes.

"When we've done you'll come back and dig enough potatoes for tonight's tea. The tools are in the shed with the chicken food."

"Tea?"

"It's tea here girl. We're too busy to eat at dinner time. Even on a Sunday. I only ever eat my main meal in the middle of the day when your mum and dad come to visit and I give myself the afternoon off."

"Do you ever get any other visitors?"

"No. And don't want them neither. I like being on my own. Well, I did. Got you now haven't I? We'll make the most of it. Dig a few carrots as well. And a parsnip or two."

She points to tell me which is which. I can tell a carrot from a parsnip but not when they are still buried in the ground.

"Use a fork," she instructs me. "But try not to shove it through the vegetables. Don't use the rake. The handle's broken and the string hasn't made too good a job of mending it."

We finish our tour with her telling me she'll teach me to milk the two cows but she'll feed the pigs because she doesn't want me giving them too much because 'food costs money' and then I go to the tool shed with Bruno at my side.

The first implement I find is the rake and I can see why I'm not to use it. The handle is completely broken in two and Gloria has spliced it together with her string. It has two wooden splints. One either side. Just like a broken leg. I lift it by the top end of the handle and the bottom half swings like a pendulum on a clock. I smile but then jump as I see a huge rat scurry across the floor in front of me. Bruno darts into action but is too slow. He's not a ratter. The rat escapes.

"Next time you go in there," Gloria tells me, later, "you take a good stick and you smash the rat on the head. They're no good and mustn't be allowed to live."

At five o'clock, I'm offered my jug of water, or half a jug to be more precise, and I take it to my room and pour it into a large bowl which sits on the worm-eaten dressing table. Beside it is a quite shiny halfpenny which is dated 1937 and has probably been sitting there ever since. I think to close my curtains before undressing but what's the point? I'm not in town now am I? I'm on a farm, or smallholding, and the nearest set of human eyes is probably ten miles away. Even as the crow flies. There are plenty of them around the farm despite the fact that Gloria shoots them with her old but trusty twelve bore shot gun. She even eats them sometimes. 'You can't turn down free meat,' she'd say.

I undress and look down at my stomach. It has filled out but so has the rest of me. I can see no sign of my baby in there as yet and don't know when I will. Perhaps in a few weeks' time?

Gloria has given me a big bar of Fairy green soap and she has told me to make it last. It's so big that I would think it would last for at least a year. We sold it in Mrs Bloomfield's shop and sold lots of bars as well. It's good for washing everything but, at home, we did have more ladylike and perfumed soap. Still, at least it will get me clean. I wet a well-worn flannel and rub the soap on it before rubbing my body. It doesn't smell too bad. At home we have bathroom mats but, in my new bedroom, I quickly learn to put a towel on the floor to mop up any errant drops of water. If they land they are going to clean that part of the rug and it will go all discoloured. Mostly dirty but with clean spots.

I haven't had chance to clean my hair since my father did what he did to me. I know the rain did wash off the worst of it but I heave a huge sigh as I dip my head down into the bowl. There's no shampoo so I have to use the soap. It's not so good but it does work.

The kitchen smells good again as the fire in the range is lit, with the door shut this time, and the smell of roasting chicken fills the room.

"Plates."

I get out the plates, knives and forks and set the table. The salt and pepper are already there. They live there and are only ever moved when the cards come out.

"That potato's yours," Gloria says, as she dishes up. "You put the fork through that one."

She says it, not in a bad way, but just in a matter-of-fact way and almost wears a smile. I say almost because I'm not hoping for too much as yet but I'm going to work on her. She takes the chicken out of the oven.

"Stopped laying," she explains. "They're no good once they stop laying. Can't feed them for nothing can we? Things have to earn their keep here. So we just wring their necks and pop them in the oven.

They're a bit tough but when they're no good that's where they have to go. Can't keep them if they're not good'ns."

She carves and dishes up.

"You can't keep anything that's no good," she repeats. "Not on a farm. They have to go. Farms are for making money. Not for keeping sickly or old things. We're no charity."

It gets dark so she relents and lights one of the three lamps above us. It fills some of the room with a warm glow and the smell of lamp oil fumes soon fills my nostrils. The chicken is tough but is surprisingly tasty. The thought of its poor little neck being wrung doesn't exactly fill me with enthusiasm for eating it but I'm hungry and there's nothing else. I can't ask Gloria for some fish and chips can I? She doesn't breed cod.

I am on my own and do wonder if I will ever see the father of my child again, but I've made the most of the day and have almost enjoyed myself. Of course, I would rather be at home and living my normal life but I can't. This is my life now and I've got to make the most of it. It hurts but I must keep that hurt to a minimum. I go to bed, satisfied that the poor girl who was in such a desperate state yesterday is already on the mend and is determined to win through.

21.

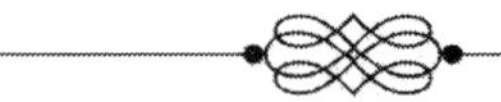

"Thanks sweetheart."

The new girl, Rachel, has just fetched me a glass of orange juice from the kitchen. I needed that. My mouth was so dry it felt like sandpaper.

"You're welcome Vera."

Vera. Gloria wouldn't call me Vera at first. She just called me girl. I was Vera before I became pregnant but, after it, it seemed I'd lost all right to a name. I was just 'girl' and that was that.

I did surprise myself with my attitude though. That poor little girl who had arrived in such a state suddenly seemed to find strength out of sadness and, on her first full day, had made up her mind to hit life in the face and beat it. Bruno still loved me. He had always loved me. I think I was the only person who had shown him love. His tail wagged automatically and madly every time he saw me.

"The singer's coming in," Rachel tells me. "And you're right. He is going to do country and western. He's called Teddy Hunt or something."

"Has he been here before?"

"I don't think so. He wanted to go to the toilet but walked into the vacuum cleaner cupboard instead."

I laugh just as Teddy Hunt comes into the lounge carrying his equipment, a couple of tall speakers, a black computer looking thing and a microphone. The efforts of carrying it all has left him sweating and out of breath and it has pulled his shirt out of his trousers. His huge and hairy belly is showing. Mine wasn't that big at nine months and it certainly wasn't hairy. He sets up his equipment, puts on a cowboy hat and starts. I'm pleasantly surprised at his voice. It certainly beats his appearance. I'm trying to talk and think but it's almost impossible.

"Can you ask him to turn it down a bit Rachel? I can't think or talk."

"Do you want to go back to your room?"

Robin flies away.

"No thanks. I want to talk and think but the music does make a change. My little Robin didn't like it though."

"No. He's flown away."

Vera sits and loses herself in the country and western songs and then, when Teddy Hunt has finished, she turns a relaxed and cheerful face towards us again. She smiles.

Do you know? Gloria did teach me how to milk the cows. It was strange at first and I must admit they did frighten me. Bluebell and Barbara she'd named them. I could understand Bluebell. That's a cow's name if any name is, but where did Barbara come from? I asked her and she told me she'd named it after her mother-in-law, her husband's mother. She said she was called Barbara and she was a right old cow for most of the time. See, when I did as I was told, Gloria was actually quite nice to me sometimes. Well, nice for her anyway. Any sort of pleasantry from her was a bonus. Even at the best of times to start with.

Heddy Tunt is leaving. Or is that Teddy Hunt? Anyway, the singer is leaving. He's finished all his Carl Denver and Dolly Parton and Willie Nelson. Somebody once told me Willie Nelson was some kind of wrestling hold. It took me ages to work that one out. I've always been slow on the uptake when it comes to the sexual side of things.

Oh hang on a minute. She's here. It's that woman who pops in to visit us. The posh one. Or the one who thinks she's posh anyway. She thinks she's wonderful as well. You know the sort don't you? Got nothing but wants us all to think she's got everything. She comes in here to visit everybody and thinks it's the wonderful thing to do. So charitable. We are so lucky to see her. Are we? I just say she's a condescending woman who's far too full of her own importance. Here she comes. She's coming over. I usually pretend to be asleep but it's too late this time. She's seen I'm awake.

"Hello Vera my dear. How are you today? You are usually asleep when I come to speak to you."

"I'm alright thanks."

"Are you over the flu."

"I was never over Flo," I reply, sarcastically. "I'm downstairs as well."

She laughs haughtily.

"Oh you are funny Vera. I love that. It's good to see a character. You've always been a character. I can see that."

She can see no such thing.

She's got a basket in her hand. A wicker one. Looks expensive.

"I've been lucky enough to go to France, the Ardenne, with my daughter, Belinda and I've purchased a few special things for you. I've got preserves and pates and pickles. I thought you could all have some with your afternoon tea."

"Got any humbugs?"

"Oh Vera. No. What would you like? How about a small bar of French chocolate? That's what everyone else is choosing."

They're not choosing it are they? That's what she's giving them. Better than nothing but I would still prefer humbugs.

"I'll have the chocolate please."

"There you are. And don't eat it all at once."

Eat it all at once? My goodness. There's hardly a bite on it once the wrapper comes off.

"It's quite rich Vera," she says.

"It's also quite small," I reply mockingly.

I shouldn't have said that, should I? How ungrateful was that? I know it was but she does get my back up with her posh voice and ways. She visits us and looks down on us as if we're animals in a zoo. Or pets to treat. Still, I suppose it makes her feel good about herself and that's something. We should all do that, feel good about ourselves. I learned to again on Gloria's farm. It took a while but not as long as I thought it would.

The posh woman doesn't stay long with me as she is so important and has to speak to everybody.

"Mustn't miss anyone out Vera," she says as she leaves my side. "I'll love you and leave you."

Thank goodness for that. She's so sickly she almost makes me want to be sick.

"Bye dear."

"Bye Vera."

She walks off and I undo my 'bar' of chocolate. Blimey it is small. I put it all in my mouth and find out she's right. It is rich as well. Got to suck this slowly and make the most of it. Someone over there has got a big box of Ferrero Rocher but I can't get to them. Can't walk but I could eat a couple of them. I think they're French as well.

Let me just finish this chocolate. It is good. Not as good as Ferrero Rocher but edible enough.

She finishes her chocolate and then wipes her mouth on her tissue.

Makes a change from wiping my eyes. I had to do a lot of that after going to see doctor Greenwood but things started to mend, on the farm. I worked as Gloria told me and I tried my hardest to keep on her good side. She did have one you know but she sometimes tried her hardest to hide it. We rubbed along. Yes. I think that's the right word too. We rubbed along and little trouble was seen. I got up, had breakfast, worked, had dinner, or tea as Gloria would call it and then I'd go to bed. There was little else. We never saw anyone else. Gloria milked the cows, and so did I, and then she made her own butter, she grew her own vegetables and fruit and we ate anything that was no longer needed on the farm. Those things that were no longer worth feeding. The ones that weren't 'good'ns'.

Even any post was left in a felt covered wooden box at the top of the lane and we only went to fetch that every three or four days. There was little of that. She had no electric or gas bills or water bills. Even her water had to be pumped up from the ground and into a bucket. It did taste good though. So cool and fresh. We did have a visit once from a man who was trying to sell encyclopaedias. Gloria wasn't interested. He came down in his little cream painted van and left in the same vehicle. Only he left quicker than he'd arrived because Gloria was chasing him with her shotgun. It wasn't loaded but he didn't know that did he? Would you take the chance? I know I wouldn't. Especially if it was Gloria who was brandishing it. She used to kill anything that wasn't wanted.

She showed me how to trap rabbits with a snare. Poor little things. They weren't needed. They tried to eat her vegetables and they too ended up in the pot. I must admit though, they did taste lovely. I just had to tell myself they were meat and not think of them as once fluffy bunnies.

We ate a lot of wild foot. Rabbits, pheasants and hares. Partridges, ducks and pigeons and even woodcock and snipe. Gloria could shoot, trap and despatch anything and all with gusto. She even taught me. I must say we did eat well and our bellies were never empty. Mine wasn't was it? My baby was growing inside me and, as the weeks passed by, I started to grow and, by the time winter set in properly, I had quite a lump. It was to be a very hard winter spent in a place where it was always difficult to escape the cold. We had a chair each and spent our free time sitting by the range. The kitchen was never totally warm that year but at least it was a few degrees warmer than the rest of the house.

22.

It's late November and is a cold, damp and foggy morning. The trees above me are just silhouettes against a grey sky, dripping with moisture. I'm a little late up this morning and am walking down the farmyard not feeling too great. I haven't actually been sick for a while but still do feel it. Bruno is up early this morning and comes out of his kennel briefly to meet me. He jumps up and says hello. His paws are cold and wet. Gloria is already in the cowshed and hears me approaching.

"No time for sleeping in girl!" comes a call as I approach. "Get in here!"

I enter the cowshed, feeling sorry for myself and my condition. Bluebell and Barbara are tied loosely, with frayed rope, to rings hanging from the wall. They are munching slowly on a mediocre amount of hay that has been put in racks in front of them.

"Ten minutes late this morning."

I nod but then remember to answer.

"You'll do extra work today to make up for it."

"Yes. Sorry. I don't feel too well today."

"You'll get over it. In a few months' time."

She laughs and I try to see the comment as a joke but my mood doesn't appreciate her unusual light-heartedness.

"Weeks you've been here Vera Hobbs and I still haven't taught you to milk a cow have I?"

"No."

She's just called me Vera Hobbs instead of Girl or Tramp. That's a small step forwards. Maybe, just maybe, one day she will drop the Hobbs part as well. She stands up and hands me her chipped white enamelled bucket.

"Sit on the stool."

I do so with some trepidation. I'm soon sitting by one of Barbara's back legs and I've seen her kick out before.

"Grab a tit girl."

I look up at Gloria. She's now standing, leaning backwards with her hands on her ample hips.

"Go on girl. Grab a tit."

I nervously do so. It's the first time I've held a cow's udder. It's quite firm and full of milk and is very warm. It's not something I wholeheartedly want to do but the warmth on a cold, damp and foggy day is very welcome.

"Right. Now nip the top off and squeeze."

I look at her again. She is still wearing the blue apron with the torn pocket. I think it's only been washed once since I arrived all those weeks ago.

"What do I do?"

"I said nip the top off and squeeze. You deaf girl?"

She puts her hand in the shape mine is with the teat and shows me.

"Nip the top of the tit and squeeze."

I do but nothing happens.

"Don't let go of the top when you squeeze. It'll go up instead of down won't it?"

I try again and am amazed as a small amount of milk squirts out and into my bucket.

"That's it."

I'm pleased with my efforts and Gloria goes over to a pile of hay under a couple of old swallows nests and takes off another tatty stool and bucket.

"You finish Barbara and I'll do Bluebell. But don't pull the same tit all the time."

The milk and the cows smell lovely and their warmth soon warms me. It was even cold in bed last night. In fact, this is the warmest I've been for about three days, nearly. A mouse scampers across a dusty beam above me and I smile. Sitting down has started to make me feel better.

Gloria's milk goes squirt, squirt, squirt into her bucket but mine only gives a squirt occasionally.

"Speed up girl!" Gloria shouts, in quite a pleasant way. "You'll get the hang of it. Pull the udder one."

I do quicken and then we change cows so that Gloria can make sure every drop has been got from Barbara.

"There'll be some lovely butter there," she says as she finally stops and puts her head into the top of her bucket and sniffs. "Come on. There's other things to do. Got to milk the chickens next."

I look at her and can't believe what I see. The woman actually has a smile on her face. A big one.

"I'll milk the cockerel," I say.

We feed and muck out the pigs before collecting the eggs. I take them indoors.

"Bring my gun. Bring both of them. Bring both of them and some cartridges. A few of the black ones and a few red ones as well. They're the smaller ones."

I know what red looks like.

Indoors, I leave the eggs in the kitchen and go to the front room. It is a room that is sometimes used in the summer but when it's cold, we spend all our time in the kitchen, sitting by the range. We can't have two fires lit at the same time and the range one is more important as it provides our food. The front room is kept cleaner than the rest of the house and you can even see through the windows because they are not covered with years of grime. I've cleaned my bedroom ones.

Behind a high backed windsor armchair stand two guns. Gloria's double barrelled twelve bore and a smaller one that only has one barrel. I put the cartridges, the black ones and the red ones, in my coat pockets and pick up both guns. Gloria is waiting by the broken and rusted metal gate that leads to a lane through a field.

"Foggy days are good days for shooting," she tells me. "We can creep up on the rabbits."

She takes her gun and I realise the smaller one is for me. I hand her the bigger cartridges and she shows me how to load mine.

"Drop the barrel, pop in the cartridge. Close the gun and you're ready to go."

Do I want to shoot anything? Could I kill anything? Gloria seems to love it.

"I kill it and you eat it girl," she says. "That's the way we've done it so far but it's about time we reversed that. Today, you'll kill something as well. Remember, it's the rabbits that eat our vegetables. And they do taste good don't they?"

I can't disagree so we set off, keeping low and close to the tall hedgerow on our right and, as we come to a slight right hand corner, Gloria stops and swiftly ducks around behind me.

"Big old buck rabbit round there," she whispers, pointing. "Your gun is loaded and all you have to do is look along the barrel, point it at the rabbit and squeeze the trigger. The gun will do the rest. Go on girl. Keep low."

I've done it at the fairground so I round the corner quietly and low and see the rabbit a few yards ahead of me. He seems huge. I know I've got to shoot it but can I? I've never shot real animals at the fair. They do eat our vegetables and they do taste lovely but can I take a life? Would that be so wrong?

"Go on girl."

She gives me a slight shove from behind and I think and repeat my instructions to myself. Look down the barrel, point it at the rabbit and pull the trigger. Can I?

I receive another shove and set to. The rabbit sits tall, calm and still, munching on a piece of grass and I point the gun and pull the trigger. The gun hits back into my shoulder and, with an almighty bang, the rabbit falls on its side with its legs flailing in all directions as if it is trying to run away but can't. I have mixed emotions running through my head. I've achieved my goal but I've just shot something that has never done me any harm. Gloria rushes passed me.

"It's not dead yet."

She picks it up by its back legs with one hand, grabs its neck with the other and swiftly pulls down and backwards. I think I hear bones crunching. It still moves slightly but Gloria assures me it's dead. She does everything in such a hard and matter-of-fact way.

"That's life on a farm," she explains. "Kill or starve."

Her words are as plain as her actions.

She then takes out a sharp shut-knife from her good pocket and opens it. Within seconds the insides of the rabbit are laying, steaming, on the ground and she has cut a hole in one back leg to tuck the other one through. It makes the back legs into a kind of handle with which to carry it.

"I used to do this with my dad when I was little," she tells me. "He had the gun and I had a stick. By the end of the day I'd be walking home with my stick over my shoulder and there'd be ten or twelve rabbits hanging from it. Heavy they were for a little'n. Carry this one and let me have a go next."

I take the poor dead creature with some trepidation and, I must admit, just a little pride as well. I know what's for dinner, or tea, tonight. There are turnips, potatoes and carrots indoors. It'll be a hot, warming and nourishing rabbit stew which will amply feed Gloria, me and my baby.

One more rabbit falls to Gloria's bigger and noisier gun, this time killed instantly, and then we head home for a cup of tea before starting work again. I sit and drink as Gloria gets out a sharp knife and quickly and deftly skins both rabbits. Within minutes they are naked and jointed and in a large bowl beside her. She then puts in water followed by a good helping of salt.

"We'll leave that 'til later," she says. "It'll help bring out the flavour."

She then puts the skins on the range fire as fuel because nothing must go to waste.

"Do you want me to peel the veg?"

"No. We'll do that later. Bluebell and Barbara need to go down to the bottom field. It's not a nice day but the grass down there'll do them good. Tell you what. I'll go and do that while you walk up the lane and see if we've got any post. We haven't looked all week."

"Ok."

Everywhere is damp and muddy and the lane is badly rutted. Not through heavy traffic but simply because it is never levelled. Gloria does drive her old Land Rover up it sometimes because, even she has to go to town sometimes. She went last week but didn't take me with her. How do you explain a pregnant fifteen year old companion? It's best for me to remain hidden.

I reach the felt topped box left there for the letters and bend down to open it just as a huge yellow and black car comes around the bend. It stops beside me and a rear window is lowered.

"And who may you be?" a highly posh voice asks from inside.

I've a pain in my belly and take time to stand.

"I'm Vera," I tell the black haired, gaunt and thin old lady. "Gloria is my aunt and I'm staying here for a while."

The lady is visibly shocked. She holds a pair of spectacles on some kind of handle to her eyes and looks down at my bump.

"Huh," she says, disapprovingly. "And the reason for that is all too plain to see isn't it?"

She's a complete stranger and my condition should have nothing whatsoever to do with her but her disapproving look says it all. My condition seems to be everyone's problem far more than it is mine. She suddenly looks ahead.

"Drive on chauffeur," she orders. "We must get away from this den of iniquity."

She looks at me again as she raises the window and I can't help but stick my tongue out at her.

"Insolent girl!" she shouts. "Your father should wipe that horrid little smirk off your face."

"Oh don't you worry!" I shout, as she stops winding the window so that she can hear my answer. "He's tried to do more than that already but he hasn't managed it and neither will you or anyone else!"

She shakes her head in disgust.

"I said drive on chauffeur!"

I stick my tongue out again as she leaves. I think living with Gloria is having a bad influence on me but I'm me and my condition is my business. All this could have taken me down but no. I'm fighting it all the way and if that means sticking my tongue out at some haughty old bag then so be it. I take two letters from the box and walk back down the muddy track with my stomach pointing out and my head held high. What am I coming to and where has that lovely sweet girl Vera Hobbs gone? I cannot answer my own question because I don't know. I don't particularly like where my life is headed but I'm growing up and am determined that, no matter where it is going, no one is going to spoil it. I later, in front of the range, tell Gloria all about my meeting with the posh lady in the posh car and she is aghast.

"That was Lady Morton," she explains, shocked at my impudence. "She owns Fairgate Hall and estate, the huge one down the road. She's the lady of the manor."

I can't help smiling.

"I only put my tongue out at her, twice."

"Twice?"

"You want to watch it girl," Gloria tells me, trying to sound cross. "That old witch will put a spell on you now. Knowing her you'll wake up tomorrow morning in a bed full of rats or frogs or something."

I look into her face and smile again. She's desperately trying to quash it but she can't stop laughing. I laugh too and, for the first time since my appointment with Doctor Greenwood, I do actually feel happy. This is only tinged with the sad thought that I have lost my Jonny. But, that aside, Gloria suddenly loses her control and lets go and we both fall about in our seats in hysterics. She puts her hand on mine.

"Do you know Vera Hobbs…Vera," she finally admits. "You're alight. You're not so bad after all are you?"

A tear comes to my eye. A happy tear this time.

"And neither are you aunt Gloria," I reply.

"Do you know," she says. "We're both a bit rough around the edges aren't we? But we'll do won't we? Yes. Do you know? We'll bloody well do you and me. Now let me dish that stew up. I've put dumplin's in. Herb ones. A touch of wild garlic as well that I dried in the summer. Just a touch. You'll like them. They're my favourites. You set the table and I'll find us a drop of cider each. Let's celebrate!"

The rabbit stew is opened and steam and fragrance fills the room. There are only candles lit tonight as the price of lamp oil has gone up again but the feeling is homely and, suddenly, that's where I feel. At home.

23.

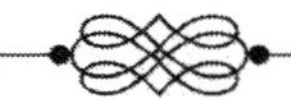

Really, a small glass of cider and slowly stewed rabbit wouldn't be classed these days as much of a celebration but we classed it as one. A huge one. A great hurdle had been jumped and a milestone had been reached. That was the best meal I've ever eaten and it was me who'd provided it. With just one shot, and a slightly bruised shoulder, I had provided meat for dinner. Or tea as Gloria would insist upon. Things weren't always that rosy and we did have a few more very minor fallings out but we had come to an understanding. An understanding of each other and exactly what made the both of us tick. For once, Gloria was enjoying the fact she wasn't on her own. She'd been on her own for far too long and had slowly become an irritable, cross and miserable woman who had a grudge against the world and most people in it. It had come about slowly but, just like the rabbit, time had worked, but the result was the opposite. The rabbit had become tender and sweet whereas Gloria had become hard and bitter. I changed all that you know. Well, almost.

The next day a man came down the lane and knocked at the door. We were having lunch.

I opened the door and recognised the man as being the chauffeur of the big yellow and black car. It wasn't difficult to do as he still had his uniform on. He told me he had been sent by Lady Morton to tell me I had to go to the hall and apologise to her. I told him he'd had a wasted journey and then Gloria joined me at the door and the man repeated the demand.

"She has to go to the hall and apologise to lady Morton," he repeated.

"I'll tell you what we'll do," Gloria said, laying an arm across my shoulders. "What we'll do, me and my girl here, is this. Us two will do nothing and you can sod off back to the old witch and you can tell her she can stuff her demands up her skinny old… I can't say it but you know where I mean don't you? It's the same place they stick them suppositories."

She was serious and he saw it so he walked back up the lane with his tail between his legs and his smart leather boots in the ruts. We shut the door and laughed together again. This may not have been the life I had wanted and dreamt of but at least it was turning into fun.

Susie's here again, with her wonky wheel. Time does fly when I'm talking to you. I like that.

"Haven't you got anybody to fix that Susie?"

"Fix what Veera?"

Hasn't she noticed?

"Your wheel."

"He off on holidays."

"Who is?"

"The man that mend things. He in Gt Yarmouth for two weeks. It long time."

"It certainly is a long time to be in Great Yarmouth," I tell her.

"You want biscuits Veera? How about Gary Baldy today?"

"No," I say. "I do prefer Hobby Nobby."

Susie laughs.

"Oh you so funny lady Veera. Coffee?"

"Black please."

She smiles.

"You want milk in that?"

"No thanks."

She pours my coffee and then off she goes. Wheel a'wobbling.

"See you later Veera."

"Yes. See you later Susie."

Do you know, I didn't really feel too well all through my pregnancy. There were days that were better than others but it did take it out of me. The whole situation should have taken it out of me but I learned something great. I learned that me, little Vera Hobbs, was a strong person. She was a girl who could deal with anything. I didn't know that before my appointment with doctor Greenwood but I soon learned it afterwards. I did like the sweet girl I used to be but the new strong one had character and bite and soon learned to face the world and punch it square on the chin. Physically during that time I did feel ill but, psychologically, I felt good. I'd changed. Or rather, circumstances had changed me.

I do feel a little ill today. Maybe I'll have an early night. But that's silly isn't it? It's only the afternoon. I feel tired and my back aches. Maybe I could leave you and go for a lie down. Yes. Perhaps I'll get to girls to take me to bed. Would you mind? I'll get snuggled down and watch the television. There's bound to be something on. Probably something about houses or gardens or antiques. I'm nearly one of them, an antique. I'm old. The trouble is I'm way past restoration.

"Rachel!"

"Yes Vera!"

"Could I go to my bed please sweetheart?"

She's looking at her upside-down watch.

"Yes. I know it's early Rachel but I've got a horrible back ache. Do you think the nurse would get me a couple of paracetamol?"

She nods.

I used to nod instead of replying verbally. I got wrong for that.

"Ok Vera. Give us a minute or two and we'll take you."

"Thanks sweetheart."

Some of the old people in here have to be lifted in big white hoist things that look like small cranes. They wrap them in this thing and up they go. They lift them up in the air and then drop them in a wheelchair. They don't really drop them though. They lower them. I'm alright though. Two girls just help me to my nearly numb feet and then they turn me around and gently lower me into my wheelchair. Last week, one girl was pushing me, I can't remember which one, and we chased another one, one of the nice foreign ones from the East, up the corridor. It was fun. We must have been doing nearly fifty miles an hour. Well, nearly anyway. I do exaggerate sometimes.

Here comes Rachel with my wheelchair. Well, it's not my wheelchair really. I haven't got my own one. I think it's one that's been left behind by a dead resident. Just like the chair I'm sitting in I suppose. They can't take their chairs and wheelchairs with them can they? They won't burn down at the crematorium will they?

Yes. I'm off to bed to watch television and rest my back now. Robin's not there. I think he's having an early day as well. I'll see you and Robin in the morning.

"Thank you girls. You do look after me."

"Don't forget your Hobnobs Vera."

"Can you bring them with us Sweetheart? I'll probably get crumbs everywhere but I'll eat them in bed."

Rachel nods.

Good night, or afternoon.

24.

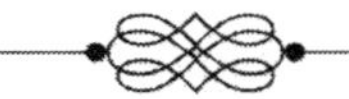

Gloria's got the radio on. I can just hear it although my head is under the bedclothes. It's been a freezing cold night again and seems to be getting worse and worse. Life on the farm is hard through the winter. Gloria did tell me that and now I'm finding out just how true her words were. I slip swiftly out of bed and into my clothes. Yesterday's clothes. They're too tight for me now as I've got quite a lump and it seems to be getting bigger every time I look at it. I can't stop looking though. It's my baby in there. Mine and Jonny's baby. I do miss Jonny and still think of him all the time. I'll find him again one day. At least, I hope I will. Baby names have been running through my head. I've settled on Penelope, Penny, for a girl and although I feel I should call a boy Jonny, I've settle on Robin instead. I do love robins.

Something catches my eye. There's a large, dark butterfly sitting, wings folded, in the corner above my bed. How did that get there? I haven't noticed it before. It must be sheltering there ready for the spring to come. It's got a long wait. I feel we've got lots of bad weather to come before we have any good.

My curtains are so frail now that I open them with great care. It's no good tearing them back as that is what they would do, tear. I open them to find thick ice on the inside of the window. I want to rub it off to look outside but decide to leave it and go downstairs where it's a degree or two warmer.

"You've got the radio on," I say, surprised at Gloria actually using her batteries.

"Waiting for the weather forecast."

"It's not looking good. Mind you, I haven't seen outside yet. My windows are iced over."

Gloria has been washing a couple of items of clothes that have probably been worn for days and dries herself on a worn blue towel which has been hanging by the range. I swear she's putting on more weight. Everything wobbles as she vigorously rubs her hands and arms.

"What are you looking at girl?"

She calls me girl but does so in a kind way these days.

"You are putting on weight," I tell her, honestly.

She looks down.

"Cheeky cow!"

She laughs.

"Well, you are aren't you? You've put on about a stone since I arrived here."

"I suppose so."

I sit in my chair by the range and she takes hers, still holding her towel.

"It's you," she says.

"What's me?"

"This extra weight," she explains, looking down over her ample proportions. "It's all your fault."

"Why me?"

"I never used to bother eating too much when I was on my own, but now you're here we seem to eat all the time."

"And that's my fault?"

"Of course it is girl. If you hadn't got yourself pregnant I'd be as skinny as a rake you bitch."

I laugh.

"Gloria. You've always been fat."

"Fat now is it? You'll be saying I'm obese next."

"You are, nearly."

She pretends to be upset.

"Go on. Ridicule a poor old lady when she's down, why don't you?"

We both laugh but then she turns serious.

"I've been on my own for far too long Vera," she admits. "It turned me into a sour old bag didn't it?"

I nod and, this time, I get away with it.

She reaches forward and holds my hand.

"You've changed me girl and I want to thank you for it. Do you know? Since my Fred died I've hardly seen anybody. I've been a whole week sometimes without speaking to anyone apart from the animals and they never reply. Then in you come to the grumpy and vicious old hag that I'd turned into and you've changed me Vera. You really have. I feel so much lighter."

"You don't look it."

"Cow!" she shouts. "I didn't mean it that way did I? And you know it!"

She starts to get out of her chair and, sensing trouble, I also get out of mine and try to get away but her towel is flicked hard against my bottom. The woman really has changed.

We sit down again. There is work to be done but we warm ourselves with a cup of tea and warm toast each before even contemplating leaving the house.

"And now for the weather forecast," a posh man on the radio says, in his best BBC voice.

We listen intently as we are told that a huge snowstorm is sweeping in from the west and should reach our area by lunchtime. At least six inches is predicted.

With the weather forecast over, the radio is hurriedly turned off in order to save valuable power.

"We'd better get out," Gloria says. "Let's quickly get everything done and then we can have the rest of the morning and afternoon here in the warm. We can get everything tucked up and warm and stay in until milking time tonight. Come on."

Long socks and wellies are put on, plus an extra jumper and my coat, hat and scarf. I wear my gloves until we are in the cowshed. Sitting by the range is lovely but I do still like the warmth and smell coming from Buttercup and Barbara and so does that mouse. He's up in the beams again, scurrying around, looking for food. I say 'that' mouse but it could be a different one. It does look like the same one though. Gloria tries to hit it with a stick but misses by a mile.

"Bloody thing! I'll get you one day!"

We take a bucket and stool each and get in position. I'm quite proficient at it now and Gloria doesn't bother to finish off for me. She knows I'll get every last drop. Soon all that can be heard is 'squirt, squirt, squirt', almost in unison, as our buckets fill and our hands are warmed.

With the cows milked and fed, we close the door and then make a plan. The ducks have a house to go into so we must put some straw in there and the geese must be rounded up and put in the shed. The pigs will be given extra straw and the chickens will be shut in their henhouse. Everything must have food. Gloria looks towards Bruno.

"He'll come indoors with us tonight," she says. "Can't have him outside in six inches of snow."

She looks to the west and sees the sky darkening rapidly.

"It's coming. Look."

We hurry around the farmyard, making ready and then Gloria realises something.

"We've got no wood in," she says. "We'll need a big fire tonight."

Eventually, all the animals are warm, cosy and protected and we head for the woodshed where an errant cockerel is sitting on the woodpile next to Gloria's scruffy old Land Rover. It makes a huge fuss as we enter and rushes noisily outside. Gloria tries to grab it but it hurries passed her.

"Bloody thing will have to find its own shelter," she says.

We fill an big old wooden wheelbarrow with seasoned logs and Gloria pushes it, seemingly effortlessly, towards the house. She's a strong woman.

"Fill the basket and then pile the rest up in the corner," she tells me. "And then we'll get another load. It's going to be a bad'n and we don't want to hold back do we?"

Her good mood is lasting well.

By the time the barrow is filled again, snowflakes have started to fall and they get bigger and heavier by the minute. And then the trees start to rustle as a light breeze turns into a heavy breeze which then turns quickly into a howling gale. Again Gloria swiftly and deftly has the barrow by the farmhouse door and the logs are stashed in a pile in the corner.

"That'll last us a couple of days," she says, closing the door to shut out the day. "If this storm is really bad then all we've got to do is feed the animals, milk the cows and keep warm."

"Bruno!"

I've just realised we've left Bruno outside so quickly brave the storm to rescue him. He isn't exactly unhappy to see me. The snow has already turned into something of a blizzard and we are both glad to get back indoors. He shakes snow off him and I shake my coat. I think I'll keep it on for a little while.

Gloria gets Bruno to lie down by the table, telling me he shouldn't get too close to the fire because it makes his ears sore and itchy for some reason. I've seen that before with Kathy's dog, Blackie.

"Want another cuppa?" Gloria asks.

"Yes please."

"Well get up and make it girl," she says, smiling widely. "I told you when you came here I wasn't going to be your servant didn't I?"

I look at her sternly.

"You did. You said lots of things."

"And can you ever forgive me?"

"No."

We laugh again.

"Of course I can. And I'll get you a cuppa as well."

"I did say a lot of things didn't I?"

I nod again.

"But things have changed haven't they? And you've really changed me."

"For the better?"

"I couldn't be any bloody worse could I? I was angry with you when I should really have been angry with myself. Like everybody else, I thought I was right and just went along with your father."

She notices I've suddenly gone quiet.

"I think we both had a lot of anger inside us Vera, me and your father," she tells me. "I can see that now but I think your father will always be angry. He's always been selfish as well. It's always been what Mr Reg Hobbs wants hasn't it?"

"Yes. And mum has always been caught up in that."

"I know."

"I think me and mum would probably still have loved each other if dad wasn't dad but it's too late now."

"Is it?"

I rub my hand over my swollen belly.

"I think so. Even after this bump has gone they're not going to take me back are they? Dad won't want me and he'll never let mum have me either. She has a life but the biggest part of her life is leading his. It always will be."

Then Gloria surprises me. She comes over to me and throws her arms around me. She pulls me close.

"Then you'll have to stay here won't you? I'm sorry but you're stuck with your old auntie Gloria aren't you?"

I look, seriously, into her eyes.

"Bloody hell," I reply, jokingly. "I don't know if I can stand that."

"Cow!" she shouts again.

Gloria's big brown teapot is filled.

"Put an extra bit of tea in today Vera. Let's have it hot and strong."

Blimey, she is still in a good mood.

I cut two thick pieces of bread and cover them with butter and jam and we sit by the range, listening to the wind howling outside. It seems to be doing its best to destroy everything.

"Do you want to celebrate Christmas this year Vera?"

I'm a bit perplexed by her question and look at her.

"I don't normally," she says, seeing the puzzled look on my face.

"You don't?"

"No. Why bother when there's only me? What do I do? Wrap myself a present up and sing carols to myself. Have you heard my voice? It's horrible."

"I know. I have heard you."

"I do sometimes don't I? I forget you're here."

I tell her that I hadn't really thought about Christmas but had just assumed that it would be celebrated as always.

"We will then. Perhaps we can have a goose. Boris is nice and plump."

I give her a huge look of disapproval and she understands my thoughts and relents.

"Ok. What about Bernard then?"

I see she's joking this time.

"No," I say. "If it's Christmas then we should be charitable and let the animals enjoy it too. Why not lash out and buy a turkey? It's not Christmas without a turkey."

Gloria looks glum.

"A turkey?"

"Yes. A turkey."

"But they…"

"Yes, I know. You haven't got any and they cost money but you're not hard up are you?"

"I am."

"No you're not. I've seen you with that big biscuit tin you keep in the bottom of your wardrobe. How much money have you got in there?'

She's silent.

"Come on. Tell your favourite niece."

"You're only my favourite because you're the only one girl. Don't get too proud of yourself."

"How much?"

"About a thousand," she mumbles. "Well nearly."

"How much?"

"Only a thousand."

"Only?"

"Only a thousand in that tin but there are a few more of them up in the attic."

"What!"

"You've got to have some put away for a rainy day Vera."

I think quickly.

"Well," I say. "It's a snowy one today so today you can make a pledge to have a turkey for Christmas dinner, can't you?"

"I'll think about it."

"No you won't."

"Yes I will."

"Gloria, you won't think about it. You'll do it and that's that."

"Oh, alright Mrs bossy knickers."

"And we'll have a Christmas pudding and decorations."

"Alright."

"And crackers?"

"Alright."

"And new batteries for the radio so we can listen to carols."

She suddenly scowls.

"I'm not prepared to go that far."

"Oh yes you are."

"Oh no I'm not."

"See. You're getting into the spirit of it already."

A gust of wind rattles the old and ill-fitting back door and Gloria goes to the kitchen window.

"Come and look out here Vera!"

I join her and peer out. It's hard to see anything at first as the snow is falling so hard but, as my eyes adjust, I see snow lying everywhere. At least four inches of it. It looks like Christmas already. It looks beautiful from inside but we know we have to go out in it later. But that's later and, for now, we are indoors only watching instead of participating and it's fun.

The cockerel appears. He's trudging up the yard, half covered in snow and is headed towards the woodshed again but he thinks differently and somehow manages to squeeze himself through the slightly opened top half of the cowshed door instead. The wind has freed it. He knows it'll be warm in there.

It's still snowing as we go outside later to check on the animals and milk the cows but it is not falling so hard. Everywhere is white and it looks wonderful. The vicious wind that has been doing its very best to destroy everything in its path has relented and all is still. Even the temperature seems just that little bit higher. Or is that my imagination?

We trudge through the snow towards the cowshed and notice a large branch has fallen from a tree by the pond.

"We'll have that later," Gloria says. "It's a lime tree. That'll burn well next year."

She enters the cowshed, grabs her stick and looks up. There's no mouse this time.

"I'll get the bugger one day," she pledges again.

When we leave, the snow is falling harder again. Not blowing a blizzard this time but falling hard and steady. It's three weeks until Christmas. I wonder if it will stay until then?

25.

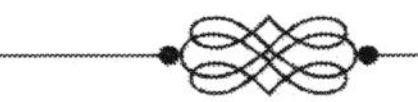

Vera's chair is empty and the robin sits outside, looking in. All is quiet in her corner but then a wheelchair appears from the main corridor that leads to the home's front door. Norma is pushing Vera.

"Oh thanks Norma. That was wonderful. I needed to get out. It's the first time I've been out since I had the flu."

One of the little girls from the East comes over and helps Norma to get my coat off and help me into my chair.

"There's my Robin. He's waiting for me. Hello my little sweetheart."

"You like that robin don't you Vera," Norma says.

"I do," I say. "I do. That's my little Robin that is. He always comes to see me. He knows it wasn't my fault doesn't he?"

They don't understand and don't ask either.

I haven't talked to you for a while have I? No. I went to bed with a bad back didn't I? That was Saturday afternoon. I stayed there all day yesterday so it must be Monday today and Norma has just walked me around the garden, or 'grounds' as the manager woman here calls them. They gave me some paracetamols but they didn't really help. Agony it was. Not as bad as giving birth but it did hurt. All that afternoon and all night it hurt. I felt a bit better when I woke up the next morning but I was washed out. I felt like I'd worked for three days nonstop or something. Oh I was tired. So I stayed in bed all day and watched television. Most of it was rubbish but you put up with that when you are ill on a Sunday don't you? It's rubbish but it's restful.

It's lovely outside though. Not too warm but I did have my coat on. It kept the chill out.

I saw Albert outside. He was working across the other side of the place where they've got a small vegetable garden. He was weeding that. He's always weeding something bless him. And he was swearing. He was swearing about the rabbits eating everything and he wants to bring his gun in to shoot them. They've told him he mustn't because it would scare the residents. I told him it wouldn't scare me because I'm used to guns and once lived on a farm where I shot rabbits, and pigeons and pheasants as well. I even shot a chicken by mistake once. He knew the area well and had even heard of that old witch down the road. We couldn't remember her name but I can now. It was Lady Morton wasn't it? The one I stuck my tongue out at all those years ago. Twice. I never did see her again but that was no hardship was it? I did become naughty, living with aunt Gloria.

Just as we had started to get on together and understand each other, the weather changed and we had a massive snowstorm. In the end there was eight inches of snow and it lasted right up until Christmas. Not all of it lasted but we did still have bits and pieces on Christmas day. The second day it fell was awful though. There was so much that we had to get spades and dig our way into the farm buildings because the doors wouldn't open. Gloria was worried about the cowshed roof. It had started to sag slightly under the snow's weight and one night, in pitch blackness, she decided we had to get ladders and climb up and used rakes and hoes to get as much off as possible. We were sure that, if we didn't, the cows would be squashed and dead the next morning. It worked. We raked and raked and got thoroughly soaked and frozen but we saved the roof and the cows underneath it. We worked so hard in the cold but we worked together and it was fun. Well, we thought of it as fun once we'd finished and were in front of the range again anyway. They were hard times but fun times. I wanted my Jonny but didn't want to go home. Yes, I would have liked to have seen my mother again but Gloria's house had become my home and she had become my friend. I certainly had no wish to see my father again, and never would. I look outside and lose myself in watching my little Robin.

"I see you've been out for a walk Vera," a voice says, disturbing my thoughts.

I turn my head to see the home manager standing beside me. She's a tall slim lady and squats down so her face is at the same level as mine. She reminds me of our old school teacher. I do wish a few more of them would do that, squat down. It doesn't really matter in the end I suppose but it is nice. It does show a little thought. She holds my hand.

"I have," I tell her, putting my other hand on top of hers. "I've been out for a walk in the grounds. Well, not exactly walking but Norma did push me around in my wheelchair. She's a nice girl."

"They all are," she says.

I couldn't totally agree with her statement because there are just one or two of them who are a little abrupt and even rude. I don't answer but just nod.

"Kenneth will be round with the tea trolley soon Vera," she tells me. "I'll make sure he has some Hobnobs."

"It'll be a milky coffee today then," I tell her.

She stands up again and starts to walk away.

"Glad you like milk Vera," she says. "It's good for you, calcium in milk."

I want to tell her I prefer mine black but it's too late. She's gone before I can get the words out.

They're putting a film on in here later. They close the doors and curtains and turn the lights off so we can imagine we are at the pictures. It's quite nice really. They bring us ice creams and even popcorn sometimes. It's a wonder the girl hasn't got a torch and walks backwards like the ushers used to. They used to do that at the pictures. I was up in the circle once with my best friend Kathy and the one in there walked backwards. She fell down the steps and flashed her knickers at everyone. Red they were. Good job it was nearly dark. She didn't hurt herself but was embarrassed, bless her.

"We're putting a film on soon Vera," Norma tells me.

"I know. What is it? Not the *Sound of Music* again is it? We had that three times last week."

"No Vera. It's *Billy Elliott* today."

"Who's he? Is he in the *Sound of Music*?"

She laughs but doesn't really know why. She can't see that I'm joking.

"*Billy Elliott* is a film about a boy who does ballet Vera."

"Does he work in a posh house then?"

"What?"

"Does he work in a posh house?"

"Why?"

She still can't see that I'm joking.

"If he's a valet then he must work in a posh house."

Suddenly the penny drops. Or is it just a halfpenny in Norma's case? She shakes her head.

"You're a naughty lady Vera Betts."

"I do my best."

They usually call me just Vera in here. Vera Betts isn't often heard. That is my name though, Vera Betts. I used to be called Vera Hobbs but I did get married. I wanted to become Vera Clitheroe but that never happened so I ended up getting married to George, George Betts. People thought I'd married George Best. My George couldn't play football. He was good at dominoes though. He was just a lonely man whose wife had died. He was lonely and so was I. He'd moved into our street and we used to meet as we passed on the hill, by where Jonny's terrace used to be. Yes. I did move home eventually but things were different then. I'll come to that later because Norma is closing the curtains.

"Don't pull too hard Norma."

She's looking at me as if I'm stupid. I am aren't I? I'm thinking about the ones in my bedroom, on the string, on the farm. Sorry Norma.

She closes all the curtains and then turns off the lights before going over to the television. I'm not the only stupid one am I? She can't see what she's doing so she has to turn the lights on again.

"Billy Elliott!" she announces, at last.

"Is he a valet?" I ask.

She looks at me, smiles, points her finger and then shakes her head again.

"Vera!"

"I'll be good," I say, putting my finger to my lips as a vow of silence.

The film is quite old these days but I still enjoy it. I've seen it before you see, although I pretended not to know what it was about.

"Is Clarke Gable still in it?" I ask Norma.

"Who the hell is he?"

She's got no upbringing, that girl.

She scowls playfully at me and I go quiet again.

It really is dark in here but let me quickly tell you about getting ready for Christmas with aunt Gloria. Or perhaps my younger Vera can do it.

26.

It's the day before Christmas eve and the snow is still managing to hold on in places. A thaw has started and has been going on for a day or two, but it's slow. The temperature is still barely above freezing and icicles hang from everywhere possible. Some of the pathways are clear but anything that has been piled up by us is still there, especially by the cowshed where we pulled it all off to save the roof.

I'm collecting the eggs. Just one or two today. I think the cold has put the hens off laying. Or is it the light? Sometimes Gloria will put a Tilley lamp in the henhouse to trick them into believing it's daylight but then she has to pay for fuel so it is a balance. We need eggs but fuel costs money. I can understand that. In winter our diets do change. No strawberries, less eggs and fresh hedgerow fruit and salad stuff but more things like apples and pears and root vegetables. Still plenty of rabbits and pheasants and pigeons though. We don't visit the butchers very often. That's an overstatement really isn't it? I never visit the butchers. I never leave the farm.

I take the eggs indoors to the kitchen. Gloria is there but is quiet.

"You alright?"

She doesn't answer me so I go over to her.

"Everything alright Gloria?"

"What?"

"You're quiet. Is everything alright?"

"Yes."

"It doesn't seem so."

"I was thinking."

"Go steady," I joke. "You did that last week and it gave you a headache."

"Sit down Vera."

I sit in my usual seat by the range which is warm and smoking slightly. I pick up the poker and give it a stir. That's better. Gloria comes over and stands with her full and wide bottom almost against the fire.

"I've got to go into town today Vera," she tells me.

"I know."

"Would you like to come?"

"What?"

"Would it hurt anything if you came with me?"

"No."

"You've been here for months now and you've never left the place have you? The furthest you've gone is up to the top of the lane to get the post."

"But what if people see me."

"They're going to aren't they?"

"And what will you say?"

"Why do I have to say anything? Sod it. It's got nothing to do with anyone else really has it?"

"But they will talk. A fifteen year old with a belly like a balloon. What are you going to tell them? Are you going tell them I've got wind or something? Or I've eaten too much porridge? I don't think they'll fall for that."

Gloria stands up, straight as a lamppost.

"Yes, sod 'em!" she says, loudly and assertively. "Sod 'em all! You're my niece and I'm proud of you, pregnant or not. We'll go, we'll do our shopping and we'll bloody well enjoy ourselves. And if they don't like it then they can stuff their opinions up, where the sun doesn't shine. Yes. Sod 'em I say. Come on girl. Get your coat. We're going to town. I might even buy you some clothes that fit. You work hard and I pay you nothing but your keep. Your father even sends me that. It's about time you had a treat."

I readily accept what is laid out as a treat and a challenge. In seconds I have my coat, hat, scarf and gloves on and we head towards the woodshed where Gloria's old Land Rover is kept, beside the woodpile. I open the door with a clunk and a loud creak, climb in the passenger seat after removing bits and pieces of straw from it and sit waiting for Gloria. She is just checking everything is sound and secure in the farmyard. Eventually she gets in beside me.

"Say a quick prayer Vera," she says. "The old girl doesn't seem to want to start without one these days."

She turns on the ignition and tries to start it but it doesn't turn over. All that can be heard is a click every time she tries.

"Give me that hammer down there Vera."

"What?"

"The hammer by your feet. I'll sort it."

I struggle to reach down but do pass her the hammer and she gets out and opens the bonnet. A few flakes of paint fall as she does so. She reaches in and then there is a large thud as she hits the engine. And then again. Thud! Thud! Thud!

"We'll try again shall we?" she says as she gets back in.

"What did you hit?"

"I hit the starter motor. Sometimes it sticks and needs a clout. My Fred used to be like that sometimes."

She turns the key again and then the engine turns over. It turns over and over and then, all of a sudden, it fires up and a huge plume of black smoke fills the shed. The cockerel does a runner again. Gloria then closes her door and puts the vehicle into gear. I laugh.

"I think you'd better put the bonnet down first," I instruct her.

"Good idea too," she replies, laughing.

The lane is a quagmire of mud but the old Land Rover seems to relish it and chugs its way to the top.

"We'll check the post on the way back," Gloria says. "Might be a letter in the box saying we've won loads of money."

"You've got enough as it is."

She smiles a satisfied smile.

"We're alright aren't we Vera?"

"We certainly are. It's a good job you like biscuits. You must have more tins than Huntley and Palmer."

"But mine don't contain biscuits now do they?"

"No. Yours are full of five and ten pound notes."

The ride becomes smoother as we reach the top of the lane and turn left onto the tarmac road towards town. The Land Rover is still smoking but it turns a light grey colour instead of black as the engine warms up. Its speed increases and Gloria struggles to find the next gear. She does it with a clunk and a grind and with no small amount of jolting and we carry on past Lady Morton's place and down the winding road with both of us happy but, perhaps just a little apprehensive, about what we are going to encounter when we get there.

The market place is three quarters full and we manage to park in a corner. A customer coming out of an adjacent shop coughs as he breathes in some of the Land Rover's fumes.

"You need to get that thing fixed Missus," he tells Gloria.

"No need," she replies. "It runs as sweet as a dream."

The man laughs.

"More like a bleedin' nightmare I'd say."

He puts on his cap and walks away.

"Right my girl," Gloria says, taking my arm. "Let's get to the butchers before they sell all the turkeys."

We walk, arm in arm, and into the butchers. We are the only ones in the shop and the butcher comes from the back room carrying a tray of sausages.

"We don't often see you in here Mrs Dunn," he greets. "All your animals been stolen or something have they?"

"No Mr Blake," Gloria replies. "Me and my niece here are spending Christmas together and we want a turkey. A good'n mind. Not something that's died of old age or rickets. How about that one hanging in the window? The one on the left there."

"But that's a twelve pounder Mrs Dunn," he points out. "You are quite welcome to it but do you need one that big?"

"Yes. We've got good appetites, and we're not hard up. What we don't eat on Christmas day we can use through the week. We love a good soup don't we Gloria?"

"We do."

"When's the baby due Miss?" the butcher asks, politely and kindly.

"May."

He winks at me.

"And I suppose it's dad is away at sea or something?"

"That's right."

He bags the turkey and Gloria pays.

"Can we pick it up in a little while? When we've finished the rest of our shopping?"

"No problem."

He laughs.

"I'll put it where the rats can't get at it."

"You'd better."

We leave the shop with Gloria putting the change from the turkey into her blue leather purse. She actually seemed to enjoy spending that money. That's a rarity.

"Right," she commands. "Now it's off to the shop to buy you some new clothes."

We head towards a large black-fronted timber framed shop. It has lots of women's clothes arranged in the window. Some folded on stands and some being shown on manikins. I'm excited as we enter the doorway and the smell of new fabric and warmth greets me. We are soon attended to by an immaculately dressed lady. She is dressed well but doesn't look over posh. She is dressed far better than me and Gloria but, then again, I don't suppose she has to milk cows and muck pigs out every day does she?

"And what may I do for you ladies?"

"It's my niece," Gloria tells her. "She's staying with me for a while and I want to buy her some nice things."

I'm almost in a dream world, looking around at this and that.

"And what size is the young lady may I ask?"

Gloria answers plainly.

"Maternity. Five months."

I turn around and the shop assistant sees the full extent of my shape. She finds it hard to speak for a few seconds.

"She's five months gone," Gloria plainly tells her. "Five months gone but get her something with plenty of room in it. She's swelling up fast."

"It…it…I…I…"

The shop assistant seems lost for words but Gloria has found herself dropped into her element.

"It's like this," she points out, plainly again. "This is Vera. She's my friend and lovely fifteen year old niece and she's five months pregnant. Nobody told her the facts of life and she didn't know what she was doing. She's having the baby and then, one day, she's hoping to marry its father who she loves dearly."

The shop assistant looks shocked and frowns a little.

"But I…"

"I like this shop," Gloria carries on, looking around and not giving the woman a proper chance to speak. "But if you have a problem with us then there is another one just down the road. It sells the same things at roughly the same price. I've got money so I either spend it here with you or down there. It's your choice."

The assistant is still visibly shocked by my condition at my age but she shakes her head, pulls herself together and speaks.

"Would you like to come to our maternity department Vera? It's this way."

Gloria folds her arms in triumph. She loves winning.

"And don't hold back with her," she orders. "I want to see her smart and warm. Get her a couple of thick pairs of trousers for winter on the farm. I'll tell you what we'll do Vera. When you've had the baby we can use them to make a pregnant scarecrow. That'll keep the birds off the taters."

"Yes madam."

We buy so many clothes that me and Gloria both go back to the Land Rover with an armful each. I think, probably for the first time ever, or at least in many years, Gloria has found life and it's one worth living.

"Hardware store next."

She shuts the back door of the vehicle and we head for the hardware shop. It's about the same size as my father's shop and sells just the same things.

"Mornin' Mrs Dunn!" greets a thin little man with a ginger pointy beard. "And what can I do for you today?"

Two other women are standing at the other side of the shop, talking. One of them points to me and whispers to the other. They don't think Gloria is looking but I know different. I know she doesn't miss a trick. She turns to them. Or should I say she turns 'on' them.

"Good morning Mrs Fanshawe, Mrs Brine. It would be a lovely day if it wasn't for the weather wouldn't it? You seem to be whispering about my niece here. Well, just to fill you in, this is Vera and, as you can see, she's pregnant. She's fifteen and she's pregnant, with child, up the spout or in the club. I don't care which one you choose but they all mean the same thing, but she is either one of them or all of them. And what she is, is her business and sod all to do with you so I suggest you sod off and keep your pointing and whispering to yourselves. Ok?"

They hurriedly shuffle out of the shop without purchasing anything.

"Sorry," Gloria says to the shopkeeper. "They didn't buy anything did they?"

He smiles.

"They'll be back. I'm the only person in town who sells this kind of stuff aren't I? What can I get for you ladies?"

If only all hardware shop owners were that sweet.

With my clothes taken out of the back of the Land Rover and then put back on top of everything else, Gloria disappears for a few minutes and then comes back with the turkey and the engine starts first time and we set off for home.

"Nearly forgot the bloody turkey Vera."

I am soon indoors, trying on everything again that Gloria has bought me.

"I'm keeping my best things for Christmas day," I tell Gloria. "Are you going to dress up?"

She shrugs her shoulders.

"I haven't dressed up in years."

"Well, the day after tomorrow you are going to, and that's an order."

"Alright Miss but don't forget we've got milking and feeding and mucking out to do first. And don't you dare wear that nice new skirt for that."

"I'm not stupid you know."

"Aren't you?"

I stick my tongue out in a playful jest and Gloria pretends to be hurt.

"What do you think my name is?" she asks. "Lady bloody Morton?"

We laugh again as Gloria pours us a small glass of cider each. Another celebration.

That evening I spend my time with paper and scissors, cutting strips of paper to glue together to make Christmas decorations which we hang in the best room. They're not bright but are brighter than nothing.

"We'll have a fire in here for Christmas," Gloria says. "It'll be the day of days. We'll keep the fire in the kitchen and have one in here as well. Sod it."

Christmas day comes and I wake even earlier than normal. I'm excited and rush out to get my work done without having breakfast. By the time Gloria joins me, Barbara is milked and I have started on Buttercup.

"My God girl!" Gloria exclaims as she enters the cowshed. "You're about early. Anybody'd think it was Christmas day."

"It is Christmas day. So you leave everything to me and go and prepare dinner."

"I can't do that."

"Why not?"

"I…"

"Go on! You haven't had a day off since I came here. Today is that day. I'm nearly finished here and then I'll quickly muck the pigs out and feed everything. You get that turkey sorted."

"Are you sure?"

"Go!"

She comes over to me and kisses me on the top of my head.

"You are a sweetheart," she tells me, sincerely.

With chores done I take my jug of water to my room and have a good wash before excitedly climbing into my new clothes and brushing my hair. For once I look into the mirror and see the old and pretty Vera Hobbs looking back at me. I then think of Jonny.

"Happy Christmas Jonny," I say, aloud.

I tell myself I can hear his reply but I know, in a real world, I can't.

Downstairs the house is warm as both fires have been lit. Pots of vegetables sit ready on top of the range and the turkey is covered with rashers of streaky bacon and goes into the oven. Then Gloria disappears upstairs. Her voice is not good but I enjoy the happiness of her singing as she washes and gets ready to celebrate. I pick up another log and put it in the range before going into the best room to check on the fire there. Gloria has put a heavy metal guard in front of it just in case. That room is hardly ever used but is so much more comfortable. It has a soft and clean settee, an almost matching chair and the high-backed windsor one that has the guns behind it.

On the wall are pictures of men on horseback, hunting foxes and a large pair of Staffordshire dogs sit on the mantelpiece, one either side of a large black slate cased mantle clock which chimes on the hour. There is no ceiling light in this room but there are two oil lamps. One on a piece of Victorian furniture and the other adorning a windowsill.

I sit, relaxed for a few minutes in the comfortable chair by the fire but then receive a huge shock as footsteps are heard on the stairs and Gloria enters the room. I say enters but, despite the extra weight, she looks like she floats in. I look at her and am completely speechless as she stands in the middle of the room wearing a little dab of make-up, clean and gorgeous clothes and has actually brushed her hair. Her cream-coloured dress looks almost new and she's wearing stockings and black high heels. Her blue apron is nowhere to be seen.

"Well, say something girl."

"Bloody hell woman!" is all I can say. "I never would have believed my aunt could look so gorgeous."

"I do try, occasionally. Very occasionally. I think the last day I looked like this was when me and my Fred went mad and went to the seaside. 1938 it was."

I jump up and hug her. She actually smells of perfume rather than pigs!

"And look at you!" she says. "You're gorgeous too. Even if you are pregnant."

We hold hands and start to go into the kitchen but Gloria stops.

"Happy Christmas sweetheart," she says.

"Happy Christmas Gloria. I love you."

She now has a tear in her eye.

"And I love you too Miss Vera Hobbs," she says. "I really, really do. You've made my bloody life you have."

We hug again.

"Now sit down again," I'm commanded. "I bought you a little something in town."

"When?"

"When I left you in the Land Rover to go and get the turkey. Just before we came home."

She disappears from the room and comes back again with a small box that is wrapped in bright blue paper.

"Here you are Vera."

I take it and eagerly pull at the paper. Inside is a small cardboard box which has the word Timex written on it in black. When I open it I find a beautiful small ladies' watch which has a silver coloured case and strap and a white face. It's no child's watch but is a proper ladies' one. It's gorgeous and it's mine. I cry and jump up to hug Gloria again. Now we are both crying.

"I haven't got you anything."

"I don't need anything. I've got you and that's enough for me."

Within minutes, the smell of cooking turkey fills the house and soon the potatoes are roasting on the shelf above it and the pots of vegetables are on the heat and steaming. It is all dished up with lashings of thick and tasty onion gravy and we sit at the kitchen table and tuck in. I'm sure that one present on that one Christmas day, with that one wonderful lady will be the best Christmas I'll ever have.

27.

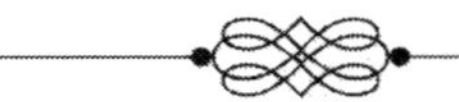

And I was right as well. There would never be a Christmas that could ever come even close to that one down on the farm amongst the trees. These days, even in here, we have things. What with the television and the Queen's speech, someone dressing up as Father Christmas and the staff doing their best to entertain us. Down the farm though, all we had was Christmas, an open fire, dinner and the wireless. We had little really, but it was still the best Christmas ever because we had each other. Me and Gloria. We had each other and we had everything, me and that once rough and miserable woman. And that turkey was gorgeous. Gloria cooked it slowly but with plenty of love and care, and onions. We ate and ate and had homemade Christmas pudding and cream for afters before settling in front of the fire, in the best room, to listen to carols and hearing other people celebrating. That evening we had cold turkey and homemade pickles and cheese and a box of chocolates. Dairy Box they were. My favourites. I loved the strawberry creams. Gloria went more for the nutty ones but her teeth weren't too good. It was as if the rest of the world didn't matter that day, and it didn't. If the rest of the world had even ceased to exist completely then, just for that day, so be it we thought. I missed none of them. Well, apart from my Jonny that is.

Oh! Who's this? She's a smart young girl. Coloured girl. I say young and she is. Everybody is compared with me these days. She looks like a teenager but she's carrying a doctor's bag. It looks like a doctor's bag anyway. Black leather it is? She's stopped in the doorway of the lounge and is looking around.

"Who are you after sweetheart?"

She looks towards me and then at a note in her hand.

"I'm looking for a Mr Ted Jackson."

"He's upstairs sweetheart," I point out. "He's got pneumonia. There are a couple of them in with pneumonia at the minute. Are you a doctor?"

"I am."

"They make them young these days."

She smiles a beautiful and true smile.

"Is he still alive then?" I ask before I realise just how stupid my question is.

She smiles again.

"I do hope so," she replies. "Or I've had a wasted journey haven't I?"

We laugh together.

"Go up the top there," I tell her, pointing in the direction of the nurse station. "The nurse is usually up there somewhere. I think she's got an office there. That's where she has her afternoon nap."

The young doctor looks at her watch.

"It's only ten thirty," she says. "Hopefully I'll catch her awake."

"Good luck sweetheart. And give my regards to Ted won't you?"

"I will. And you are?"

"I'm Vera," I say. "But I don't think old Ted will remember me much. He can't even remember what he's had for dinner. I can. But only if it's sprouts."

She walks off with her bottom wiggling in her tight white trousers and has perhaps one too many buttons of her blouse undone. I hope she doesn't try and take old Ted's blood pressure. That'll be high for sure. Knowing him he'll go off like a firework on November the fifth.

I can hear Susie coming back with her wheel wobbling.

"You got enough milk in your coffee Veera?"

"Yes thanks Susie. I like it black and milky."

She starts off towards the kitchen. Won't be long before lunch is ready. I wonder what it is today. Maybe I can catch her.

"Susie!"

She turns back.

"Yes Veera. What you want?"

"What's for lunch today?"

"We have toady hole."

Sounds like a disease to me.

"And stewed cabbage again?"

"I think so Veera. We do have cabbage with toady hole."

"Can you ask the cook not to kill it too much today?"

"I will."

There she goes again. Three wheels on her wagon and she's still rolling along.

It's good to hear old Ted's still kicking. Mind you, he has got the doctor in. Can't be too good. Thinking about it though. Haven't I had the doctor in or was it two? Why was it two? I haven't been well have I? But I'm better now. I've had the flu you know. I remember that. I felt dreadful. Do you know, if that strange old man with the scythe had come by my bedside and said it was my time to go I wouldn't have minded. I did feel that bad. I would miss my granddaughter I suppose but even she doesn't come to see me very often these days. That's the problem when you get old. You become a nuisance and a burden and visiting you becomes a chore. People don't like chores these days. They'll be here when I'm gone I suppose. Her and her mum. They're not bad people in any way but they won't say no to what's left in the bank after all my fees here are paid will they? I pay a lot of money for my room, meals, help and this chair but there will always be plenty left over. I inherited the lot eventually, you see. It didn't matter too much to me but I did. I got the lot. There was dad's shop with the flat above, our house and four cottages. Then there was the money from selling

George's house when he moved in with me and I even inherited aunt Gloria's farm. I was a wealthy woman after they all died and I know it may sound corny but I honestly would have swapped it all to be with my Jonny again. Every last pound note. I was, and am, a millionaire. Or should that be millionairess? They do change everything these days. Millionaires and millionairesses. Actors and actresses. They'll be calling chickens cocks and cocks next.

Me and George. We were alright I suppose but the spark inside me had gone out. I always knew that it was only my Jonny who kept that flame kindled. Or was it like that? Perhaps I just wouldn't let anyone else set a match to it again. I don't know. I was a wealthy woman who had nothing. Does that make sense? I think it does. I had everything and yet I had nothing. I sold the shop and flat as soon as they were mine because they reminded me too much of my father but I kept everything else for years and years and lived very comfortably on the rents that came in. Me and George had a big green Jaguar and we used to travel everywhere and in comfort. Places like Wales and Scotland. Dorset was nice too. We stayed in a posh hotel there several times. I can't remember what it was called but it was lovely. Right on the seafront is was and we had a big room overlooking the sea. We booked the same room all the time when we could.

They were good times but I was still sad. I know that was my own fault. I should have made more of it all shouldn't I? And I do regret it but I had lost the two things most dear to me and, to tell you the truth, I never did get over it.

Vera is crying and wipes her eyes again.

Do you know? I'm stupid. I've wasted far too much of my life wanting things I hadn't got and could never have again. I've spoiled it all really haven't I? Why didn't I just let go? Why didn't I just let go of Jonny and what I wanted with him? I was stupid and it was stupid, and still is. I still do it you see, even now when it's absolutely hopeless. I was fifteen the last time I saw him for goodness sake. That was five sixths of my life ago. See, I'm still good at sums.

All this time I've hung on. Futile. Is that the word? Futile? I think it is. I've wasted a life, wanting to live a dream. But a dream is all it ever was wasn't it? What chance have I got of even hearing his name now? Or seeing him across a busy street? I've got no chance of ever hearing his voice again or seeing him smile have I? So why do I hang on? I'm just a silly old bag who's wasted her life when, with a little common sense, I could have been happy. Jonny's probably six foot under by now and his hair is probably still not combed. I bet it's sticking out of his coffin. Bless him.

Come on Vera. Get over it you silly old sod. You've got your Robin. Isn't that enough? It is something isn't it? He's not there at the minute. Perhaps he's round with Albert in the vegetable garden. Albert's probably feeding him worms again. He does need his goodness. Even worms are good for you when you're a Robin.

28.

"The swallows are back in the barn Gloria," I say, excitedly, putting eggs on the table. "And I just saw a blackbird looking for nesting material."

"She'd better not be nesting in the Land Rover again this year."

Gloria is washing dishes. The house hasn't always been clean but she is proud of her crockery and glass. She holds a glass dish up to the window to make sure it's spotless. It is put aside on the draining board with a smile of satisfaction.

"It's been a long old winter Vera," she replies, happily. "But we've come through, you and me. Look at it out there now. Lovely. It's hard to believe we had all that snow just a few weeks ago. Must go and check on Betty a little later. I think she might be getting ready to give birth. She looks ready."

She looks at me.

"And she's not the only one is she?" she adds.

I take a seat for a few minutes. I'm huge and even just collecting the eggs has made me puff. My belly feels tight and everything seems to ache. I'm not a large girl and this body doesn't seem big enough for both of us anymore.

"There is work to do," Gloria advises. "But you take it slowly. You've only got a couple of weeks or so. I used to manage on my own before you came here and I can do it again if necessary."

"Thanks. I am struggling."

Gloria turns to me again with a huge look of sympathy.

"Tell you what," she suggests. "I'll get you a nice cup of sweet milky tea and you sit there for a minute or two and then perhaps you can dry the dishes while I go and plant some potatoes. Got some lovely King Edward seed potatoes from town. They'll be a bit late but they'll do. Potato planting's no work for a girl who's nine months gone. When we've done that we'll go and check on Betty. I'm sure she'll have her piglets today. I can feel it in my water."

I smile.

"Feel it in your water?"

"I know. Silly isn't it? But that's what I say. I've been around animals for so long now that it all becomes instinctive. Is that the word? And I bet I'm right as well. She'll have her babies today. You mark my words."

She dries her hands on the same, almost threadbare, blue towel that has been hanging around for weeks and then she leaves the house.

"You rest for a little while Vera."

"Thanks. I will."

I sit and sip my tea and all I can hear is the loud ticking of the large wood cased wall clock that hangs in the corner. It's always reliable and sounds like a metronome with its precise timekeeping. It's been hanging there for as long as I can remember and the winding of it has always been Gloria's first task in the mornings. I remember uncle Fred saying it was a clock that belonged to his grandfather and had never lost a minute in its life. It strikes ten o'clock and, as it does, I feel I should get up and do some work. Living on a farm is a busy life and you do start to feel guilty if you sit and rest for too long. Come on Vera.

The weight of my baby is playing havoc with my back and I can feel everything tightening and pulling. About a quarter of the way up my spine is a bone that feels like it is being crushed and the pain is bad. I take a deep breath, hold my belly and push down on the arm of my chair in order to stand. The effort makes me wince with pain and gasp for air.

"Look what you've done to me Jonny Clitheroe!" I say, loudly and with a smile as I eventually stand somewhere near close to upright.

I do wish he could see what he's done to me. I do wish he could. Bless him. I wonder where he is and what he's doing? Is he waiting back at home for me? I don't know, but I hope he is. I was cross with him the last time I saw him and it does worry me that he thinks I don't want to see him again. I do want to see you again Jonny. I do still love you.

Perhaps I could get in contact with him somehow. Do you know? I hadn't really thought of it before. I may be over thirty miles from home and have no transport or telephone but I could write him a letter couldn't I? I was unceremoniously dumped here and felt that was that. I'd betrayed my family by making a baby with Jonny and had simply just accepted my excommunication. I had been weak and had let everyone deal with me as they wished but I'm not weak now am I? I'm Vera Hobbs and I've changed. I have writing paper, envelopes and a pen. What an idiot. Why haven't I done it before?

I smile to myself and resolve to write a letter to Jonny tonight. Maybe, if I time it right I can give it to the postman when he comes to leave our letters in the box at the top of the lane tomorrow. Better not tell Gloria though. We are getting along so well. Mustn't do anything to spoil that. I know where she keeps a stamp or two. It may be dishonest but I'm going to have to borrow one without telling her. I'll make it up to her somehow.

Eventually I feel a little better and am moving easier. The dishes are soon put away and I go out and let Bruno off his chain. He's not too unhappy about the fact and immediately runs towards the pond and the ducks. They're too fast for him again though and they quickly take to the water. Bruno hates water and decides to cock his leg up against the cow shed instead.

"How are you doing?" I shout to Gloria as she wipes her sweating cheeks on her blue apron. It has been washed.

She's on the vegetable garden behind the house.

"Nearly done! I'll meet you down at the pigs!"

"Ok!"

Two sows, Betty and Bramble are having babies but Betty is to be first. She's laying on a bed of straw by the far wall and is breathing quite heavily. Like me, she looks uncomfortable. Gloria likes her Bs for names. There's Bruno the dog, Bluebell and Barbara, the cows and Betty and Bramble, the sows and then there's geese, Bob, Boris and Bernard and chickens called Belinda, Bramley and Buckle. Even Gloria doesn't know why the three geese have boys names when they are all girls but she likes it. It makes her happy. She says the geese don't know which are boys names and which are girls ones anyway so why worry?

I think she just calls them the first 'B' name that comes into her head. She once had a pig called Breakfast. And that's what it became. Gorgeous bacon.

I sit on a bale of straw in the pigsty and watch Betty. We are going through the same thing and I sympathise totally. She moves, trying to get a little more comfortable and groans as she does. Then she turns her head and looks toward her rear end, seemingly knowing that something is happening.

Gloria makes me jump with an unannounced entrance.

"How's things?"

"I think she knows her time is near."

Gloria sits down beside me.

"We'll stay here a while in case we are needed."

We are needed sooner than we think as, with another grunt or two and more looks towards her rear end, Betty puts her head down and shuffles again, before giving quite a loud squeal as the first piglet comes hurriedly into the world. Gloria goes to it, looks down and checks it over.

"That's a good'n Vera," she says, joyfully, as the piglet seems instinctively to try and make its unsteady way to a teat. "A few more like that will be lovely."

A few more like that do come, seemingly one after the other in almost a timed sequence.

"That's six now," Gloria announces. "And here comes the seventh. He's a quick one."

He is quick because he's quite small. They call them the runt of the littler but this one is not just a runt. It is quite deformed.

"He's not a good'n," Gloria says, sadly. "We always seem to get a runt or two but that one's a bad'un. Look at him Vera. He's all bent up and his back legs don't work."

"What will you do with him?"

I needn't have asked. Gloria picks it up and takes it away from its mother. She then drops it into some straw in the next pen.

"He's not a keeper Vera."

Five more piglets are born and, thankfully all the rest are fit and healthy. Gloria quickly checks Betty over.

"She's fine."

Before long, all the new-borns, apart from the one, are merrily attached to a teat each and mum relaxes after her ordeal, content in the knowledge that she has brought new life into the world again. She lays on a lovely bed of soft straw and grunts almost blissfully with her family attached.

"Lovely sight isn't it Vera?"

I nod.

"That'll be you in a couple of weeks' time I reckon."

I smile.

"Not with that many I hope. One will do. Not ten."

"Eleven."

I'm enchanted and almost entranced by the sight before me but then I think of the other poor little piglet. The one with its problems. The one that has been dumped in the next pen.

"What about the other one?"

Gloria looks over to it.

"As I say. He's not a keeper."

She goes over to the wall and picks up a length of old two by two wood. It's about two and a half feet long.

"Can't keep bad'ns Vera," she says. "No money to feed what won't grow. We've got all them good'ns. They'll do. Can't have the poor little bugger suffer neither."

She calmly walks over to the helpless little creature, looks down at it for a second or two, and then the piece of wood is raised and coldly brought crashing down upon it with a sickening thud. There is no noise from the piglet as it is killed instantly. There is no compassion on Gloria's face either. I look at her glumly.

"Can't keep badn's Vera," she tells me again, forthrightly. "I know it seems hard but this is a farm.

Not a charity. That poor little bugger would have died in a few days' time anyway and it would have suffered all that time as well. We'll get a spade and give it a nice burial. Perhaps you could pick a few nice flowers for it."

"Is that what you always do?"

"I always have to end it for them but I don't usually bother with flowers. You can though. It'll be nice for it won't it?"

She laughs a little.

"Come on sweetheart," she says, putting down the wood, picking up the piglet and holding her free hand out to me. "I know it's hard but it's life isn't it? Don't worry. We're not having pork tonight."

I'm sad for the piglet but know Gloria is right. I do feel, though, that perhaps she could be a little less callous about it.

"Brian," I say.

"What?"

"I'm calling him Brian. It is a boy isn't it?"

"Doesn't usually bother me what sex they are," Gloria answers. "Just look at the geese."

She doesn't usually bury her dead baby animals either. I know that because I've seen them dumped on the muck heap. But this time, and just for me, we will.

"Fetch the spade from the veg garden Vera."

I do and meet her at the back of the pigsty.

"Here will do. In the sunshine."

"And at least it will be near the other pigs."

Gloria digs a hole and the piglet is about to be dropped in.

"No Gloria," I say. "Let's do it nicely."

I go to the shed and fetch a hessian sack.

"Wrap it in this."

We do and then lay it in the hole before covering it over. I think to say something sweet but can only think of the Lord's prayer so say it like we used to in school.

"That'd be a good job for you Vera."

"What's that?"

"Undertaker."

"I don't think so."

"We'll check on Betty in an hour or so. I think she'll be alright. She looks well and happy."

We do and her and all her new family are thriving. They look so happy and comfortable in their lovely cosy home. It's just so sad that one didn't make it.

The rest of the day goes by and I am eager to go to my bedroom to write my letter to Jonny. I still can't really think why I haven't done it before but this is my chance now. My chance to contact him and, perhaps, see and hold him again. I lift the front cover of my writing pad, which has a passenger ship on it, drawn in blue, and open the writing pad. It's new and not even one page has been used. I thought to bring it with me so why did I never think to write on it?

I think what to write.

Dear Jonny.

No. That's not right is it?

My darling Jonny.

I didn't leave you because I didn't want to see you anymore. I left you because my mum and dad sent me away to my aunt Gloria's because I'm having your baby. It must be a shock for you but it's true. The baby is ours. Yours and mine. If dad finds out I've written this letter he will kill me but I have to tell you I am well and I do still really really love you so much. The baby is nearly due now and I would love you to come and see me. I miss you terribly.

Aunt Gloria's farm is miles from anywhere but perhaps you could get a ride with someone. The address is at the top of the letter. Scatters Farm.

It was horrible being sent here Jonny and Gloria wasn't nice to me at first but she's lovely now. We really get on together. What she'll do if you turn up I don't know but I need you to take that chance Jonny. I really do need you to. I'm having your baby and I need us to be together. We are young, I know, but our love is real isn't it? I know it is.

Come to the farm my sweetheart. Please come and see me.

Will love you always Jonny.

Your Vera. (Yours forever.)

XXX

Tears fill my eyes and one falls onto the paper and smudges my words slightly. At first I see it as an annoyance but then I change my view and see it as a kind of seal that shows my love. I fold the paper carefully and gently slide it into an envelope already addressed to Jonny Clitheroe, 3 Bailey's Terrace. The stamp that I borrowed on the way upstairs from a box in the best room is placed in the corner and then I lick the envelope and seal it, thinking and hoping that this is my way to freedom and a new life. One with my Jonny. My dear dear Jonny. Jonny Clitheroe.

It's bright and early the following morning and I hurry as fast as I can up the rutted lane. It's dry now but the ruts are still there. I'm a little late and my heart is pounding. I need to get my letter to Jonny and don't want to miss the postman. It may be days or even weeks before we go to town again and I can't wait that long. The letter is written at last and I need it to be delivered. The postman is my best bet. But what if there are no letters for us and he goes straight past? I can't miss him so I hurry more. I'm puffing and the exertion is making my belly hurt but I must get there.

Luckily I reach the top on the lane just as his van stops and the postman gets out.

"Morning Miss!" he greets. "I haven't seen you here before."

"I'm staying here for a while," I manage to say between gasps of breath.

He looks down at my belly which is about to pop.

"And I can see why," he says, smiling. "But it's nothing to do with me is it? My wife's expecting. July it is."

"Can you take this please?" I ask, holding out the letter. "It's important."

He looks at it and does.

"Anything for a lady. And here's one for you," he replies. "Looks like a bill."

"If it is," I tell him, "my aunt will probably burn it."

'Will you be ok walking back down the lane?"

I look down the track.

"It's downhill on the way back," I say. "I'll be fine. I'll just take my time."

"Nice meeting you."

"And you."

"Best of luck."

He gets back into his little red van which starts with a rattle and a rumble, then he waves and leaves. I look down the track. It is downhill and I'll be fine. I'll be even finer when my Jonny comes to see me.

There's a robin sitting on a post as I reach the farmyard and he, or she, has got a little caterpillar in its beak. He's probably got a family somewhere. I hope me and Jonny will be one soon.

29.

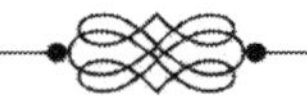

Aunt Gloria. That's it. I was with Aunt Gloria wasn't I? She died years ago, when I was about twenty five. Heart attack. Just like her husband, Fred. It was her second one. They say it happened quickly but my pregnancy didn't. I stayed with her for months and months and although I was with her it seemed, for most of the time, at first, I was on my own but then, one day, she shocked me. She actually laughed. A belly laugh it was. Do you remember them? Times when people couldn't help but enjoy themselves? Do they bother these days? Neither of us had anyone but then, just like that, we had each other and it turned into something quite wonderful.

Underneath her gruff exterior, Gloria was actually quite a lovely, if a little rough, lady. She was very matter-of-fact and even callous sometimes but that was how she had to be. It was how she survived. That was life there on her farm. Everything was basic and raw. Is that the word you'd use? Raw? I suppose it is. Everything was black and white and there were never any other colours in between. If a duck was ill it either got over it or it didn't. If a chicken was ill it was in the pot, sometimes with the duck. If it didn't lay it was in the pot. If Auntie Gloria was ill she just got better. Never a doctor. Mind you, she was never ill really. Dirty sometimes maybe but never really ill. Not until she had the heart attacks that is. She wasn't ill again after that. Just dead. Bless her.

Time went on and we did start to get along well. In the countryside sunshine, things even started to get quite lovely. She looked after me and became a friend. I even called the farm home. I worked hard but liked what I did. I liked the animals and they seemed to like me. Feeding the chickens and collecting the eggs was my favourite. They'd run over to me and cluck and cluck, knowing I was about to give them a treat. The pigs were lovely as well. People say pigs are stinking animals and they can be a bit smelly but if they are kept right they can be beautiful. And Gloria did keep them right. They were her favourites. Having babies for them was just the same as with anything else though. The ones that were healthy survived and the ones that weren't were simply 'got rid of'. Aunt Gloria would say she ran a farm, not a charity. If she couldn't treat them then she wouldn't bother anybody else. 'Bothering others cost money'. 'If they're not good'ns they go'.

I was with the pigs one day when I started to get pains. Eleventh of May it was. About seven months since my visit to Doctor Greenwood. When I'd got pregnant I'd had no idea how it got in there. I had no idea how it got in there but I quickly knew it was about to come out so I went in to the house where Aunt Gloria was making sausages. She stopped winding the handle of the sausage machine and got me upstairs with a cup of very sweet and milky tea. It was her elixir for everything. According to her it was the best cure for everything, coughs, colds, headaches, piles and even a broken arm. I didn't believe her of course but I did drink it. Who was I to argue? I couldn't upset her because I knew full well I was about to need her totally. She was there and it was plain to see that no one else was going to be called. We were on our own and in it together. Ours was a world away from everyone.

"Would you like a bath today Vera?" Norma asks.

"Would I?"

"We'll have time in about half an hour. Is that alright?"

"That'll be lovely."

I like Norma bathing me and washing my old back with her rough hands. My back has been bad you know. I think the hot water will do it good. Although, I must say, it has been better today.

"I haven't had a bath for weeks," I joke.

"Yes you have Vera Betts," she says, smiling and pointing at me. "You had one just a few days ago didn't you?"

"I don't remember."

I do remember really. I can remember smelling that stuff they wash me with these days. You know what it is don't you? Not soap. Fairy or Lifebuoy. That other stuff. What is it called? Yes. Shower gel. That's it. That's what they use these days. It's shower gel. Smells lovely too.

Fire. Why am I seeing a fire? Ah, that's it. I'd gone into labour hadn't I? I was going to sit by the fire but Gloria helped me upstairs. She told me it would happen quickly. She seemed to know but for what seemed like ages I lay there and then Gloria washed her hands and put the kettle on. It was instinct. She'd seen so many births in her animals that she seemed to know instinctively when it was actually about to happen so she washed her hands for the first time that day, took mine to reassure me and then pulled back the bedclothes. She'd put towels under me. She'd never been exactly house proud but she said she didn't want her sheets to get messed up because they had been wedding presents and it looked like rain the following day and she wouldn't get them dry.

Eventually I undressed from the waist down, or the feet up, and laid on the bed with the pain coming nearly all the time and I could feel that the baby really wanted to come out. It was agony but I suppose a lot of you hearing my story will know that already won't you? Men won't know will they? They don't have babies. And if they were the ones that had them I think the human population would soon disappear. Don't you?

There's a chap arrived in a wheelchair. Just seen him being taken through. Tall man. Well, he would be tall I think, if he could stand up and walk. Tall and big man. Looks a funny old bugger. Bald head and a lump on it. Right in the middle. Almost looks like he's wearing a bobble hat, bless him. Pleasant looking chap though. Well, he's smiling anyway. That's more than some of them do. Miserable load of old so and sos some of them are in here. He must be the new man. He's headed towards old Mr Trafford's room. Yes, it had to have been him who died. I did hear the back door being opened early the other morning. Must have been the undertakers. They use that door. Hope they took his false leg.

Sorry, I was telling you about me having my baby wasn't I? I was wasn't I?

Aunt Gloria asked me what I was going to call it. She said she liked Agnes as a girl's name. I said I liked something a bit more modern like Penelope and she didn't disagree. We didn't talk too much more as it really did want to come out by then and she went into action stations and started to shout 'Push! Push!'. I never heard her shouting that to any of the pigs. I did push and then out it popped, eventually. Well, not quite that easily.

30.

Betty and her piglets are doing well. They're two weeks old now and are hardly recognisable from the little squealing scraps that were born. They're running around and playing with each other and all seem healthy and happy still. It's a shame the little one had to go but I have managed to get over it, nearly. I actually had a dream, or nightmare, about Gloria hitting it so hard with that piece of wood and woke up in a sweat. In real life the piglet died but, in my dream, it suddenly became taller than her and started eating her. It was horrible.

I've been having pains in my belly all morning. Ever since I woke up and I even seem to remember them before I really woke up and.... Oh.... and here comes another one. Let me just sit down on a straw bale until it goes. The pains come and then they go and are happening about every twenty minutes or so now. They seem to gradually be getting closer together. I'll time the next one. I look at my watch. It's eleven twenty.

Coming out of the pigsty on what has turned out a gorgeous day after overnight rain, I see the robin heading towards the shed where the tools are kept so I follow it. It's got food in its beak again. The shed door is closed but it doesn't fit too well these days and the robin flies in, with ease, through a gap between the door and the frame. I don't want to frighten it so I wait outside with my back flat against the wall. My back may be flat but the rest of me isn't. Gloria is looking from the house and she sees me.

"Everything alright Vera?"

I put my finger to my lips as a sign for her to keep the noise down and then, as I do, the robin flies out again so I go in to investigate. Where is the nest? With my little knowledge of wildlife, I know it wouldn't be too close to the ground because of predators so I look up but see nothing. Where can it be?

There are old wooden boxes and tools, both good and broken. Gloria won't throw anything away. There's the one with its handle tied together with string. My search is fruitless as there are so many possible nesting places so I decide to hide in a corner and let the robin come back in. It does and doesn't seem to be bothered when it spots me there. It sits on a fork handle, looks at me, looks around and then flies up onto a dusty old shelf and into a metal watering can which is lying on its side. I can hear the voices of baby robins, excited for food, as they are echoed around the inside of the can. The food is delivered and the robin leaves to hunt again. I'm about to leave when another pain hits me. It's eleven thirty two. Twelve minutes this time. That's quick! I'd better tell Gloria. She's still in the kitchen with the window open.

"Gloria!"

"Yes?"

"I'm having pains like you said I would."

"How often?"

"I timed the last one. Twelve minutes."

"Come indoors Vera," she says, already rolling up her sleeves ready for action.

I start walking but then stop and look at Gloria again.

"What's wrong?"

I look down.

"I think I've just wet myself."

She laughs.

"This is it girl," she says, quite excitedly. "You haven't wet yourself. Your waters have just broken."

She's told me about that as well but I'd forgotten. At least I haven't wet myself.

I go in. Gloria is making sausages and she stops winding the handle of the silver machine which is clamped tightly to the draining board.

"Let's get you up on your bed," she says, picking pieces of sausage meat from her hands and putting them back in the bowl before wiping the rest off with her blue towel.

The fire is burning and the kettle is steaming. I was thinking about sitting in front of the fire but no. We climb the old wooden stairs and I'm about to lie down.

"No. Not yet."

I'm not feeling good and really do want to lie down.

"Stay there."

"Why?"

She doesn't answer but disappears and comes back with an armful of old towels. I say old but some of them look far better than the ones we use every day. I look at my one, draped over the back of a chair. It's so worn you can almost see through it.

Gloria pulls back the covers and lays the towels over the sheets.

"Don't want to ruin them," she says. "They were a wedding present from Fred's mother."

I smile.

"And when was that?"

"A year or so before you were born."

"And they've lasted all this time?"

"Yes. So far."

"And you're still worried about spoiling them?"

"They've got a few years left in them yet," Gloria asserts. "And anyway, if I have to wash them they won't get dry will they? They've forecast rain again. You get your bum on those towels and don't argue Miss Hobbs."

I start to carefully get on the bed.

"Going to have your baby with your knickers on are you?"

She's right.

"I bet you never had your knickers on when it got in there did you?" Gloria adds, laughing heartily.

I shake my head.

"Strip from the waist down Vera."

"Waist down or feet up?" I try to joke.

Gloria does laugh but tells me this is a serious time.

"You're about to give birth girl. You won't be joking in a little while. Believe me, this is going to hurt and I know. I've been through it, remember?"

She has been through it. I remember coming to the farm and playing with little Leonard, or Lenny as they called him. He died when he was five years old. Caught a cold and it turned into pneumonia. It was three weeks between him catching the cold to being dead. Sweet little boy he was. A mop of thick blonde, almost white, hair. Gloria never did have any more children.

The pain again. I look at my watch. Just over nine minutes.

"It was nine minutes that time Gloria," I struggle to say.

"It'll be a good while yet. What I'll do is go and make you a nice cup of…"

"Sweet milky tea?"

"Cures everything you know."

"I'm sure it does."

Gloria leaves the room and I strip to the waist as she has told me to and lie on the bed, making sure the towels are arranged neatly beneath me before I pull the covers over me. Not for warmth as it's such a beautiful day outside but just out of modesty and dignity. I know both of those will fly out of the window soon but, for now, it feels right. It feels proper.

Gloria soon returns with a tray. A cup of tea each and some biscuits.

"Everything alright Vera?"

"Yes."

I sit up and take the tea. It seems extra sweet and extra milky. It tells me I'm in for a rough time.

"I was thinking about your Lenny, bless him," I say.

"I think about him all the time," Gloria replies. "He'd be coming up for fifteen now. August the eighth. Me and Fred were happy we had someone to leave the farm to. We hoped Lenny would carry on with it and look after us as we got old but no. It wasn't to be was it?"

"Why didn't you have more children?"

Gloria looks very thoughtful.

"It just didn't happen Vera," she explains. "I don't know. We planned Lenny and it just happened but then, after he died, there was nothing. We did try but nothing happened. Were we trying too hard? I don't know. I don't know how it all works. How come you can have one, just like that, and then nothing?"

And then she shocks me.

"I'm going to see the solicitor next week," she tells me, seemingly out of nowhere. "The farm will be yours when I go."

"Mine? Why me?"

"Because I love you Vera," she says, holding my hand and smiling totally sincerely. "Because I love you and you're all I've got. There's no one else is there? Fred and little Lenny are gone. I think your father's hoping he'll outlive me and get it but he's got enough already. Let's skip a generation and give it to you. That'll upset the old so and so."

She smiles a bigger smile.

"But I'm not ready to go yet young lady," she assures me. "So don't get your hopes up."

"I won't. Thanks."

She has just sealed the closeness of our relationship.

Another pain and then another and another. They're coming quicker and quicker.

"More tea?"

"No. No tea Gloria. Just hold my hand."

She doesn't speak straight away but holds my hand for a second or two and then starts to remove the bed covers.

"You can't give birth all covered up can you?"

I feel my dignity is gone and my modesty is severely dented as I lie there semi naked. I look down but can only see my bump. It moves before another pain hits me. This one does really hurt.

"Bloody hell!!"

"You shout all you like," Gloria says, scanning me with her eyes as a type of examination. "I'm sure I've heard it all before. Your father never holds back does he?"

I don't answer as I have no wish to talk about him.

"Won't be long now."

Suddenly, and for a few minutes, everything seems to stop and we both look at each other, wondering what has happened. I immediately start to worry. Can this be normal? Should everything simply stop like this?

"Is everything alright?"

Gloria seems worried too. She cannot answer my question or hide her concerns.

Two or three minutes later and still nothing. No pains and no movement.

"Gloria?"

Still no answer.

I look down at my bump and pray in my mind for it to move or do something, anything but nothing happens.

Gloria puts her hand on it and squeezes gently.

"There's nothing happening Vera," she says, sadly and dropping her head.

Another minute goes by and my worries run to a nightmare but then…

"Aaaargh!!!!!"

Another pain rips through me and I can feel movement. I scream again.

"Bloody hell!!!!"

Gloria puts a hand on each of my knees and eases them apart. No dignity now but no matter either. I can feel my baby wants to come out. I think it has moved down. I'm sure it has.

Gloria lowers her head to look where the baby is coming.

"Give a little push Vera."

I do and she lowers her head further. Then she lifts it again and smiles.

"I can just see the top of its head."

All goes still for another minute or so and then another pain.

"Bloody hell!!!" I shout again, gripping onto the sheets either side of me.

But then I think. Better not grip too hard. They were a wedding present you know.

"Push Vera!! Push!!"

I do. I can't help it. I have to push. I've no choice. I push and it hurts like hell. I nearly cry out for my mum and do think it would be nice if she was here but I've got Gloria and she's seen it all before. I'm no pig or cow but I know I'll be ok.

I hold my breath and push with all my might but feel myself going faint and clammy and don't like it so I ease off a little.

"You don't look good girl," Gloria says, handing me a wet flannel. "Give your face a bit of a wipe. It'll make you feel better."

I do and it does.

"It didn't seem to move much that time," Gloria tells me. "So you're going to have to do it all again and again. I know it's not nice. Do you think you can manage?"

"I've got no choice have I!" I shout as the pains start again.

"Push Vera!! Push! Push! Push!"

"I'm bloody trying aren't I?"

Gloria smiles and looks down again as I push with all my might. The wet flannel seems to have worked and I don't feel faint and clammy this time.

"That's it my girl! That's it! It's coming this time."

Another pain and another monumental effort and Gloria seems ecstatic.

"Its head is out Vera!"

A final pain whips through me and Gloria takes hold of my baby's head and tugs gently to assist it as I push. The worst of it seems over and I feel a huge release as my child is finally out of me. It has been growing in there all these months but is finally a baby instead of just a bump.

"Is it alright?"

Gloria is busy sorting out its umbilical cord and wiping it. She doesn't answer.

"Gloria. Is it alright?"

"Yes. It's fine. Quiet, but fine. It's breathing nicely."

She smiles.

"Ten tiny fingers and ten tiny toes Vera. You're a mother now. It's a bouncing baby boy."

She eventually finishes what she's doing, wraps him in another towel and hands him to me. I look at what me and my Jonny have created and cry with joy and relief. I knew nothing of what I was doing when we made him but we have made him and he's all mine. I lay him on my chest and sob and sob. I wonder if Jonny got my letter?

"He's called Robin," I say, as he finally starts to cry a little.

"And I'm not surprised," Gloria replies. "You like robins don't you?"

I nod and look down at him. He's beautiful. He hasn't got his dad's hair yet thank goodness.

Gloria washes me and then covers me up.

"You look good down there Vera," she reassures me. "No problems. You'll be fine. Why not try and feed Robin?"

I undo my top and try to put him to my breast but he'll have none of it.

"Is that alright?"

Gloria reassures me again.

"It's fine," she says. "Some do start straight away. Others take ages. He's been through a traumatic time you know."

I suppose he has.

He goes quiet again and just lies still on my chest. I go quiet as well and do the same. I've been through a traumatic time as well.

Gloria leaves the room and comes back a couple of minutes later carrying a wicker cradle and stand.

'This was Lenny's," she says, sadly. "I kept it. Thought it might come in handy one day. I thought it would be for my next baby though. Never yours. I've got clothes as well. Even bought little Robin some in town."

"Thanks."

She leaves the room again and comes back with soft baby blankets and sets up the cradle beside my bed.

"Want me to put him in for you?"

I look down at Robin.

"No thanks. I'll just cuddle him for now. He's beautiful."

"Tell you what then," Gloria suggests. "I'll leave you to have a sleep and I'll go and finish the sausages. I'll come back and see you soon. Is that alright?"

"That will be lovely. I'm worn out for some reason."

Gloria laughs.

"I don't know why," she jokes.

She leaves me and, after counting what blessings I had, I drop into another world, a world of much needed sleep. I don't think much of this giving birth lark I can tell you.

I awake two hours later and look at my little Robin. He has his eyes open and is looking at me.

"Hello gorgeous," I say. "I'm your mummy. I'm only young but I will look after you."

I am his mummy. It has just dawned on me. That's what I am now, a mother. I touch his tiny hand and look at his even tinier fingers. They're so small but so perfect. I look at his fingers and then look at mine. They're exactly the same but in a different size. I'll try to feed him again. I do but still he isn't interested.

"Gloria!"

She hears me and comes up.

"He won't feed Gloria."

"Don't worry," she says, smiling. "He's only just born. He'll be alright. All new mums worry but there's no need. He'll be fine. He is a handsome little fellow isn't he? Is his dad handsome?"

"Very. Apart from his great mop of hair that he won't comb. Yes, he's lovely."

Evening soon comes and the sky darkens. Robin is laid quietly in his cradle and, before I know it, we are both going to sleep. I have no expertise with babies but should he be this quiet and contented? Shouldn't he be screaming the place down? I'm still tired though, despite my sleep earlier, and drift off again. Robin cries once through the night and I try to feed him again without any success.

"He's had a very quiet night," I tell Gloria the next morning. "He only cried once and that was just a cry. More of a whimper. Not a scream. I tried to feed him but he wouldn't take it."

Gloria picks Robin up and cuddles him. He gives a murmur and a gurgle.

"He seems content enough," she says. "Look at him. He'll be fine. He's a good'n."

She then looks into his eyes as they open and her face changes.

"What's wrong?"

She hesitates in answering.

"N…Nothing. I think he's just got wind."

"Wind? He hasn't eaten anything."

"Try him again."

I do and, this time, he does latch on to my breast and starts to suck a little.

"There we are," Gloria says, triumphantly but still holding something back. "He's fine. Look at the little mite. Bless him. He'll be running around in no time."

At lunchtime I get up. Little Robin is sound asleep in his cradle and I wash and dress before picking him up and taking him downstairs for the first time to see the home he has been born into. Getting out of bed was not too bad but I do find the stairs a bit of a struggle. Things are sore still.

The house is filled with the smell of cooking and a sizzling is coming from a frying pan on the range.

"I'm doing us a sausage sandwich for dinner," Gloria says.

It was always the same. I call it lunch and she calls it dinner.

"I'm having raw onions in mine," she adds. "You'd better stick to ketchup as you're feeding. Is he feeding?"

I'm heartened by the fact that he has started.

Gloria makes my sandwich and takes Robin as I eat it. She cuddles him and shuffles around the room and to the window.

"That's your farm out there young Robin," she says to him, as he takes her finger in his little hand. "It'll all belong to your mum one day when I'm gone. But I'm not going to go just yet. I'm going to stay here and look after you. Look out there. Everything will belong to you and your mum. Every sagging roof, broken door and rusty Land Rover. I think your mum will sell it all though and I don't blame her. It's a lonely old life running a farm. I was lonely until she came along."

She looks down at Robin and has that serious look on her face again.

"What's wrong?"

"Nothing. Just wind again."

"Again?"

She puts Robin over her shoulder and gently pats his back. He still seems content but no wind comes up.

I finish my sandwich and then prepare Gloria's for her before taking Robin from her so that she can sit down and eat.

"Feed him again Vera."

I sit in my chair and do. This time he latches on well and I'm sure he's getting some.

"That's better," Gloria says with a chuckle. "He'll do."

I take her at her word but, deep within me, she has installed a niggle. One that I try to dismiss but can't.

"Why is he so quiet?" I ask.

"He's just a contented baby."

"Is that the only reason?"

Gloria does her best to convince me.

"Most mothers could only dream of having one that good," she tells me. "Look at him. Fed and clean and cuddled up to his mum. He's had his goodness. What more does he want?"

I'm almost convinced.

The day goes by with nappy changing and feeding and cuddling and cooing. Gloria spoils me in every way. I do my best to feel as happy and contented as Robin seems but my brain is bothering me. But I've been through labour and have given birth. I know that takes its toll. I've been asleep but am still tired. I tell myself not to worry.

The next day I feel much brighter and wrap Robin well and take him for a walk around the farmyard to introduce him to all the animals, most of whom have names beginning with B.

"There's Bruno and there's Buttercup and Barbara and the pigs Betty and Bramble," I tell him, in a mother to baby voice.

The geese, Bob, Boris and Bernard are nowhere to be seen but I can hear them down on the bottom field. A rat scurries across the farmyard.

"I won't tell you what B Gloria calls that one," I say.

Again that evening, Robin is quiet but Gloria insists he is just contented. He does seem to be feeding, but only just. Is he getting enough goodness? I start to take him to bed on his second full day and then hesitate.

"Tell me Gloria," I say, seriously and concerned. Almost in tears. "Tell me honestly. You've noticed something haven't you?"

"I'm sorry Vera but, being totally honest, I have to say yes," she admits. "It may be nothing. Nothing at all but when I look into his eyes I see something's missing. Perhaps it's just me being stupid."

"But you aren't stupid are you?"

She shakes her head.

"He'll be alright Vera. You take him to bed and, if I'm still at all concerned in the morning, I'll go and fetch a doctor. I know you've been hidden down here but that doesn't matter now does it? You've had him and we'll look after him. First thing in the morning I'll check him and, if I'm bothered still in any way whatsoever then I'll go to town and fetch him."

I'm worried now but reassured at the same time. I can't simply dismiss Gloria's thoughts and submissions because she knows so much about life and babies. It doesn't matter if it's a pig or poultry or even my little Robin. She knows because they're all much the same and she's had the experience. I go to bed, feed my baby, change him, cuddle him and put him in his cradle. He's still contented but how I wish he wasn't. I wish, from the bottom of my heart, that he would scream and scream all night. Just to let me know he's normal.

"Come on my little Robin. Please scream for your mummy. Your mummy loves you with all her heart and she would love that. She really really would."

He doesn't. Instead, he just looks at me through his pretty little eyes that could so easily belong to his father, closes them and drifts off again. I check his breathing. It's strong and fine so I leave him and get into my own bed, somehow dreading falling asleep. I lay thinking about him and watching his cradle. I pray for him to scream. Sleep is not what I want but I do eventually and, later, have the piglet nightmare again which wakes me in the early hours of the morning.

Robin is quiet still so I get out of bed and go to him. Bless him. He looks so cute and contented but, slowly, I realise something is wrong. Something is quite wrong, dreadfully wrong. I go to pick him up. He's been covered up but he's cold. He's been contented but now he's completely still. A huge realisation hits home. One which fills me with an abject horror. My baby is cold and still. I'm suddenly unable to breathe and tears well up from deep inside my tight chest. I'm completely frigid with fear and realisation. I don't want to admit it but I step back in horror. Surely I'm still having my nightmare. It can't be but it is. I try to scream and eventually do but it takes time.

"No!!!"

My baby has died.

"God!!!"

My oh so precious little Robin, the one thing I have that's mine, has passed away in the night. My whole being is in a dreadful panic. I've touched him and want to again but step another pace back instead. I can't touch him again. I just stare. He's cold, pale and still. He's gone. I scream at the top of my voice and that scream is repeated over and over again until I fall to my knees in despair. Tears flood from my eyes. His life has been extinguished, taking mine with him, completely and utterly.

"Gloria!!"

She rushes into my room, lifts me and holds me, giving only a slight glance towards Robin. She knows what's happened and obviously expected little else.

I can only point. I'm too numb now to do anything else.

"My baby!" I say, after a struggle.

"I know."

"My little Robin!"

"I know sweetheart."

She helps me to the edge of my bed and cuddles me again.

"What was wrong with him?"

"I don't know."

"But you saw something didn't you?"

She nods.

"What did you see?"

She puts a hand on each of my shoulders and turns me towards her.

"He weren't a good'n Vera. That's what I saw. That's all I saw sweetheart. I hoped I was wrong. I really did."

I look into her completely loving and sincere eyes and fall into her arms.

"He was my little Robin Gloria," I sob, uncontrollably. "He was my little Robin and now he's gone. I want him back!!"

"Sorry sweetheart but you can't have him back. He has gone."

"What can I do?"

"There's nothing you can do sweetheart. Nothing at all."

"But I have to do something Gloria. He's… He's my baby. My little Robin."

I seem to almost drown in my own tears. I shake with grief. I have no baby inside me and, suddenly, only a vast emptiness dwells there. It's an emptiness that I know can never be filled again. My life may as well be over too. I look towards his cradle and do honestly wish I could join my little baby in whatever world he has gone to. It can't possibly be any worse than this one.

"He's my baby. I've got to do something."

"You'll do nothing sweetheart," Gloria tells me, holding me closer still. "You just leave everything to your auntie Gloria."

31.

It was a boy and I realised I couldn't really call him Penelope. 'It's Robin', I told Gloria as she passed him to me. It's Robin and he's beautiful. I had always planned on Robin. I was crying and, to my astonishment, so was she. And there he is look. Outside, sitting on the fence. My Robin. He'll come down in a second or two. He knows it wasn't my fault.

When it was all over and I'd sat myself up in bed a little, I took my little Robin and cuddled him so close to me. He was quiet and seemed quite contented and I cuddled him like I'd never cuddled anything in my life before. Apart from Jonny, his dad, that is. I'd cuddled him a few times. Bless him. For so long I'd had nothing but Aunt Gloria and the animals but suddenly I had the most precious thing any female could ever hold. Her own baby. My own beautiful child. I had him but how I wished I could have had his beautiful and dear father as well. How I wished I had my Jonny. I didn't have him and couldn't have him but I did have my Robin. He laid on my chest and I fell asleep. I didn't know if my Jonny had received my letter to him but I'd heard nothing back.

But then it all changed again didn't it? I couldn't have my Jonny but I did have his son and that was a great substitute but it didn't last did it? Just the three days.

I hear a call.

"You alright Vera?!"

"What?"

"I said are you alright?"

It's Norma and she's got her blue rubber gloves on.

"I'm ok thanks. I think so anyway. Haven't seen the new man again. Has he died already?"

"No," Norma replies. "He's having a lay in bed Vera. He's not feeling too bright today. He's come in because he's had a stroke and he's still not too good. They wanted him out of the hospital bed. Maybe he'll be about again later. Or tomorrow."

"You ready to give me my bath?"

She looks down a little.

"Do you mind if we do you in a little while? Got an emergency one going."

I smile.

"Someone else shot themselves have they?"

Norma laughs.

"Something like that Vera," she says. "You're a good'n you are."

"My Robin wasn't."

"He's there," she replies, pointing. "He's outside look."

"There he is. Bless him."

"I'll be back in half an hour Vera. Is that alright?"

"Fine sweetheart. You carry on. Try not to drown anybody."

A nurse comes along, the dark one, and Norma walks off with her.

I honestly thought my life had ended that day when I lost my little Robin. And it did in a way. I didn't have my Jonny or my Robin and I didn't even have a proper home really. Although I did call the farm home it wasn't really my home was it? I'd been sent there for being a sinner who would bring a bad name to my family if I'd stayed at home. Surely your own family should be more important than the thoughts of others. Would you do it? Send your daughter away because you didn't tell her the facts of life and she got pregnant because of it? Of course you wouldn't but then, as I've already said, times are different today aren't they? Times have changed and some things have changed for the better. Not everything but some things have haven't they?

Vera is emotional and weeping slightly. She lifts her glasses and wipes her eyes again.

I'd lost my baby and had also lost my mind. It's hard to tell you just what happened and how I felt exactly because, to be honest, I was so far gone at times I don't even remember myself how I felt. Poor

Gloria was heartbroken and tried her best to look after me but the trouble was I wasn't me was I? I was an inconsolable wreck and a blubbering idiot. I did have good reason to be that way but that didn't help the poor woman who was doing her best despite my continuous crying and general hysterics. Do you know, I've never been one to get ratty. I've always tried my hardest to stay calm, polite and kind. I've made a point of it, but not then. I shouted and screamed at Gloria on many an occasion but it wasn't her fault was it? It just happened she was the only person there to listen. And she did listen, bless her. Not once did she raise her voice in return. I was horrible to her and, do you know, she never even batted an eyelid. She was a good'n alright.

She took care of Robin for me. I couldn't do it. I was distraught for over three weeks. I was hungry but I wouldn't eat and I was dirty but wouldn't wash. I was tired but wouldn't sleep and I was alive but wanted to die. Gloria was there all the time but could do nothing apart from deal with my dead baby. My son. I found out later, when I started to come to my senses again, that she'd made a nice box, lined it with a blanket from his cradle and had buried him deep, next to the dead piglet, behind the pigsty, in the sunshine. She'd even made him a nice wooden cross but the nail she used to fix the two parts together wasn't strong so it had bent over when she hit if with the hammer. String came in useful again to bind it properly. You wouldn't do it today, bury a baby in a farmyard but, as I have just said again, these are different times. I thought to have him moved later but that posed a huge dilemma for me. Should I have him buried in a churchyard or should I leave the poor little love in the only place he had ever seen? The place that he, and I, knew as home. I decided to leave him and let him rest in peace. Poor little Robin. His body is still there, in the sunshine. I know it's not right but, in truth, what the hell is?

She wipes her eyes again.

Do you know? I fancy a cup of coffee and a biscuit. Where's that Susie with the wobbly wheel?

32.

"It's been three weeks now Vera," Gloria says as she sits gently on the edge of my bed and lays an arm around me. "I know it's been a rough old time sweetheart. A rough old time for both of us but it's happened and we can't turn back time can we? It's not possible. We've got to move on you know."

I nod.

"I know we have to Gloria," I say, still very sad and not even really wanting to talk. "I know but I don't know if I can."

"You were so strong before weren't you?"

"I was. I know. I grew strong when I came here but this has killed me now. It's all gone Gloria. I've lost my son, my Robin and it's all gone."

"No it hasn't. You're still young and with a life in front of you."

"But I don't want it do I? I don't want to live it."

"Yes you do."

Gloria changes tack slightly. She knows a weak spot of mine.

"And your little Robin wouldn't want to see you sad like this would he? You were his mummy and you loved him. He knows it wasn't your fault doesn't he?"

"Wasn't it?"

"Of course not."

I look into Gloria's eyes.

"It wasn't was it?"

She lifts my shoulders from the bed I've been lying on for most of the past three weeks and cuddles me.

"Of course it wasn't your fault Vera sweetheart. Nothing was. There was nothing you could have done. He wasn't a good'n and that's that. It's sad but that's the fact of it. I was going to get help that day but it wouldn't have made any difference would it? He was going to die no matter what we did. No matter what anyone did. And I'm sure he'd be so angry now if he saw you like this. He'd want you to be strong again Vera. He lost his life but he would feel dreadful if you gave up yours as well. He would feel so guilty if he knew he had caused all this; if he's hurt his mummy."

"I know," I say, through yet more tears. It's amazing how many tears you can cry before they all run dry.

I look at Gloria again.

"I am sorry."

"You've nothing to be sorry for have you?"

"But there were times when I was horrible to you for no reason. I upset you didn't I?"

She holds me away from her and raises her voice slightly, appearing to be angry.

"I don't know who you think you are Vera Hobbs," she says, almost indignantly. "Don't you ever think you're so special young lady. I'll have you know I've been upset by far better people than you in my time."

For the first time in three weeks a smile manages to force itself onto my much troubled face.

"How about you get up? I'll get you a jug of hot water and then you can wash and get dressed while I go and check the post box."

"Hot water? In the morning? We don't normally wash in the mornings."

"But you've saved me loads of hot water my girl. You've hardly washed in three weeks. You can have some this morning and you're welcome to it. Now come on. Up, washed and dressed by the time I get back and then we'll go and see your little Robin."

"Ok."

Gloria stands up and starts for the door and stairs.

"I am really sorry," I tell her.

By the time she is back from the post box I'm downstairs, making a pot of tea, still with shaky hands. She comes in with a letter in her hand. She has a concerned look on her face.

"It's for you Vera."

"Is it from Jonny?"

"I think it's from your mother. It looks like her writing."

I sit down by the range and open the letter. I read it.

Dear Vera,

You probably really hate me now and I cannot blame you if you do but I have to write and tell you that your father has died. He died on the eleventh of May of a massive bleed on his brain. He was in his shop, serving customers. The authorities have told me it was an aneurysm that burst. It's a weakened blood vessel. We never even knew he had one.

I know we've both treated you so badly and I do hope everything is alright now. Have you had the baby yet? Your father did hate you for what you did but my hate only came from his attitude. I know I've always sided with him and have always gone along with his feelings but mine were not like his Vera. Please believe me. You were still my little girl. You didn't deserve all that did you? I should have been there for you, not against you.

I do still love you Vera and I know in no way do I deserve you in my rotten life but I do need you. If you could find it in your heart to possibly come home and see me I would be so grateful but if you never come anywhere near me again then I will understand. I cannot expect to treat you as I did and yet still have you want me but I do want you. Please come and see me and bring my grandchild if it has arrived.

Yours,

Mum.

I put the letter down on my knee and look at Gloria. I've read it out loud to her.

"What are you going to do sweetheart?"

"I don't know. I don't think I'm strong enough to go yet. I don't know if I'm strong enough to do anything at the minute."

"But you do want to?"

I nod.

"I've got to Gloria, really. I've got to go back. I need to see mum. And I need to find Jonny. I can now can't I? My father's gone."

"You've got me Vera," Gloria says, sincerely, holding my hand once more. "But I'm no substitute for your mother am I? And I'm certainly no substitute for Jonny."

"She'll never be as good as you. No one could ever be that good," I tell her.

"Don't be daft girl."

"I'm not. It's true. You are one in a million and I love you so much."

Then a thought runs through my mind.

"Do you know?"

"What?"

"My father and little Robin died on the same day. How ironic is that?"

For the first time, Gloria suddenly thinks of the part about my father dying.

"I should be horrified shouldn't I?"

"About what?"

"That's just it. About what? We've just heard that my brother has died and I've just cast the fact aside as if it doesn't matter. To tell you the truth Vera, it doesn't. Is that bad of me?"

"Well, at least you haven't gone to pieces for three weeks like I did. And a good job too. I wouldn't put up with all the rubbish you took from me."

Gloria stands up and holds out her hand.

"Come on sweetheart. Let's go and visit your Robin. We'll have a drop of cider tonight to celebrate his life and then I'll run you home in the Land Rover tomorrow."

"Only a little drop of cider I suppose?"

"Well, his was only a little life wasn't it?"

"Bless him."

I stand up and lay my letter on my chair.

"And do you think the Land Rover will get us as far as home?"

"Who knows? But I do know something."

"What's that?"

"You're not pregnant any more girl so if it breaks down you can push."

"Thank you."

On unsteady legs I make my way, guided by the hand of my guardian, to the back of the pigsty. I'm terribly nervous but what am I expecting? I'm not going to see his little dead body again am I?

We reach the spot and I almost feel guilty because a tiny smile does cross my face. It's the string. Gloria has thoughtfully made a nice cross for Robin and it is tied together with bailer twine, her favourite material. It is set into a small mound of freshly dug soil and, in front of it, lays a lovely bunch of spring flowers. The sun is shining warm and bright on us and my lost child. I say the Lord's prayer again.

I'm not right but do realise little Robin is at peace. Over the past three weeks all I wanted to do was join him but I realise now that is no plan. Life must go on, somehow.

The next morning, feeling slightly brighter and after actually eating breakfast for the first time recently, the old Land Rover is started after a bash with the hammer again and we are soon on our way home. But what is home? Where is it? I don't know now. Forty minutes later we are in town and heading downhill, past the water tower and towards Jonny's terrace but where is it?

I'm stunned.

"Stop the car Gloria."

She does and I stare, agog at what is before me. The whole row of cottages has been flattened and the site has been all but cleared. His house has gone and my Jonny too. I've been so excited about knocking on his door but even that has disappeared. Where is he?

"You alright Vera?"

"No. He's gone. No wonder he didn't reply to my letter."

We turn left and climb the hill that, in my father's mind, separated the classes and are soon entering our drive. His car is there and it makes me creep to see it. I remember that awful time I last rode in it.

Gloria places a hand on my knee.

"The car may be there Vera sweetheart," she says, "But he's gone hasn't he?"

"Yes."

"Come on."

I get out nervously and go to the front door and think to knock, but no. I've got a right to go in. Every right. It should be my home so I just open it instead of knocking first and the smell of polish fills my nostrils for the first time in many months.

"Mum!" I call very half-heartedly.

All is quiet as we walk towards the kitchen but then the back door opens and closes.

"Mum!"

"Vera?"

I hear her voice but don't truly know if I welcome it or not. She has recognised mine but seems very nervous in making her short reply. We meet at the kitchen door together and just stand, staring. Neither of us knowing a single word of what to say.

"Mum," I repeat eventually.

"Vera."

She throws her arms around me and all the sobbing starts again. In all my years this is the first time she has actually thrown her arms around me. Why couldn't she do it before?

"I'm so so sorry Vera," she utters through a torrent of tears. "All this should never have happened."

She draws herself away from me and looks down at my form.

"And my grandchild?"

"A boy mum," I tell her, sadly. "Robin. He died mum. Three days old. He died the same day as dad did."

Dad. That word is hard to say.

"She's been suffering Connie," Gloria tells her, plainly. "This poor little girl, the loveliest thing to come into my life for years, has been to hell and back. Twice. Once when you and Reg dumped her at mine and now again with her baby dying. She needs you Connie. She's had me and I have done my best, believe me I have but I'm not her mother. You've got a good'n there and I suggest you make it up to her in some way. Saying I love you and have missed you would make a start."

Mum nods now.

"I do love you Vera. I always have loved you. And, believe me, I have missed you every single day we've been apart."

"And you would still be apart if Reg hadn't died wouldn't you?"

"Yes."

"You sucked up to that man for far too long Connie."

"I know I did and I know I should have been stronger."

"I've got her things in the Land Rover," Gloria says. "I'll miss her, just like you did, but she's home where she belongs now. She still has a home at mine as well though and she's welcome back any time. More than welcome. She's a big girl now and I think it's about time she chooses for herself where she lives. In future nobody's going to force her either way. I'm going to leave her here for now but do you know what I'm going to do as well?"

"What?"

She looks at me.

"I'm going to pay to have the phone put in at mine so she can ring me whenever she wants. Then, when she's had enough of being here all she has to do is ring and I'll come and collect her."

Gloria then goes outside to unload all my things. She places then in the hallway.

"Thanks for your help Connie," she says to mum, a little crossly as she drops the last article. "You never were too good at practical things were you? Everything's there. Some of it may need a wash though. Things are not always too clean on a farm."

"Would you like tea?"

"No thanks. Leaving Vera is going to break my bloody heart and the sooner I do it the sooner I can get over it. I'm off. I'll ring you as soon as the phone is put in Vera."

I run over to her.

"Thanks Gloria. I don't know what I'd have done without you. You're wonderful."

She tries to walk away but can't.

"Come here girl," she says, turning to me.

She grabs me and actually manages to hug me so much my feet leave the ground.

"Life is going to be a bitch without you Vera."

"At least it begins with B."

We laugh but mum doesn't get the joke.

"I love you Gloria."

"And I love you too sweetheart. And always will. You've changed my bloody life you have and now I'll go home and get all hard and miserable again."

She knows differently.

I hold her hand as she goes out to her car. This time it starts without the hammer. But only just.

"I'll ring you Vera."

"And don't forget."

"Don't you worry. I'll never forget my Vera Hobbs."

She leaves with a bang and a puff of smoke and I turn to go indoors but decide not to.

"I'll be back in a little while mum."

"Where are you going?"

"I'm going to find Kathy."

"Can't you do that tomorrow?"

I can't. My father's gone and my life is my own at last. I'm free. Free to do what I want and when I want to do it. I do still love my mum and think I may live with her from now on but she did hurt me badly and I feel I cannot fully forgive her just yet. I'll find Kathy today and try and start to forgive mum tomorrow.

"Won't be long mum."

I walk down the hill and under the cherry trees that are ladened with tiny fruits. Blackbirds sit in the branches as if they are waiting already for the Autumn. A coal lorry chugs down passed me. It's Ernie the 'cool man'. It still says so on the side.

I reach the spot where the cottages were and stand where Jonny's gate once was before going onto the site to look for anything familiar. Very little is left apart from bits and pieces of brick, wood and plaster. Nothing is recognisable but then, just in front of my feet I spot something. A piece of plaster with a discoloured flap of wallpaper on it. I pick it up and study it. Could it be? It is. I hold it close to me. If only that piece of wallpaper could talk? It would have so many stories to tell. The things it has seen and heard.

Eventually, and after such reminiscing, I leave the site and head a little further down the hill. I hear a bicycle behind me. It passes by but then stops and the rider turns her head and looks at me.

"Vera? Is that you?"

'Kathy?"

She has come from her aunts and stops and jumps off the bike. She lets it crash to the ground before running over to me.

"Vera!!! Where have you been?"

"I had to go away Kathy. I was pregnant."

I'm crying again.

"I know you were. It took some time but we all worked it out in the end."

"I've been on my aunt's farm."

"The one in the trees?"

"Yes."

"So where's the baby?"

"He died Kathy. Three weeks ago. The same day as my father."

"That old bastard?"

"I wouldn't call him that."

"Only because you never swear."

She sees my piece of plaster.

"Whatever have you got that for?"

I laugh. I still don't feel too happy but I do laugh.

"It's from Jonny's bedroom wall," I tell her. "I'm keeping it as a souvenir. It used to hang there and flap all the time."

"All the time you were doing it?"

"Yes."

"So it was Jonny's baby?"

"Of course it was. I loved him Kathy. Still do. Where is he?"

Kathy looks at me with serious concern written all over her face. She puts her arm around me. She has been so pleased to see me that she has only just noticed I'm still not well.

"Your father went to see him," she explains, holding me close to her. "He went after him and told him he had upset you and you didn't want to see him again. He told him to stay away. He said if Jonny tried to contact you in any way he would come again and beat him up. Even if his brothers were there. He was so angry."

"So where's Jonny?"

"A few weeks later, he realised you weren't around and took it that you had dumped him so when somebody offered him a carpentry job in London that paid good wages he went. He did really love you Vera. He was hurt bad."

"I know."

"Is he still in London?"

"I think so."

"And the terrace?"

"It was always bad wasn't it?" Kathy explains. "But one night, about three months back, the end wall fell out of the first one and the rest had to be condemned. Nobody was hurt. The council took them down and is going to build new council houses there. Four of them. Two pairs."

I feel really really sad again but try not to show it. I know I look a mess and don't want to make myself look any worse.

"So my baby's gone and so is my Jonny."

"Sorry Vera," Kathy says, putting her arm around me again. "It's been a rough old time hasn't it?"

I nod.

"It has."

"Have you come home now?"

"I think so. My aunt Gloria has given me the choice. Here or at hers. I'll see how things are with my mum and then I'll make up my mind."

I then see an almost perverse and funny side of things. I look down at the piece of plaster which I still have in my hand. I then look at Kathy and force another smile.

"I've lost my baby and my Jonny Kathy," I repeat, smiling through tears. "But at least I've got his flap of wallpaper haven't I?"

33.

And that's what I had for all my troubles, a flap of old and discoloured wallpaper. Life can be rubbish sometimes can't it? But at least I did start to feel stronger again and felt my life was mine to live. All I had to do was find something to live for again. I did find my George later but I even feel sorry for him. I still feel really guilty. He's dead too now and but I still feel sorry for him. I wasn't a good wife was I? No good wife can be in bed with her husband and be thinking of somebody else instead can they? I did. I always did. To put it plainly, as Gloria would have done, I was having sex with George while I was thinking of Jonny. Every time I did it. Of course, I never ever told him that but it was true. He must have noticed my mind wasn't on him but he said nothing. He never did have much of a flame inside him and I certainly never ever let him rekindle mine. Only my Jonny could ever have done that.

Oh, by the way, the new man in here did replace old Mr Trafford. I thought I hadn't seen him lately. He used to only have the one leg. He said he'd lost the other one in the war. I told him to be more careful where he left it next time. I said it's silly, losing a leg. He did laugh. Nice old man but he'd turned a bit gaga. He used to sit in the corner over there. Yes. You've guessed it. By the rubber plant that never gets watered, but that young Rachel's going to do it later isn't she? He used to sit there looking out of the window all day and think he was waiting for the bus to Peterborough. It never came.

Vera shuffles slightly in her seat and runs her hand along its arm.

This is a nice seat. Nice and soft but you do get uncomfortable sometimes when you sit here all day and you can't move too well. I seem to lose the feeling in my bottom. It must go numb. Either that or I am dying from the feet up. I can see them but I can't really feel them. It's hard work being old but then again it has to be better than being dead doesn't it? I suppose so anyway. I didn't always think that way.

Vera falls asleep.

"Sorry Vera," comes a voice. "Sorry to wake you but I've got more tablets for you."

"What are they? Sleeping tablets?"

It's the nurse lady with her tablets and her trolley and jug of water for us to down them with.

I look across and then tell the nurse something.

"That man keeps looking at me," I say to her. "Staring he is."

"Don't worry," she says. "It's the new man. He's probably just feeling a bit awkward and wants to settle in. Would you like to talk to him?"

"No thanks. Not likely. He looks a funny old bugger. Looks like he's wearing a bobble hat."

She laughs.

"You are naughty Vera."

I laugh as well and the nurse pushes her trolley away and over to the next tablet taker. I suppose we all are at our age. I look at the man again. He's a big man with a big head and is almost bald but he has one or two long wisps of hair left and they poke out sideways. Funny looking old chap he is. He looks again and then they take him towards the toilet. I think he's had a stroke because his left arm seems to be hanging and laying heavily on his lap.

I'm glad he's gone and just look outside. It's a nice day. I may go out again tomorrow.

He's back again now. The new man. That was quick. They've sat him beside old Tommy Harris, the one from Market Harborough. That's what he says anyway. That's what he says today but yesterday it was Middlesbrough and Scarborough the day before that. He doesn't know where he's from but at least the borough bit is consistent.

He's looking at me again now. No. Not Tommy Harris. The new man. He's looking at me. Why's he looking at me? I've never met the man and he doesn't know me and yet he's looking at me. He's staring now and that's rude. I'll just ignore him.

Oh, that's good. The new girl. The nice one. Rachel. That's it. She's been talking to him and has got the handles of his chair again and she's moving him. I can't sit here with a strange man staring at me all day can I? It's unsettling. Maybe she's taking him for a bath or something. Maybe he's come from somewhere dirty and they're going to have him fumigated or maybe he missed when they took him to the toilet and he's wet his trousers. Oh dear. Maybe she's bringing him over here. No. Please don't. I really don't want company. Not now. Especially the company of a funny looking old bald man with a lump on his head that I've never met before.

Rachel smiles a beautiful warm smile as she parks the man by my feet without even asking permission. He's still looking but, this time he's looking into my eyes. I don't like it.

"This is the new gentleman," she says. "I want him to meet everyone and he especially wanted to come and talk to you first Vera. That's nice isn't it?"

"Lovely, I'm sure."

"Cheer up Vera. Be nice."

"But I was talking to…"

"Talking to who Vera?"

"Oh, never mind."

"Hello Vera," the man says softly, leaning forwards and taking my hand.

What? What's he doing? I panic. I'm not having a strange old bald man with a silly lump on his head grabbing hold of my hand in broad daylight.

"Nurse!"

I try to pull my hand away but, for some reason, it won't move. He starts to cry. The silly old bugger actually starts to cry. Whatever is going on and why did I squeeze his hand instead of pulling away? It wasn't just because he was crying was it? I feel strange and almost look around and call for help again, but no. What's happening? Should I call the nurse, or Rachel? This is wrong. Or is it? I don't know if it is wrong or right or what the hell it is.

"N…?"

He has had his head bent down slightly but he looks up again and into my eyes.

"Hello Vera," he says again, emotionally and wiping his eyes with his good hand. "Long time no see."

I give him a tissue.

"What do you mean long time no see? Do I know you?"

I look at him inquisitively,

He smiles through his tears and yet despite them, he almost giggles a bit at the same time.

"It was a long time ago sweetheart," he says, quite sweetly. "A long long time ago and you probably wouldn't even remember me anyway but I remember you. How are you these days V?"

"V? Only my Jonny ever called me V."

Bloody hell!

I didn't recognise him but then, for the first time, and with that one little letter being uttered, I look straight into his eyes and a massive realisation hits home. Then all hell lets loose in my mind followed by my heart almost stopping and tears burst out. I'd given him my last tissue but suddenly need dozens of the things myself.

"Jonny?"

All he can do in answer is nod and shed more tears.

"Yes," he eventually manages to say. "Yes. It's me V."

"My Jonny? Fuck me."

The shock is so great I've just used a bad swear word for the first time in my whole life but I feel the situation deserves it.

"My Jonny?"

He nods again and reaches over to hold both my hands in his good one and then we just sit there, looking at each other, neither of us knowing at all what to say or do next. But that doesn't matter. Who need words when we've got each other.

"My Jonny? Jonny Clitheroe from the terrace?"

He nods again.

"That's me."

Rachel comes over and kneels down beside us.

"What's wrong?" she asks. "You both look dreadful."

We both look at her and then at each other again. We say the same thing at the same time.

"Nothing's wrong sweetheart."

"Nothing's wrong at all," Jonny adds.

"This is my Jonny," I tell her. "I thought I'd lost him forever but I haven't have I? He's here. He's come back to see me. Just like my…our little Robin. Can you get me some more tissues sweetheart? I think I….I think we both need them. We haven't seen each other since we were fifteen."

She gives me some tissues and then, out of respect and realising we have decades to catch up on, she leaves us alone.

"Look," I say, pointing. "That's Robin out there."

"Who's Robin?" Jonny asks me.

I point out of the window again to the robin who is poking around in the soil for worms and nibbles. Jonny hasn't seen him.

"There he is. That's our Robin," I say, through another tear. "That's Robin. Our little Robin."

"A bird?"

"He is now," I tell him. "But he was our Robin. Our baby Robin. Our baby. Yours and mine. That's why I had to go away and leave you."

Jonny's confused but his ageing brain does catch up somewhat eventually.

"You had a baby?"

"Yes. It was ours."

"But they told me you didn't want to see me anymore and had moved away."

"Didn't want to see you Jonny?" I say, trying my hardest to move my frail old body towards his. "I did want to see you. I really really did. I loved you. I wrote you a letter. I've wanted to see you for the last seventy years nearly but they took me to my aunt Gloria's place and I was shut away. I was pregnant with your baby and was a disgrace that had to be hidden so they hid me in the middle of the woods where nobody could see me."

"And the baby? Where is he?"

Jonny is still a little confused about the whole baby and bird thing.

"Robin?"

"Yes."

"He was born there Jonny, in the woods and there was only me and my aunt. Nobody else knew. Nobody else even knew I was there apart from a stuck old woman from down the road and the postman who took my letter to you. Gloria never had many visitors and even when she did I had to hide up somewhere out of the way while she chased them off with her shotgun."

I laugh, remembering the encyclopaedia salesman.

"What happened to him? Robin."

"He died Jonny. Poor little thing. He died. Three days old he was bless him. Died the same day as my father did. Maybe he could have lived if he went to hospital but he couldn't go could he because nobody was to know he was even born let alone ill. When he was born he looked so cute and quiet and beautiful but he wasn't quiet because he was contented. He was quiet because he was ill Jonny, very ill. We didn't know that. Me and aunt Gloria did our best with him but nothing worked. She said he wasn't a good'n. He was ill and he wasn't feeding properly. He wasn't getting any goodness. You need goodness. You could see it in his eyes Jonny. He had your eyes but his weren't right. There was definitely something missing. Something not right at all. To be honest, I don't think it was something that could have been mended even if he did go to hospital. I don't know. We'll never know. He was so cute but we could see he wasn't a good'n. He did have your eyes. I woke up one morning and he'd passed away in his cradle in the night. Just like that. Gone. He hadn't made a sound all night and then, there he was, dead. His little body was still, stiff and cold. He was dead and was 'got rid of'."

"Got rid of?"

"That's what she did with dead things, Gloria. She got rid of them but he's out there now, look."

Jonny looks outside but still can't quite see the connection. Or he can see the connection but he can't believe it as I do. Does he think I'm stupid? Am I? I am aren't I?

"I've always loved you Jonny," I say, squeezing his hand firmly. "Years later I met and needed a man, George, and he needed me. He was a decent man and he'd lost his wife. I was alone and so was he. We got married and rubbed along ok but I didn't love him did I? I only ever loved you."

"Did you have any more children?" Jonny asks.

"No."

"Why not Vera?"

"I couldn't. Me and you were having sex for ages before I got pregnant weren't we?"

Jonny smiles broadly.

"We certainly were," he answers. "I remember the haystack."

"And I remember the flapping wallpaper."

"And the dodgy stair rail. My dad never was good at fixing things was he?"

"They later said it was a miracle that I ever got pregnant at all," I tell him. "I shouldn't have done. There was something wrong with me that said I couldn't ever but I did just that once. George died ten years ago. All that time and all those years I suppose I was happy enough with him but I've only ever loved one man, Jonny Clitheroe. My Jonny. Did you get married?"

Jonny manages to lean forward in his wheelchair again and I just about manage to meet him. We kiss lightly but painfully as our old joints are stretched almost beyond their frayed tolerance. Jonny holds my cheek momentarily.

"Remember the picture of the old lady that used to hang in our hallway?"

"She used to hate me."

"I did get married," he says, in answer to my question. "When I was twenty eight. When they told me you didn't want me I thought about it and realised there was nothing left in the town for me so, although

I was still young, I went to London. Took my tools and did carpentry there. It worked out for a few years and I met and married Cynthia. She worked in the corner shop. A bit like you did. I've got a son and a daughter and three grandchildren. I'm about to have my first great grandchild. Life was quite good really but a big spark was missing. A huge one really. You were that spark Vera. Vera Hobbs was no longer in my life and it couldn't possibly ever be the same without her."

"And Cynthia?"

"We divorced just after my John's wife had their second child. Cynthia became temperamental and even aggressive and I couldn't cope. I should have coped but couldn't. We found out later she was suffering from a clinical depression. I couldn't cope with her and she couldn't cope with life. Poor woman. They gave her tablets to help with her condition but she took them all at once. They did help then. She didn't suffer any more."

I look at him again and all those features seem so familiar at last. Especially the few strands of sticky out hair. He has changed but, in a way, he hasn't changed at all. Apart from losing most of that hair and the big lump on his head that is.

"You used to have brown hair and now it's grey," he says.

"At least I've still got some," I answer.

Jonny smiles.

"I think I lost mine because I combed it too much," he adds.

We smile and for a while no more words are said and we just sit looking at each other and then we look outside. I squeeze his hand again as my Robin comes up to the double glazed window.

"I've got my Jonny," I say. "I've got my Jonny and I've got my Robin. At last I've got my family and now, one day, I can die in peace. No hurry though. I'm not going yet. Not yet thank you God."

A rattily trolley comes along. It's Susie with the funny wheel.

"Oh I see you have new friend Veera," she says.

"This is my Jonny."

"I say hello Jonny. You like tea or coffee?"

"Coffee please …?"

"It Susie."

"Coffee please Susie. Black."

I smile a huge smile, knowing what is to come.

"Jonny. You want milk in that?"

"Yes please."

We all laugh. I do love my Jonny. Jonny Clitheroe. Jonny from the terrace.

Jonny goes quiet for a few seconds and just looks into his lap. He's thinking.

"Vera," he says, slowly lifting his head and looking directly and totally seriously into my eyes. "Will you marry me?"

I don't have to think too hard to find an answer.

"You daft old sod," I reply, happily and squeezing his hand. "Of course I will. I've waited bloody long enough haven't I?"

*

Good bye and thanks for listening to my story. I do like a happy ending.

THE END

Printed in Poland
by Amazon Fulfillment
Poland Sp. z o.o., Wrocław